Look for More Titles by Cassandra Chandler

SCIENCE FICTION ROMANCE

Cygnian 7
NUAR
KRAL
LAR
DORN
BRON
TARN
ROM

The Department of Homeworld Security
Gray Card
Resident Alien
Business or Pleasure
Tied up in Customs
Entry Visa
Duration of Stay
Duel Citizenship
Invasive Species
Export Duty
COALITION RECKONING
Import Quarantine
Homeworld for the Holidays
Nothing to Declare
Rate of Return
Trade Secrets

—

PARANORMAL ROMANCE NOVELS

The Forbidden Knights
FORBIDDEN INSTINCT

—

PARANORMAL ROMANCE NOVELLAS

Court of the Yuletide Fae
The Yule Cat
The White Stag
The Krampus

Court of the Springtime Fae
Jack Frost
Prince Charming
The Oak King

—

SCIENCE FICTION - HORROR ROMANCE

The Blades of Janus
PACK
PROGENITOR

PARANORMAL - HORROR ROMANCE

The Summer Park Psychics
WANDERING SOUL
WHISPERING HEARTS
LINGERING TOUCH

—

COLLECTIONS

The Department of Homeworld Security
THE DEPARTMENT OF HOMEWORLD SECURITY OMNIBUS 1
THE DEPARTMENT OF HOMEWORLD SECURITY OMNIBUS 2

Courts of the Fae - Duets
WINTER AND SPRING

Whispering Hearts

The Summer Park Psychics
Book Two

Cassandra Chandler

Copyright Page

This book is pure fiction. All characters, places, names, and events are products of the author's imagination or used solely in a fictitious manner. Any resemblance to any people, places, things, or events that have ever existed or will ever exist is entirely coincidental.

Whispering Hearts
The Summer Park Psychics, Book Two
Copyright © 2016 by Cassandra Chandler
Print ISBN: 978-1-945702-53-2
Digital ISBN: 978-1-945702-50-1

First eBook edition: January 2016
Second eBook edition: May 2017
First print edition: January 2016
Second print edition: May 2017
10 9 8 7 6 5 4

cassandra-chandler.com
P.O. Box 91
Mission, Kansas 66201

Cover by Cassandra Chandler

Dedication

For those who listen with their hearts.

*Don't miss out on any of
the eerie romance in Summer Park.
Subscribe to Cassandra Chandler's newsletter at
cassandra-chandler.com now!*

Prologue

Rachel hung from the chains that held her to the wall, her arms splayed like a dismal butterfly. Her wrists were searing points of agony, her knees throbbing from the cold cement beneath her. Holding still helped keep the pain at bay.

Nothing could help with the voices.

"The exhibit is opening tonight."

The peculiar echo that accompanied the voices of the dead sent a chill down Rachel's spine that had little to do with her circumstance. This one she recognized as Veronica. Her voice was higher than the others'. Gentler.

"They won't know. All those people looking at our portraits, and they won't even know what they're seeing."

"He'll kill her afterwards."

Pragmatic, forceful. That would be Anna. Rachel wondered if any others were present. From the conversations she had overheard, half a dozen spirits haunted Michael's garage.

"I can't watch him kill another one." Veronica's voice rose in volume, the echo growing with her distress. She let out a long, high wail.

Keening was the worst sound Rachel had ever heard. She couldn't stop the shuddering sob that wracked her body. She only hoped the ghosts didn't figure out it was more from their conversation than anything else. They couldn't figure out that Rachel heard them. She hadn't given up hope yet. If she made it out of this alive, she didn't want the dead to know that she was clairsentient.

Nicole joined the conversation, her deep voice distinct from the other two. *"At least she won't suffer as long as we did."*

"We should be here to help her in case she doesn't cross over," Anna said.

"There's nothing we can do to help her."

No one had a rejoinder for Nicole's statement. Finally, a moment of blessed silence.

Except for the thoughts churning through Rachel's mind. Garrett was always at the forefront—with his easy smile and gorgeous blue eyes. Garrett who always showed up whenever and wherever she needed him. This time, she was afraid he'd be too late.

She might never see him again. The idea tore at her heart, but at the same time, she wondered if he would be better off. No more need to rescue Rachel from her poor decisions or step in as her emergency date. No more mixed messages.

She did wish that she had kissed him. But she knew it wouldn't have ended there. If she had ever opened that door, he would've walked right through to meet her and been doomed to a lifetime of this—living with the dead. Knowing they were everywhere. Wondering every time her attention strayed if they were truly alone.

Keeping Garrett at arm's length had been a good choice. She only wished her judgment had been as sound with Michael.

There had been so many things she had explained away. The way he kept scaring Elsa by showing up at her house uninvited. The way he had talked about her friend, Dante.

Rachel had finally ended their relationship. Michael had seemed to take it well. When he'd asked her to sit for a portrait, she'd been too flattered to resist. That vanity might cost her everything.

She had ignored the voices, tuned out the whispers when she walked into Michael's house—even though she could tell there were so many of them. How could she have been so stupid?

Oh, right. Years of practice.

"I'm going to the gallery."

Rachel jerked her arms, startled by Nicole's voice close by. Her wrists sent lightning strikes of pain along her arms, punishing her for her loss of control. She feared the consequences of her lapse would be greater than that momentary increase in suffering.

Several moments of tense silence followed.

"Did you see that?" Veronica's voice. Right next to

Rachel's ear. *"You don't think she can hear us, do you?"*

Rachel closed her eyes and focused on the pain. It was an easy distraction, with her nerves clamoring for attention. If the ghosts decided to test her, to shout at her or try to startle her, she could ignore them. When their attempts failed to get a response, they would decide she couldn't hear them.

Please let them decide she couldn't hear.

Light struck her retinas, burning through her eyelids. That was new. Rachel flinched away. She couldn't help herself. It was so bright.

"Rachel? Rachel, it's Elsa."

The voice was solid—no unearthly echo. And it was accompanied by touch. Soft, but firm.

Rachel opened her eyes. The bright lights made them burn, and she blinked several times, trying to bring the room into focus. The shelves and workbenches crowded into the garage filled her view. She turned her head and saw a small blonde woman next to her.

"Elsa?"

Elsa was kneeling on the floor at Rachel's side. How was that possible? Only one theory presented itself.

"Oh no. Did he get you too?" Michael had talked about Elsa after chaining Rachel to the wall. He had told her Elsa was his next "model".

"No, sweetie. We're here to rescue you."

"Oh thank God." Rachel trembled as another sob

escaped. She leaned against Elsa and looked around the room, her eyes finally adjusting. No one else was in view. "How are you going to get me loose?"

Dante's face appeared above the workbenches. The fluorescent lights washed out the red scars covering his right cheek and arcing across his forehead. "Do not be afraid. I will have you free presently."

"Dante?"

"Did you not recognize me with my new look?" His tone was playful, but Rachel could see the strain around his eyes, the tightness to his smile. He was wearing one of the new outfits that Rachel had bought for him. Dante's exhibit was opening tonight as well.

Rachel's heart seemed to freeze in her chest. Dante and Elsa were supposed to be starting a new life together—a life Rachel had helped him create. She had walked blithely into this nightmare, and now her friends were being dragged into it as well.

Metal clanked and rattled as Dante worked the winch that controlled her chains. Elsa helped support Rachel's arms as enough slack was let out for them to drop to her sides.

The winch was lined up so that Rachel could see Dante work. He was using the crowbar arm of a tire iron to try to pry loose the moorings that attached her chains to the floor. Michael always had a sick smile on his face when he let out slack or pulled them tighter, delighting in watching her suffer.

There was no way Dante could get her loose with that tool. Michael wore the key on his necklace. Rachel had asked about it when they'd just started dating. He'd said it was the key to his success. She shivered at the memory.

A pins-and-needles sensation in her arms let her know her circulation was returning. The burning would be nothing next to her wrists when more feeling returned there.

Rachel didn't care.

How many times was she going to let other people save her? How much longer could she play the fool before someone she loved was hurt trying to help?

She didn't know how they had found her, but Rachel couldn't let Elsa and Dante continue to endanger themselves. They needed to leave and call the police.

Rachel moaned. "That will take forever. Dante, you have to get Elsa out of here."

Elsa pulled Rachel closer, stroking her hair. "It's okay, Rachel. I'm not leaving without you."

"You don't understand. He wants you too."

"Well, he can't have me. And he can't have you, either."

Rachel had said such awful things to Elsa the last time they spoke. Yet here Elsa was, risking her life for Rachel. She gripped Elsa's arms, more sobs shaking her, listening to the rattle of the chains as Dante worked to get her free.

Elsa hugged Rachel tighter. "Dante…"

"I know. I am hurrying."

The voices began to whisper something, the echoes distorting their words, but not their urgency.

"Run."

"Run."

"Run!"

There was a brief pause, then Dante shouted, "Elsa, run!"

A sharp pop and the sound of breaking glass joined the sudden keening of the ghosts. Blood sprayed the shelves as Dante jerked back, then fell to his knees behind the workbenches, out of Rachel's sight. Elsa scrambled toward Dante as Michael stepped into view.

Rachel saw his gun first, then that horrible smile. Michael had them caught. He knew it. And he was enjoying every moment of their pain.

A hand appeared on top of one of the workbenches. Dante pulled himself up to stand, leaning on the heavy table. Rachel couldn't see his face. She knew that was a mercy. She could see the trail of blood still running down his neck, staining his shirt red.

Michael leveled the gun at Dante, stepping further into the garage. "This is more than I hoped for. I get Elsa hand-delivered, and the freak thrown in for free."

When he laughed, Rachel heard a faint echo from the ghosts—a grieving moan.

"I think I've made an improvement on your face," Michael said. "I can't believe that Jazz wanted me to share the opening with you. I'm a true artist. Not like you, with your boring little landscapes. How much are you willing to sacrifice for your art?"

Dante's voice was strained. "Art is about creation, not sacrifice."

"There is no creation without sacrifice. I'm willing to give up what I love most. Over and over again. I imbue the canvas with their essence. It's how I immortalize them."

"No, no, no…" A loud screech pierced Rachel's ears. She shook her head, but couldn't block out the sounds, no matter how hard she tried. Echoes, moans, sobs, prayers.

"And how many women have you immortalized?" Dante asked.

"How many paintings have I done?"

"Don't kill him!" the voices shrieked.

Rachel heard a thud, then something skittered toward her beneath the workbenches. The light glinted off of Michael's gun. Another thud brought her attention back to where Michael had been.

Without thinking, Rachel picked up the gun as she stood. She walked between the benches, ignoring the pain searing through her wrists as the chains rattled along behind her.

Dante was on the ground again, pulling himself toward Elsa. Michael was on top of her, his hands around her throat.

"No, please no. Don't kill him!" The voices were so distorted that Rachel couldn't tell who was speaking.

"She's going to free him!"

Michael was strangling Elsa, screaming at her as he did. "You think you can make a fool out of me? You're mine! You belong on my canvas. All of you!"

Elsa was fighting, but Michael was too strong.

"Don't kill him!"

"She'll set him free!"

Michael straightened his arms to avoid Elsa's fingernails as she clawed at his face, giving Rachel the opening she needed. She lifted the gun and pulled the trigger.

Red bloomed on his chest, spreading in a circle from the bullet hole. He looked down at the spot, then up to Rachel. His eyes were wide, full of surprise. Then he fell to the floor.

Rachel kept the gun trained on Michael's body. She wasn't sure if he was dead. Even with his eyes staring blankly at the room, it didn't feel as if he was dead.

"Run! Run! Run!"

The voices blurred together, growing fainter. Michael's presence remained strong.

Elsa was coughing, but that meant she could breathe. She rolled away from Michael's body as Rachel approached.

He needed to die. Why wouldn't he die? Rachel pulled the trigger again. And again and again. She kept pulling it even when all the rounds were spent.

She still felt him in the room.

Elsa stood and staggered toward Rachel. That wasn't right. Dante should be Elsa's main concern. But Elsa hugged Rachel instead, one hand sliding down her arm to the gun.

She let Elsa take it. Rachel didn't care. There was nothing more it could do to help them.

She wondered if it had really helped them at all.

Chapter One

Two months later

Garrett was about as happy to walk into the Montgomery household as he'd be going in for a colonoscopy. He'd encountered Rachel's mom a time or two at social events and always felt the need to shower afterwards. But Rachel was inside and no one had heard from her in a week.

He sat in his car for another moment psyching himself up, then murmured, "Into the lion's den."

Lioness, really.

The cool air from inside the car rolled past him as he opened the door, leaving him to poach in the steamy summer. Heat from the asphalt hit his legs like he was stepping into a blast furnace. The muggy humidity made his shirt cling to his skin. Sunlight reflected off the white sidewalk, blinding him even through his sunglasses.

Ah, Florida.

Wearing slacks and a long-sleeved shirt wasn't his idea of comfortable, but shorts and a T-shirt wouldn't fly for a visit to Chez Montgomery. It was bad enough that he had opted for his light brown boat shoes. He wasn't even wearing socks.

Scandalous.

The house in front of him was immense, set back from the road on a jewel-green lawn that must cost a fortune to maintain. A few palm trees framed the white two-story mansion, accenting the view of neighboring dwellings just as large.

Garrett was happy with his country home. Summer Park wasn't as heavily populated as much of the state, but it still had tons of people running around. He preferred the quiet outside of town.

Living half an hour or more away also helped him avoid the demands of making too many social calls like this one. If he really wanted out of something, he could always say that gators had crawled up to sun themselves on the one road that led to his neighborhood, blocking his way to the city.

Not that he would ever do such a thing. He let out a tense laugh as he made his way along the front walkway.

At the door, he bent his knees a bit to see his reflection in the narrow window that gave people inside a view of who was calling. He ran a hand through his hair, brushing it back past his collar. It was longer than he would ever have let it grow when he worked the ER. Back then, it had been uniformly brown. The sun had added highlights everywhere. Being a man of leisure had left its mark.

Quitting his job had definitely changed him. After two years, he wasn't sure if it was for the better. He had enjoyed having time to read and think about things at first. But self-reflection was tipping over into brooding and that had to stop.

He'd been spending too much time lately thinking about the reason he left the crazy hours and the constant stress. She was somewhere on the other side of the door.

Damn, he should have shaved. He wiped his hand over the darker stubble that covered his jaw, then shrugged. At least it was in fashion. Hopefully Rachel's mom wouldn't be too offended at his scruffiness and send him packing.

As he stood straight again, he rang the bell and forced himself to smile. Time to turn on the Southern Charm and make his mama proud.

"Yes?" The woman who answered was wearing a maid's uniform. Her eyes widened as she stared at Garrett's chest. She tilted her head back farther and farther to look up at him.

This was the best part of being six-seven. The expressions were always priceless by the time they reached his face.

He upped the voltage on his smile and took off his glasses, letting his southern drawl thicken when he spoke.

"Good afternoon. I'm Garrett Wolfstrom. I'm here to call on Miss Montgomery."

The woman blinked a few times, then smiled back.

"Oh! Doctor Wolfstrom. Please come in."

The staff knew he was a doctor? That meant the Montgomerys must have mentioned him before, even though this was his first visit to the house. Maybe Rachel had spoken of him.

"If you would wait here for a few moments..." The woman nodded to him, then walked briskly from the foyer toward the back of the house.

A mix of emotions churned within him. Worry and hope battling in his chest. He couldn't wait to see Rachel—to know she was all right.

Well, physically, at least. Mentally and emotionally, she had to still be reeling from what had happened to her, no matter what her psychiatrists said.

When she was discharged from the hospital, she had seemed fine. Too fine. People didn't swing from a psychotic break to *everything is roses* after a few weeks of therapy—no matter how intensive it was.

But she had her doctors convinced the medicines were working. Garrett wasn't sure she was taking them.

He had noticed her working on the doctors at the hospital. Doctors with heavy caseloads and light experience when it came to one Miss Montgomery. She had pulled out all the stops. Nobody could turn a head like Rachel. With her vibrant personality and warm smile, her natural charm beat his best efforts by a million miles. To make things worse, she was insanely gorgeous, eyes the pale blue of a morning sky and hair as gold as the sun.

Yeah, he had it for her pretty bad. At least he owned it.

"Mrs. Montgomery will see you in the tearoom."

"I was hoping to talk to Rachel."

The woman was already walking back through the house. Garrett followed.

"Miss Montgomery is resting currently. But her mother would love to speak with you."

Garrett felt a trickle of sweat run down his back that had nothing to do with the heat wave making this summer even worse than usual. How did anyone stand living in the city?

He ducked to avoid smashing his head on the door's lintel as he took the single step down into the tearoom.

Mrs. Montgomery was sitting at a small round table covered by a pristine white cloth. She was holding a tiny teacup and matching saucer, which she set on the table with practiced ease.

Everything about her was fake—from the long, perfect nails on the ends of her fingers to her sculpted and dyed hair. Blonde, of course. Her eyes weren't altered, though. They were the same pale blue as Rachel's. Seeing that bit of Rachel in Mrs. Montgomery fortified him for the encounter.

"Dr. Wolfstrom!" She extended a hand to him, the faintest hint of a Southern accent lacing her voice. "It's so good of you to call on us."

"Ma'am." He took her hand and bowed over her, kissing the air near her cheek. "I apologize for not letting you know I was coming."

"Don't you worry about that. We're always happy to see you here."

Garrett didn't doubt it. Rachel's jokes about her mother wanting a doctor for a son-in-law had been reinforced every time he met Mrs. Montgomery. Too bad Rachel wasn't interested. Whether it was an act of rebellion or just a personal choice in Garrett's case was a mystery. A mystery too painful to try to unravel.

He sat at the table feeling like a full-grown gator in a ten-gallon fish tank. Mrs. Montgomery was built like a porcelain doll, tiny and delicate. It just made him feel worse.

Rachel was taller than both her parents. And she worked out. She had muscle to her and an athletic frame, though she usually dressed to hide it. Usually.

When they had been working together fixing up his house, she'd mostly worn shorts and tank tops. He hadn't been able to ignore the tempting curves and lines of sinew on her body. Or the way her smile hit him all the way down to his toes.

He cleared his throat and pushed the memories from his mind. Now was not the time.

"I was hoping I might have a word with Rachel."

"I'm sure you can have several, but not until I'm done

with you." She gave him a flirty smile. He hoped the one he forced in response was convincing.

"It is rather important. None of her friends have heard from her in a while."

Mrs. Montgomery's smile faltered enough to give Garrett a glimpse of the real woman. The cold, reaching woman beneath the surface of civility she projected to the world. He wanted to leave, but couldn't until he knew Rachel was all right.

"She's been resting quite a bit," Mrs. Montgomery said.

"That's good. But she shouldn't be isolating herself. It isn't healthy."

"I don't think she's isolating herself." Mrs. Montgomery lifted her cup and saucer again, slowly and deliberately. "Rather, she's moving on."

"What do you mean?"

She took a sip of her tea, only glancing at Garrett from the corner of her eyes. He hated the social dance she was playing at, but knew she wouldn't give him answers if he didn't match her moves.

"I hope you're not planning on leaving Summer Park," he said. "The Montgomerys are an important part of the city."

It was a bald-faced lie, but stroking her ego might help to loosen her tongue and get him to Rachel faster. Mr. Montgomery was a defense attorney. If Mrs. Montgomery had her way, he would eventually be President.

"Don't you worry, my dear." She set down her teacup again. "Our plans keep us in Summer Park for a little while longer. I have to say, I would very much like to see Rachel settled down before we move on." She gave Garrett a pointed smile.

He wanted to shrug and say, "I'd be game if she'd stop shutting me down," but didn't think that would end well for Rachel.

Adding to her stress in any way wasn't a good idea. Pressuring her about marriage right after what had happened with her latest boyfriend would be downright despicable. How could Mrs. Montgomery even allude to such a thing?

She tilted her head to the side as she raised her shoulder to meet it—a dismissive shrug Rachel had picked up and used too often. "Unfortunately I don't see that happening if she keeps associating with those friends of hers. Present company excluded of course."

Garrett was stunned. "Rachel needs her friends, Mrs. Montgomery. Now more than ever. They can help her get over what happened with—"

Mrs. Montgomery waved her hand in the air and shook her head. "We mustn't speak of that unpleasant matter."

"Unpleasant?"

Rachel's boyfriend had kidnapped her. Tortured her. He had planned to kill her—and she wouldn't have been his first victim. Not by a long shot. But Rachel had survived.

She had survived and gunned the bastard down while he was trying to kill two of their other friends.

"She needs to talk about what happened," Garrett said. "Especially with the people who went through it with her."

"They did, didn't they? Doesn't that seem a bit odd to you? That so many of her little group was involved?"

Garrett took a deep breath and held it to keep from yelling. When he trusted himself to speak, his voice was tight and clipped.

"Mrs. Montgomery, I don't know what you have been told, but Dante and Elsa were present because they were trying to rescue Rachel."

Mrs. Montgomery's perfectly shaped eyebrows rose on her forehead. "And how did they know she needed to be rescued?"

Explaining that would give away secrets that Garrett had sworn to keep. He doubted she would believe the truth anyway.

When he didn't respond, she looked back to her tea and said, "Weren't they all associated with that gallery owner Rachel fell in with? That Asian woman with the ridiculous name and reputation for *creative* marketing tactics?"

Garrett clenched his hands into fists on his lap. It wasn't only what Mrs. Montgomery was saying but how she was saying it. He had never had the urge to shake someone before.

"Mrs. Montgomery. Elsa was strangled and Dante was

shot trying to help your daughter."

"Only one person suffered gunshot wounds." She shifted in her chair, the first sign of unease since Garrett entered the room. "I read the police report quite thoroughly. Mr. Lucerne's injuries weren't sustained from a gunshot."

"You read the report?"

"Of course." A bit of an edge crept into her voice. "Since our family was involved, we thought it best to be well informed on the matter. My husband is a lawyer, you'll recall. Which brings me back to Mr. Lucerne."

She took another sip of her tea, then set it on the table.

"I believe he's just launching his career as a painter." She leaned forward slightly and narrowed her eyes. "Doesn't it seem a bit coincidental to you that he was injured only on the side of his face where he was already disfigured?"

Garrett could barely speak. Was Mrs. Montgomery talking to Rachel like this?

"This wasn't some publicity stunt."

"But it was publicity. The worst kind. We can't afford to be involved in such a scandalous event with Edward's political campaign starting so soon."

She was about to get another scandalous event. Garrett was going to lift up her tiny table and chuck it through the window. He stood so quickly, when the backs of his knees hit his chair it went flying across the room.

"Garrett?" Rachel's voice swept through his adrenaline-charged system. His skin felt electrified.

Glaring at Mrs. Montgomery, he let her see his outrage. He couldn't speak his mind at the moment, but he wanted her to know that what she was saying was not okay.

Her eyes widened and her mouth fell open. She leaned back in her chair, one hand clasped to her chest.

He took a few deep breaths to calm himself down. He didn't want Rachel to see him so angry. He made his voice cheery and plastered on his best smile as he turned around.

"Rachel, it's good to see—" He froze, a lump forming in his throat too big for his words to squeeze past.

Rachel stood in the door to the tearoom, eyes unfocused like she was looking through him. Her hair was dull and clung to her scalp in lifeless strands. Her skin was pale, her lips bloodless and chapped. For some inexplicable reason, she was wearing a tennis outfit—complete with wristbands. The white fabric caught and reflected the light in the room. Her skirt was wrinkled as if she'd slept in it for days, and her feet were bare.

Mrs. Montgomery made a tsking sound behind him. "Rachel, how can you let a gentleman caller see you in such a state? Go to your room and clean up."

Rachel hovered in the doorway. "Sorry."

She tended to fade next to her mother, like a flower folding in darkness, but this took it to a whole new level. He was used to her being vibrant, lighting up a room with her conversation and charm.

"It's all those dreadful medicines they have you on. Hurry up and change, dear. And do something with your hair."

"Yes, mother."

Garrett's chest felt tight—too full from everything he was having to process, all the things he could imagine that woman saying to Rachel when no one else was around to hear.

"Don't trouble yourself," he said. Rachel had trouble enough.

She opened her mouth as if she was about to say something, but her mother spoke over her.

"Are you leaving so soon then?" Mrs. Montgomery's tone was smug. She thought she had won some victory. Garrett was through playing her games.

"Yeah. And Rachel's coming with me."

Rachel's gaze came into sharp focus as she started to back away. "I won't go back to the hospital."

"You don't have to. But you can't stay in this toxic environment."

"Excuse me!" Mrs. Montgomery must have been taking another sip of that damned tea, because he heard the cup and saucer clink on the table.

Garrett rounded on her. "There is no excusing the things you just said to me. And if that's how you talk to company, I can't imagine what you've been saying to

Rachel since she came home."

He turned back to Rachel, approaching her slowly to be sure he didn't scare her. He didn't want to bring up memories of the nightmare she had endured just two months ago.

The urge to protect her was overpowering. When he was close enough he rested his hands on her arms.

She looked up at him, eyes shimmering with unshed tears. "Where would I go?"

"We'll figure that out." He kept his voice as soft as he could manage, barely above a whisper. "But you don't have to stay here. Please let me help you."

She pressed her lips together tightly. He knew that look. She wanted to argue. But she nodded instead. She must be worse off than he thought.

He let out a breath of relief, only then realizing he was dusting his thumbs back and forth over the soft skin of her arms. He stopped and said, "Go and pack a bag. Holler from the front door when you're ready."

Mrs. Montgomery rose from her chair. "I will not be disrespected in my own home!"

She started toward Rachel, but Garrett turned and crossed his arms, shifting so that he entirely blocked the door to the small room. Sometimes being a giant was very useful. He let himself be intimidating.

"If you think I'm going to let you near Rachel again, you are very much mistaken. Sit down and finish your tea."

Mrs. Montgomery raised her voice enough for Rachel to hear. "If you leave now, don't bother coming back."

The stunning lack of compassion left him speechless. He looked over his shoulder at Rachel to see how she would take the callous remark.

Rachel paused at the base of a staircase, one hand on the bannister. Without turning to even glance at them she said, "I won't."

Then she vanished up the stairs.

"How dare you come into my house and cause such a disturbance!"

Garrett turned back to the livid woman before him. "How dare you treat your daughter like this?"

Mrs. Montgomery snorted—a sound he never expected to hear from her. Then she narrowed her eyes and smiled.

"She'll come crawling back, eventually."

Garrett laughed and shook his head. "You have no idea, do you? Those friends that you seem to have such a low opinion of? We all *love* her. Every single one of us. We would die for her. Two of us damn near did. She has homes with us all, places where the people will care for her and treat her right. Speak to her with the respect and compassion that she deserves." He tried to stop himself, but he was too angry and kept going. "But you? You deserve to live a long, lonely life. Because that's what you're making for yourself. That's your choice."

She gave him a strange smile, like she knew something he didn't. Then she shook her head and walked to the table, a casual stride instead of her usual elegant glide. It unnerved him.

By the time she sat down, her mask of fine manners had swept back over her face. She took a sip of her tea, once more the proper lady.

"You want to take her off my hands? Fine." Her voice was low and somehow menacing. "But you will find, Dr. Wolfstrom, that my little girl is never alone. And you might not appreciate the company she keeps quite as much as you think."

Chapter Two

Socks, underwear, jeans... Rachel gathered the things she would need, stuffing each into her backpack as she checked them off her mental list. A few button-up shirts followed, then a pair of sneakers on top.

Shoes. Right, shoes.

She shoved her feet into some sandals before she forgot she was barefoot. The pavement would be hot and she didn't want anything to delay her in getting the hell out of here.

Was she really doing this? Leaving her sanctuary?

She had wanted to leave. Of course she had. But her room was safe. The one spot in the world where she knew she could actually be alone.

She glanced around at the powder-blue walls, the white slatted closet doors and canopy bed that had barely changed since she was a child. The stuffed animals and boy-band posters were gone in a vain attempt to make her room look more like an apartment.

Instead it was stark. Barren. Like a prison cell.

This was no way to live.

She told herself she was staying with her parents to

help with their political aspirations. Photo-ops were much more effective with the entire family embracing and smiling at the cameras. The pictures were just another kind of lie.

In truth she was terrified—afraid to make the simplest changes in case it somehow opened a crack in her defenses. Even when studying Interior Design in college, she hadn't changed the color of the paint, added different furniture, or even put in area rugs. She kept everything the same.

She couldn't stay here anymore, listening to her mother's daily barrage of deprecating statements and watching the help avoid her or make the sign of the cross when they thought she wasn't looking. A lifetime of that scared her more. She could make other places safe.

She walked to the window and put her fingers behind the plain white poppet hanging there—a tiny doll with no distinguishing features aside from its hominid form. A medley of herbs were inside along with the cotton stuffing that gave it its shape. The few times people caught her making them, she said it was her take on potpourri sachets.

It wasn't.

"Salt." She spoke as if the little doll could hear her. "I'm going to need salt." She let it go and watched it swing back and forth in the window for a moment.

No more time for dallying. She ran to her bathroom and opened her medicine cabinet. The door was plain wood—

she had removed the mirror decades ago. She grabbed the large cylinder of salt that was inside, along with her hairbrush. No way she was leaving stray hairs around. The brush and salt went into the top of her backpack, which was lying open on her bed.

There was a medium-sized suitcase in her closet that already held most of what she needed. Books, notes, a few necessary supplies. Hidden away where the staff—and her mother—wouldn't get at them.

She pulled it out, then wheeled it to her bed and opened the zipper so she could shove in a few extra things like toiletries and…more books. She dropped to her knees and pulled her best book on psychic self-defense from under her bedside table.

The tattered thing was wrapped in cloth to prevent further damage to the binding. Rachel had slept with it under her pillow every night for as long as she could remember. Each morning, she hid it in the thin space between the bedside table and floor. She placed it in her suitcase with reverent care.

From the drawer in the small table she grabbed scissors, thread, needles, and white fabric—the basic materials to make new poppets—then shoved them in her backpack. Wherever she was going, she hoped they had a well-stocked kitchen. She would need fresh herbs.

"You about ready?"

When she heard Garrett's voice, she let out a little yell

and fell backwards onto her bottom. He ran to her and knelt at her side.

"I'm sorry. I didn't mean to startle you."

He put his hand on her shoulder. Large, strong, warm. The hair on her arms stood on end as a shiver of pleasure swept through her body.

His eyes were dark blue. Deep and rich, like the ocean. But warmer than the waters she had known.

He was ridiculously gorgeous. His face had the perfect symmetry of a model, his jaw and bone structure as strong as a superhero's. And he was *built*. Broad shouldered and barrel chested, but not too bulky.

When he hugged her, he enveloped her. It made her feel safe.

The ideas that sprang into her mind when he touched her were the hardest to handle. Her imagination tortured her with a future she had no right to think about. At least when it came to him.

"How are you here?" she asked.

Garrett was always there when she needed someone. Even when she didn't ask. He always knew.

"Well, it took some poking around, since none of the staff was of a mind to help me. But if I stayed in that room with your mom another minute…" He let out a sigh through his nose, his lips tight. "Let's just say I might have turned ungentlemanly."

She couldn't imagine Garrett being anything but gentle.

Case in point, he cupped her elbows and helped her to her feet. Her hands wound up resting on his chest. She couldn't stop staring into his eyes.

He grinned, the lopsided smirk making her heart feel like dandelion seeds. The two of them could float away on a trail of gossamer white to a place where they could put down roots, enjoy the warm sun, press themselves closer together...

"You keep looking at a guy like that, you might give him the wrong idea." His smile vanished as pain and worry shoved it aside. "I'm sorry. I shouldn't have said that. I forgot for a minute..."

"Forgot?"

Oh right. Her ex-boyfriend, Michael. The ex-person, thanks to her.

Her hands curled into fists and she dropped her gaze to Garrett's feet. She started to pull away, but he gently tightened his grip on her elbows. Just enough to get her attention and make her pause.

"Have you been taking your medicine?"

"It's right there."

She pointed at the bedside table, to the army of bottles containing the exact amount of pills she should have left based on the instructions her doctors had given her. She disposed of several every day in case someone counted.

"That doesn't answer my question."

She managed to look at him, then. "The longer we stay

the more likely something will happen to keep me here. Please, Garrett. Can we just go? I want to go."

He nodded and let his hands drop from her arms. "Yeah. But I'm going to want to talk later."

"That's fine."

She ran to the table and threw the bottles in her backpack to reassure him. They took up precious space, but getting away quickly was most important. If they took too long, the yard would be crowded with spirits by the time they made it outside. Everyone wanting something from her. She wasn't sure she could handle that.

In a moment, she'd have nowhere left to run to.

"Can you get the glass ball that's hanging in the window?"

He did as she asked, detaching her witch's ball from the swag hook in the ceiling. He stared for a moment at the chords of blue-green glass that had been created inside the sphere. The strands were meant to catch and confuse spirits trying to enter the room.

Taking down her witch's ball would weaken her boundaries. She wasn't sure how much. But she would need it wherever she ended up.

Her heart pounded as they removed the strongest part of her defense. Leaving the others in place would buy her enough time to leave in peace—she hoped.

"It's pretty handy, being tall. You want this thing too?" He reached for the poppet.

"No!"

She took a few steps toward him, but stopped when he jerked his hand back from the doll. His puzzled look turned to concern. She would deal with that later too.

"Rachel?" Her mother's voice carried down the hallway.

"Rachel..." The echo came from her closet.

Rachel's heart leapt to her throat. That was fast. Too fast.

She grabbed the glass ball from Garrett and stuffed it in her backpack with her clothes, cushioning it as best she could. Her hands were shaking as she zipped everything shut. She grabbed her purse and a spray bottle full of saltwater from her desk.

"Can you get the suitcase?" She slung her backpack over her shoulder.

"Sure." Garrett lifted her suitcase by the handle rather than wheeling it around. He nodded toward the spray bottle and said, "What's that for?"

"I'll explain later. We have to go. Now."

The door to the bathroom slammed shut and they both started at the sound. It reminded her of the popping noise Michael's gun had made.

"Is there a window open in there?" Garrett asked.

"No." There were no windows in the bathroom at all.

Too fast and too powerful.

Rachel grabbed Garrett's hand and pulled him toward

the hallway. They needed to leave immediately. For that level of manifestation to take place so quickly…

They must have been waiting for her. Waiting for her to let down her guard even a little. Like they had warned her they would.

Her mother was already in the hallway, her small frame somehow taking up the entire space.

"It is highly improper to have a gentleman in your bedroom."

Rachel froze. Her mother was a master manipulator. All she had to do to destroy Rachel was tell Garrett that the voices Rachel had heard in the hospital—the ones that made everyone think she was crazy—hadn't gone away. Rachel doubted it would help if Garrett knew they had always been there.

Voices of the dead.

Garrett was a doctor. He would think in terms of pathologies and cures. He would take her back to the hospital, where the rooms and halls were filled with wandering spirits. She wasn't sure her sanity would survive another stay.

"Don't let it trouble you." Garrett squeezed Rachel's hand, pulling her along. "We're leaving."

He shouldn't be the one facing off against her mother, but Rachel didn't know if she was strong enough to do it herself. She knew what her mother was capable of and was terrified of the woman.

In that moment though, she hated herself. Hated her weakness.

The past few weeks were a gray blur of pain and despair. Her mother's words only seemed like an anchor pulling Rachel deeper into the abyss. An abyss that was calling out to her.

"Rachel…" she heard again.

"And where are you taking her?" Rachel's mother asked.

"You don't deserve to know," Garrett said. Rachel had never heard him sound so angry. His hand was trembling, his grip tight. "I can't believe you're more concerned about bad publicity than your own daughter."

"Don't leave us." The voice was louder, closer. Then another spoke. *"You're supposed to be with us."* And another. *"You were never supposed to leave."*

The voices were right next to her. Her skin erupted in gooseflesh as she felt a breath of icy cold air on the back of her neck. She quickened her pace, but her mother followed along as Garrett led Rachel down the stairs into the foyer.

"My daughter has already been abducted once," her mother said. "I think that's quite enough."

"Mother!" Rachel didn't recognize the shriek that came from her mouth as she wheeled around. Her entire body was shaking. "Don't you dare compare this with what happened to me," she said. "Garrett is trying to help, which is more than you've done since I came home."

Wherever Garrett was taking her had to be better than this—as long as it wasn't back to the hospital. She was fine with whatever he had in mind. She trusted him.

She didn't trust anyone else in the house with the knowledge of where she would be. Why did her mother even care?

Wait—she *didn't* care. She was a merciless, vengeful woman. Rachel's cheeks tingled as she understood her mother's plan.

Either get Garrett to say where he was taking Rachel, letting the spirits in the house overhear and seek her out to torment, or even better, watch Rachel slip up and mention the voices in front of him.

It didn't matter that her mother knew they were real from first-hand experience. Rachel had inherited her ability from her mother—not that the woman would ever let anyone know she was psychic. Without the moonstone earrings she always wore that somehow blocked the voices, her mother would hear the ghosts too.

No, she didn't want to know where Rachel would be. Her mother wanted to punish Rachel for leaving—like she'd punished Rachel for befriending spirits as a child.

Rachel's rage became a living thing inside her demanding release. Thoughts and feelings she had stifled for days, weeks, her entire life pressed against her lips. For one brief moment she wanted to know what it felt like to be free.

She stepped in front of Garrett, walking right up to her mother. She had never noticed how small the woman was.

"That's the first time you even admitted that I was abducted," Rachel said.

She dropped her purse and the bottle of saltwater so she could pull the sweatbands off of her wrists.

"I'm done. I'm done being a marketing prop. You want a picture?" She threw down the wristbands and held up her arms, revealing the shining red and white scars Michael had left behind. "Take one now!"

Her mother's mouth dropped open, but nothing came out. Rachel would remember that sight for the rest of her life. She felt a thrill of victory. Lillian Montgomery, speechless.

"That's why…" Garrett's voice was almost a whisper, so soft Rachel thought at first it might be one of *them*.

"That's why she had you wearing the tennis outfit," he said. "To match the wristbands. So no one would see and ask questions—no one would know what happened to you."

"It doesn't matter." Rachel bent down to pick up her things. "We're leaving."

"It does matter!" Garrett stepped toward Rachel's mom, glaring balefully. "What the hell is wrong with you?"

She knew Garrett had seen through Lillian's act the first time the two spoke. It was one of the things Rachel loved about him. Her mother had never been able to fool him.

Rachel had been watching him all night at the fundraiser, unable to pull her eyes away. She'd caught the look of revulsion on his face as he walked away from his exchange with her mother. Their gazes had locked across the room.

He'd looked nervous, but Rachel smiled and rolled her eyes at him, then shrugged. His smile had been hesitant—the first one he'd directed at her. Butterflies had swarmed up from her stomach, words sticking in her throat.

She had left early to avoid talking to him.

Rachel put her free hand against his chest. Her voice was shaking. "Garrett, please."

"Where are you going, Rachel?" a voice said. Another whispered, *"Where are you going?"*

Rachel's heart lurched at the sound—at the low, even tone of the women's voices—vaguely familiar. Three people in the hallway. Five voices.

Garrett looked stricken as he gazed down at her. Rachel struggled to appear at least a little bit calm.

"She's your mother," he said.

Rachel cast one last glance over her shoulder at the woman who had given her life and then proceeded to make it a living hell.

"Not anymore."

Lillian stiffened her spine, getting ready to light into them again. "I will not be spoken to in such a disrespectful manner in my house!"

Garrett opened the door and tugged Rachel's hand. "How about in your yard? Because we're heading outside and if you want to follow us and keep being a royal bitch, you'll have to come along."

Rachel wished she could laugh at the scandalized expression on Lillian's face. But all she could think about was getting away.

"Where are you going, Rachel?" The voice was in front of her.

She ducked behind Garrett and quickened her pace, almost stepping on his heels as he led her down the front walkway.

She was reminded of the tale of Orpheus and Eurydice. Garrett was braving the underworld to bring Rachel back to the world of the living. She had a feeling Hades was kinder than Lillian.

Rachel kept her gaze on her feet and softly chanted, "Don't look back. Don't look back."

She matched Garrett's pace until she felt the heat-soaked asphalt nearly scald her legs, burning her feet around her sandals. She walked a little faster.

He led her to the far side of his car, into the green grass along the verge of the road. How long since she'd breathed fresh air?

He set down her suitcase, then dug in his pocket for his keys. The car beeped as he hit the button to unlock it. He opened the back door and set her suitcase on the seat.

"Let me help you." He lifted her backpack from her shoulder.

"Be careful."

"I will."

He stared into her eyes and she knew they weren't talking about her bag anymore. He set it in the car and closed the door without looking away.

Her heart had been thumping like a jackrabbit since he asked her to come with him. The thumping turned to thunder as she realized he was still holding on to her hand. His grip was tight, as if he was afraid she would slip away.

She had tried. Tried to stay out of his life—to leave him alone so he could find a nice normal woman to settle down with. But every time she thought he was moving on, something happened that brought them back together. Like now.

Looking back at the house, she saw her mother standing in one of the front windows, arms crossed and condescending smile firmly in place. Hopefully that smile would fade when she realized that Rachel wasn't coming back. One way or another, she was never coming back.

Rachel stood a little straighter, determined to leave with her head held high. She tried to compose herself while staring at her mother—Lillian—before turning back to Garrett.

The sun glared off the top of his silver car, blinding her

for a moment. The car's window reflected back the palm trees behind them, the open sky and white clouds above… and the two dead women standing over her shoulders.

Blonde hair, blue eyes. Michael had a type.

"Where are you going?"

For a moment, Rachel could only stare in shock. Both women were gaunt, their skin absolutely white, which made the dark circles under their eyes stand out like livid bruises.

The spirits lifted their arms for her to see. Their wrists were mangled, bloodied and torn in the same places Rachel's had been.

Michael's victims. Two of the spirits who had begged Rachel not to kill him.

"I'm sorry." Rachel closed her eyes tight, tears spilling down her cheeks. Hearing the women Michael had killed was bad enough. Seeing them was unbearable.

"Hey," Garrett's voice was so gentle it hurt. She felt him dust his knuckles over her cheeks, wiping away the tears—even though more quickly followed. "There's no reason for you to be sorry."

"You have every reason to be sorry!" One of the ghosts shouted right next to Rachel, a blast of cold hitting the side of her neck.

Her eyes snapped open as she pulled away from Garrett, lifting her spray bottle. He held up both hands and backed away as if she was holding a gun.

She wanted to laugh, but knew she would sound hysterical.

"Didn't we suffer enough, Rachel?" one of them asked. *"You barely suffered at all!"*

The other said, *"We told you what he did to us. We warned you not to kill him."*

Rachel tried to ignore the voices. She knew she must look crazed to Garrett. Taking action would only make things worse.

"You killed him anyway. You let him reach us," the first one said.

Rachel shook her head and tried to cover her ears without setting down her spray bottle.

"Rachel, what's going on?" Garrett asked. "Talk to me."

A voice hissed into her ear. *"But now we can reach you!"*

Icy cold pressed against her wrists and around her neck. The spirits hadn't figured out how to cause real damage yet. But they were trying.

"Don't touch me!"

Rachel started spraying in the direction of the voices, saturating the already salty air with concentrated saltwater. Any spirits in her immediate vicinity would be disrupted for a few moments at least—time she needed to use to her best advantage.

She threw open the door and jumped into the back seat,

spraying everything. The windows, the seats, the floor, the ceiling. She reached into the front and did the same thing.

Garrett stood outside the car, eyes wide, mouth hanging open. How was she ever going to explain this?

That was a problem for later.

"Get in!" she yelled. "Get in and drive! Please!"

As she slammed her door shut, he ran around to the driver's seat. He slid behind the wheel and started the car, then peeled away from the curb. Maybe he was trying to get her to the hospital as quickly as possible.

She would jump out of the car if it came to that. She wouldn't go back to a place packed with spirits, with environments she couldn't control. The vengeful spirits from her mother's house would probably check the hospital first anyway.

Rachel didn't want to jump out of the car. She wiped the tears from her cheeks and sniffed.

"Please don't take me back to the hospital. They don't know how to help me."

"I don't know how to help you, either."

His tone was flat. Hopeless. He was trying to help her and it was hurting him. Like always.

She'd need a hand and he would appear and make everything better. In the process, the attraction between them would flare like a star, and she would bolt right before anything happened—before a real connection could be made.

If she had explained why, he would have moved on, seeing her for the freak she was. He could be married by now. With kids. She knew that was what he wanted. She wanted it too, but how could she pull someone she loved into the chaos that surrounded her? How could she ever start a family when her life was full of death?

Her tears kept falling, but she ignored them. She shifted in the seat to see him without looking in the rear-view mirror.

"Dante and Elsa are staying in the city. Maybe I can stay at their place in the country with Winston?"

That would be perfect. The lower the population density, the fewer ghosts would be hanging around. Then she could focus on dealing with the ones that were after her specifically.

"Winston's with them in the city."

"Even better. I need to be away from everything. Far from people."

"I'm not letting you be alone."

"There are too many people here, Garrett. Too much history. I can't deal with it."

He nodded, then accelerated again. "Okay."

Maybe he thought she was talking about Michael or her ordeal at the hospital. She didn't care, as long as they kept heading out of town.

She threw herself back against the seat, closing her eyes and taking deep breaths, so grateful he had come for her—

was helping her. She would keep herself in check this time. No lingering stares or light touches. No raising his hopes.

Garrett would take care of her. She knew it. She just had to make sure it didn't cost him too much.

Chapter Three

This was the stupidest thing Garrett had ever done. Instead of the hospital, he was taking Rachel to his home.

It made a sort of sense that she didn't want to go back to the hospital. She associated that place with her abduction and mental breakdown. The only memories she had of his home should be positive—painting rooms, cooking, looking at the stars with the telescope she'd picked out for him.

At least, he hoped his house would be filled with happy memories. He wasn't completely sure, with the way she had dropped out of his life.

She had renovated his house—living with him for months—helped him host a few dinner parties after she moved out, and then abruptly stopped visiting. No warning, no explanation.

They had never been more than friends, but he had still been so messed up about it that his friend Jazz had tried to set him up with her best friend Elsa. Jazz said the pairing was destiny, since the two of them even lived right next door to each other. It was a nice sentiment, but not meant to be.

At least Elsa had let Garrett be part of her life after dating didn't pan out. Rachel and Garrett's paths only seemed to cross anymore when she needed help. Sometimes she'd call. More often he'd just stumble into things.

He glanced in his rearview mirror, which he had adjusted so it was mainly focused on the back seat rather than the road. Rachel was sitting with her head against the window, her eyes vacant as the lush scenery sped past. She didn't perk up until Elsa's driveway came into view.

"You're taking me to Elsa's after all?"

"No." Garrett's drive was just past Elsa's. He didn't dare look to see Rachel's expression. He would read too much into it, no matter what it was.

"Don't go into the garage," Rachel said. Her voice was tight.

Damn. He should have thought of that. It was the first reaction she'd had that made sense.

Michael had kept her chained up in his garage. That was where he had tortured her.

Garrett stopped the car in front of his house. He waited for a moment before killing the engine.

What was he doing?

He heard Rachel open the door and kicked himself into gear. Movement shook his thoughts loose.

He was helping his friend. That was what he was doing. He would sort the rest out later.

By the time he was out of the car, Rachel had already slung her purse and backpack over one shoulder. The spray bottle she had nearly drowned him with was tucked into the strap of her purse. She was just starting to drag her suitcase out of the back seat when he reached her.

"Let me get that."

"Thanks."

She turned and stared at his house—modest compared to her family's or even Elsa's. Garrett didn't need much and didn't want to have to keep up with a big place. It was just him most of the time.

When he'd bought it, he had still been working in the ER with hours so crazy he barely slept at home. Rachel had been delighted to find all the walls blank, the place sparsely furnished, and a budget that let her imagination run wild.

Even with that freedom, she'd kept Garrett's comfort in mind with every choice she made. She had contractors turn all his square doorframes into arches so he didn't feel like he was about to whack his head any time he left a room. The only thing on the windows were blinds, which kept them nice and open and made every room seem more spacious.

He would never have thought to do half the things she had done that made his house feel like home. The memory of her living with him during the renovation was a big part of that, though.

"It's been a while since you've been here." He didn't mean it as a dig, but she winced. Great job making her feel welcome.

He pulled out his house key as they walked to the front door. Once inside he said, "Come on. I'll make us some lunch while you get settled."

"I'd rather cook." There was an urgency to her tone that didn't make any sense. She must have picked up on it because she tried to laugh it off. "It's the least I can do with you taking me in."

"This isn't going to work if you aren't honest with me."

"What do you mean?"

"I know you. I know when you laugh for real and I know you use the fake ones to throw people off your trail. I want to help you, Rachel. I really do. But I can't do that if you aren't honest with me about what you need—what you're going through."

She let out a snort of a laugh. Unladylike and real. It didn't carry any mirth, but it was better than the fake twittering of a trained socialite.

She cleared her throat, then said, "I think I need to work up to that."

"Fair enough. But in the meantime, we need to call your doctor. He can come here to talk, maybe have sessions over the phone."

"I don't need a doctor."

Garrett let out a sigh that he felt all the way to the soles of his feet. "From what I've seen today, you do."

"Can't you be my doctor?" Her voice hitched and grew small. She sounded scared.

He wanted to tell her he could make everything better, but he couldn't. "That isn't a good idea."

"You treat Elsa and Winston. And you consulted with Dante's case. Even Jazz calls you when she's sick."

"That's different."

"Why?"

"You know why." He stared at her. Harsher than he should, probably. But he was carrying a lot of pain. Pain he knew she was aware of.

He never had figured out why Rachel played dumb with everyone else, but he had seen the woman behind the pretense. The brilliant, funny, caring woman he'd lived with for three months. He was crazy about her and she knew it.

Her lips parted. Some of the color had returned to them already. They were still cracked and dry. He might not be able to treat her as a doctor, but he could treat her like a friend.

The first thing she needed was to settle in. He wanted to comfort her, give her a place of solace.

"Let's get your things put away." He hefted her suitcase again and headed for her room.

Technically, it was a guest room, but he always thought of it as hers. It had been empty when she started redecorating his house. White walls and beige carpet.

Now, it had light brown hardwood floors made of bamboo, walls of warm gold, and a queen bed with matching dresser, table, desk, and a comfortable chair for reading near the window. The lamps were art pieces—ceramic sculptures that caught the light and matched the colorful paintings on the walls.

She had stayed here during the months she was renovating his house. Months when Garrett had found himself questioning his career for the first time in his life.

Back then he couldn't wait to get home and didn't want to leave for work. She'd said she wanted to immerse herself in the environment and oversee everything personally. To really get a feel for how he lived.

What she'd done instead was show him what he was missing. He would come home to gorgeous dinners, usually in the fridge since he worked such long hours, but sometimes Rachel would wait up to eat with him.

She helped him with his schedule, building him a workout room when it became obvious he never had time to get to a gym. She talked to him, really listened, and used that knowledge to transform his home.

Every day he was comforted by things she had done for him. Every day he was reminded of how much he missed her.

During the renovation, Garrett had started to come up with more things he wanted to fix to keep her around longer. When she left, he wanted to ask her to stay, but she'd already made it clear that they were just friends.

That was all she wanted. He would be that for her now.

"I really appreciate you letting me stay here." Rachel set her backpack and purse on the chair, then set her spray bottle on the dresser nearby.

"I'm glad to help." He set her suitcase on the floor next to her bed. "Feels like this thing is full of rocks. What do you have in here?"

"Books. I'll put them away later."

"Whatever you need. I suggest you start with a hot shower and a change of clothes."

He couldn't believe her mother had her wearing that ridiculous outfit to cover up what had happened to her. But it shouldn't surprise him. Her family had covered up the whole thing. He was amazed at how little media coverage there had been. Rachel's name was never mentioned. Lillian Montgomery probably didn't want anyone to see that her daughter's life was anything but perfect.

He felt sick. His eyes burned and he wanted more than anything to put his hand through a wall. Any wall. He turned around quickly to hide his anger. She'd seen enough of that with Michael.

She shouldn't have to be going through any of this. He didn't want to make things worse, so he walked to the window and looked outside at the palm trees that lined the small canal behind his house.

"It's okay." Her voice was close. She must have come up behind him, quiet as a mouse.

He turned around and shook his head. "No it isn't. None of this is okay." He brushed a lock of her hair behind her ear without thinking. She didn't seem to mind. "At least it's over."

Her lips parted on a brief breath and her eyes filled with tears.

If it was over, why did she look so scared?

Maybe she was remembering something. He couldn't change what had happened to her, but at least he could help her process it. He desperately wanted to help her feel safe.

He pulled her against his chest, wrapping his arms around her and burying his face in her hair. She wound her arms around him, grabbing the back of his shirt, pressing herself closer. Her body trembled, and he felt the front of his shirt grow damp.

How could this have happened? Rachel was the brightest, most carefree person he had ever met. Always happy, always smiling. She was the last person he would ever think would get caught up in a nightmare like this.

And yet she was at the center of it—the storm blowing around her. He wouldn't let it pull her away.

He didn't know how long they stood that way and he didn't care. Eventually he felt her grip loosen, her hands flatten against his back.

"Tell me what you need. Anything, and I'll do it. I'll make it happen. You need to cry or scream. You need somebody to wail on…"

She leaned back and laughed, wiping her nose on her arm. Her mother would be mortified. Garrett smiled.

"I need a shower."

"That one's easy. The bathroom's right where you left it."

"Could you…"

She clamped her mouth shut and looked away.

"Could I what?"

With a sigh, she said, "Could you stay outside the door for me? I'm…scared."

"Sure. Sure I can." Hell, he'd sit inside the room if she needed it. Eyes shut, of course. He was pretty sure he could manage that.

"Thanks." She smiled at him, then pressed a hand against his cheek. "Thank you. For everything."

He gripped her hand in his, squeezed it, didn't trust his voice to speak. He would give her everything. Everything he had, everything he was. He would give anything for this to have not happened to her. But that was outside his power.

Instead, he nodded and let her hand slip away as she headed to the bathroom. She paused by the chair and unzipped her backpack, then pulled out the pretty blue-green glass ball Garrett had taken down from the window in her bedroom.

"I don't suppose you could hang this up for me while I'm in there?"

"I think I can manage that. There's a hook in the ceiling and everything."

"Thanks." She gave him one last smile before picking up her backpack and heading into the bathroom. She left the door open a crack behind her.

Garrett waited till he heard the water start before hanging up the globe. Strands of molten glass formed crisscrossing patterns inside, connecting the sides of the ball like pathways.

The light caught and reflected from its surface and the little tunnels within. It was pretty and interesting. He'd never seen anything quite like it. The tiny doll in her window was new to him too. He'd ask about it later and why she had flipped out when he touched it.

That reminded him of the other weird thing she'd brought along. The spray bottle.

He walked to the dresser and picked it up, inspecting the cloudy water inside. It probably wasn't toxic, with how she had liberally sprayed it in his car and all over him.

He sprayed some into his hand and smelled it. Nothing.

Rubbing his fingers together, he detected a bit of grit.

He touched a fingertip to his tongue. Salt overwhelmed his taste buds. He wiped his mouth on his sleeve. Yeah, they were a bastion of manners, he and Rachel.

Putting back the bottle, he tried to come up with a rational reason that she would spray his car with saltwater. She treated the thing like it was some kind of weapon—like it was vital for her survival.

The list of questions he wanted to ask her grew, as did his concern. He should call her doctors, but knew what they would say. They would want her to come in for another assessment.

She would never go for that. He didn't want to find out what she would do to avoid it.

He moved her purse to the dresser, then sat in the chair. His head ached and he rubbed his temples to try to ease some of the tension.

At least Rachel was here with him. She was safe and he could take care of her. Scratch that. He could make sure she took care of herself. Help her while she got back on her feet and sorted things through with her actual doctors.

There were too many blurry lines. Too much gray space between them. They were friends, but could have been more. She needed a doctor, but Garrett couldn't help her in that way—not in good conscience. And she knew it.

But when she was at the hospital, she had still asked for his help—even cried out for him. She had begged him not to leave her side.

And she had come with him today without hesitating. She trusted him. He couldn't betray that trust by carting her off to the hospital right away. Not until they had talked and he could ease her into the idea.

The delay might cost her, though. Like when Garrett waited to listen to Finn's voicemail the day after she was abducted.

Finn was Garrett's best friend and a private investigator. He had been working on a case for Garrett—a case involving Elsa and Dante, not Rachel. And Garrett had called Finn off, asked him to stop digging.

He had done it for Elsa. She had been terrified when Garrett told her that he had hired Finn. But instead of barging in and taking charge of things as usual, she asked Garrett to take care of it. She had never trusted him to do something like that before, and he didn't want to let her down.

Now he knew that she'd been afraid that Finn would discover that she had a psychic power. And she was right to be afraid. Finn had ferreted out her secret—and Dante's.

Garrett should have known Finn wouldn't be able to walk away from that case. Still, when Garrett had noticed the voicemail, he'd thought it was nothing—an invitation to a jazz club, Finn calling to give Garrett a hard time about something. He never thought it could be so important.

His stomach cramped at the memory. He had gone over the details hundreds of times, thought of the different ways he could have spared Rachel from even a moment in Michael's garage or kept Elsa and Dante from being hurt.

Garrett had done the math, figured out when the call came in and when Rachel was taken, when Elsa and Dante showed up to help her.

Garrett had been consulting with another doctor when Finn called, but could have listened to the voicemail right after. Instead Garrett had gone home to get ready for the new exhibits opening in the gallery. His stomach had been upset all that day and he'd felt weirdly out of it, but he had wanted to see Rachel again—even if she was on another man's arm.

Jazz had happened to drive past him while he'd been walking from his car to her gallery. She'd slammed on her brakes and nearly ran into another SUV, cutting him off on the sidewalk, then she screamed for him to jump in. When she'd told him what was happening, he'd never been so scared in his life. Not since…

He shook aside a memory that was even darker.

He *would not* lose Rachel. He wouldn't let her slip away.

Chapter Four

Steam surrounded her, clinging to her soapy skin. Rachel stood in the tub and let the hot water pound on her back.

She hadn't been able to shower for a week. She couldn't bring herself to be naked in her parents' house. She felt vulnerable enough as it was. Sloughing off all that grime and oil felt as decadent as a full body massage.

Knowing that Garrett was right outside, she felt safe for the first time in months. Safe and awful.

She was taking advantage of him. She knew it. He cared about her. More than cared.

No matter what was going on in her life, he was always there for her. And every time she walked away, she saw how much it hurt him. Every time, it was harder for her to leave.

She couldn't pull him into the chaos and darkness of her life. Helping her out from time to time was easier to handle than living with what she could do, with what she knew.

She had to get on her feet—and out of his house—as quickly as she could. To spare him from getting his hopes up. To spare them both from their connection starting to build, only to be severed again. But where could she go?

Jazz's apartment was in one of the most densely populated parts of the city. It would be thick with ghosts. The same went for Elsa and Dante's loft.

Their house was a different matter. And it was next door.

Rachel could run over, cleanse the place, put up poppets, and hide until she was strong enough to tune out any voices that didn't belong to the living. If she waited long enough, maybe word about her among the spirits would quiet down.

Right. Like that was going to happen. The only reason they had left her alone for this long was because her friend Hiram had been around to convince the other ghosts that Rachel's powers were fading as she grew up. Hiram was gone. He had crossed over decades ago.

Elsa and Dante's house was still her best bet. If she could convince Garrett to give her the key, she could leave him in peace. She might need to borrow a laptop till she could get one of her own. Then she'd be able to order everything she needed without leaving the property.

But she would be isolated. As much as she wanted to avoid the dead, she knew she needed the living. Being alone reminded her of the time she had spent chained up in pitch darkness while Michael had her in his power. The memory made her shiver.

Garrett wouldn't go for it anyway. He was set on her not being alone. Knowing him, he wanted to keep an eye on her, to watch for signs that she was a danger to herself or others. He would want to keep her close, to help her heal. To protect her.

She didn't deserve it. She was lying to him—to everyone. People she loved had risked their lives to save her without really knowing who she was. All they saw was the socialite's daughter, the role her mother had raised her to play.

If they knew what she could do, would they still care about her? If they knew she was a coward?

She had hidden herself away from ghosts for as long as she could. Then she had run. And she hadn't even managed that on her own. Garrett had come to her rescue again.

At least she had finally stood up to her mother.

Lillian. Saying terrible things about Rachel was one thing, but Garrett... Apparently Rachel reserved causing him grief for herself.

The only thing that made staying with him bearable was that she loved him too. She turned around, eyes stinging as her tears mingled with the hot water.

The numbness that had enveloped her over the last few days fell away, leaving her heart flayed and bleeding. Not from shock or horror over what had happened to her, but from the loss of what could have been between her and

Garrett. If she had been born normal.

But Rachel wasn't normal. She never would be. And Garrett deserved better. It was bad enough he was saddled with her as a friend.

She shouldn't keep him waiting. She finished cleaning herself quickly, then turned off the water.

After wiping the excess moisture from her skin, she looked for a towel. Several were stacked on a shelf built into the wall just beyond the sink. Which presented a problem—she hadn't thought to cover the mirror when she entered. She had ducked her head and raced for the shower.

The mirror was fogged with steam. And Garrett's house was far enough from the city that she hoped there were no haunted places nearby. Unless *she* was haunted now, and that was a very distinct possibility.

Michael's other victims had not been happy with Rachel when she killed him. They were very clear on that point, even before they were certain she could hear them. They were afraid of what would happen when Michael's spirit was no longer trapped in his body.

She didn't want Michael to be able to hurt anyone, living or dead. But she hadn't known what else to do. She'd had to stop him, to save Elsa and Dante. In that moment, she had made her choice.

As soon as she had been discharged, she'd started working on helping the spirits of Michael's victims.

Luckily, her parents had gathered all the information they could on *the incident*—including what had been done with Michael's body.

No family had come forward to claim it, so it had been cremated. Rachel felt a sigh of relief flow through her every time she thought about that.

With no earthly remains to link him to the physical plane, his spirit would be forced to move on to whatever came next. She had that on excellent authority, and her research corroborated what she'd been told.

Michael couldn't be the reason the ghosts at her mother's house were angry. Not directly, anyway. She didn't understand why they were so upset that she had escaped and they hadn't, why they hadn't moved on when Michael died. What was keeping them here?

They could want Rachel's help, like many spirits did. Tying up loose ends that had been left unraveled when they died.

She wasn't a stranger to ghosts trying to scare or bully her into helping them. That was the norm rather than the exception. It was a big part of why she did her best to ignore them all. Even the ghosts who were comparatively nice were just too numerous. It was overwhelming.

She shuddered as she remembered her mother's harsh lessons about toying with the spirit realm.

"You want to play with ghosts? Fine. Here are some new playmates."

Yeah, her mother was going to Hell. Except Rachel didn't believe in Hell. Or Heaven. She knew there was something *after*, but didn't think she could conceive of what it was like.

People made their own Heavens and Hells right here on Earth. Both the living and the dead. Whatever the reason, it wasn't right that Michael's victims were still suffering. She had to do something to help them.

She would check her books. She would find a way. But first she had to give herself a safe sanctuary, a place where spirits couldn't enter without her permission. To do that, she had to leave the bathroom.

She looked toward the mirror again, but couldn't bring herself to move. The AC was running and the water left on her skin began to evaporate, chilling her.

If she called to Garrett and asked him to cover the mirror, it would be one more mark against her, one step closer to him giving up on her and taking her to the hospital. She was shocked he hadn't done so already. She sank down in the tub and curled into a ball to stay warm while she thought of a plan.

She could crawl out of the bathroom. No, too weird.

Close her eyes as she passed? Her reflection would still appear in the mirror, making it that much more likely a ghost would find her.

She could just deal with it. Walk out and say, "Hi," to anyone who might be in the room with her. Not brave enough.

Just the thought of talking openly to a ghost made her tremble. Too many memories poured through her mind.

Whispers in the night, shadows flashing across any reflective surface, wicked smiles as they reached for her, let her know that they were touching her, even if she couldn't feel them—and worse, the ones she *could* feel.

Closing her eyes, she shook her head. She wasn't that terrified child anymore. Was she?

"Rachel?"

She shook her head harder, pressing her hands over her ears.

"Rachel?"

"Stop," she said. "Stop talking to me."

She felt a hand on her shoulder and jumped sideways, her shoulder slamming into the tile of the shower.

"Rachel! Are you okay?"

Garrett was kneeling next to her, leaning over the tub. He wrapped his arms around her and pulled her up against his chest.

"I'm getting you all wet," she said.

"I don't care. Come on." He helped her stand, then tried to ease her out of the tub.

"Wait."

He stopped, staring into her eyes. The pain she could see there would be etched on her soul forever. How could she do this to him?

She should tell him. Just explain everything.

But that would buy her a one-way ticket back to the hospital.

His gaze briefly wavered, a deep red blush coming to his cheeks. He looked away, but kept his hands on her arms.

"What do you need?" he asked.

"A towel."

He nodded and released her. The room was small and he was huge. He only had to take a step to reach the towels. He turned back to her with one in hand and offered it to her, averting his gaze from her body.

"Thanks." She wrapped it around herself, then pointed at the mirror. "Could you cover that, please?"

"The mirror?"

"Yes. I—" Inspiration hit and she said, "I don't like looking at myself since…it happened."

Her heart was pounding painfully against her ribs, as if it wanted to punish her for the half-truth. She had *never* liked looking in mirrors and only used a compact so she could control what she saw.

He stared at her for a few moments, the lines on either side of his mouth deepening. It was obvious he wasn't buying her story. But he picked up another towel and draped it over the mirror anyway.

"Thanks." Tears pricked her eyes again.

He helped her from the tub. His hands didn't linger this

time and he pointedly avoided looking at her. Since he had just seen her naked, that kind of made sense. He was also keeping his body as far from hers as he could.

She was used to them gravitating toward each other, especially in close-quarters like these. Her heart squeezed painfully at the absence of that contact. It was the least she deserved for putting him through this.

"Are you going to be okay if I step outside while you get dressed?"

"Yes. I'm fine, really."

He looked at her then, pinning her with his gaze. "No you're not. And you don't have to be. Not with me. But you will be okay. You're going to get through this."

He lifted his hand as if he was going to touch her, but stopped himself and let his arm drop back to his side. He stepped out of the room again, pausing in the doorway.

"I'll be right outside."

A lump formed in her throat and she could only nod. After he pulled the door mostly shut, she stood still for a few moments while she composed herself. If she could pull herself together, maybe she could keep Garrett from being hurt again. More than he was already hurting.

She grabbed another towel to blot her hair. She dried herself, then threw the towels in the hamper.

She'd do the laundry while she was staying with him. And the dishes. And cook. Cooking would give her inconspicuous access to the spice cabinet, which she would need to make a new poppet for the window in her room.

Her bag was already open on the floor. She pulled out a pair of pale jeans, a deep blue button-up shirt, and her brush. Within minutes she was dressed and presentable. She put on her best smile as she opened the door and stepped into the guest room.

"Thanks so much. I feel worlds better after that."

Garrett was sitting in the reading chair, glowering so intently Rachel could almost imagine storm clouds over his head. His hands gripped the arms of the chair and his lips were pulled into a deep frown. Creases at the edges of his eyes cut grooves where she was used to only seeing laughter.

The quips she was hoping would lighten the mood dropped from her mind. She wanted to tell him not to worry about her, that she didn't need it or deserve it. She wanted to throw herself into his arms and kiss him until they both forgot all their troubles.

Instead, she walked to the bed and sat near him. She folded her hands in her lap and stared at the floor.

"You are not okay," he said. "You are not taking your medicine. And there is more going on here than you're telling me. More than you're telling anyone."

Even her psychiatrists were convinced that Rachel was on the mend and doing well. Garrett could see right through her. He always knew when she put on her fake smiles and hollow laughter.

He knew because she had been weak and let him in—let him see through the masks she wore for her parents and friends. She'd felt safe with him and let him get too close. He'd been paying for her mistake ever since.

"I am not okay," she said. "I am not taking my medicine. I'm grinding it up with a mortar and pestle and mixing it with coffee grounds and throwing it away. I didn't want them to get into the water supply."

He snorted, then leaned his elbow on his chair, rubbing his eyes with one hand.

"Well, at least you considered that." He let out a deep sigh before looking at her again. "Did you consider how not taking your medicines would affect you?"

His question wasn't patronizing or condescending. He didn't even sound angry or concerned. He asked it as one doctor might ask another during a differential, trying to get to the root of the problem—her.

"I did."

No one had all of the facts except Rachel. Her doctors gave her drugs to stop her hallucinations, but she knew that what she heard was real. She had never met a doctor she thought might believe ghosts existed, let alone that people could perceive them. Even if she opened up to someone, the more she shared, the crazier she sounded.

Garrett leaned forward, hands steepled between his knees as his long arms rested on his thighs.

"I know you wouldn't make this choice without a reason. A damn good reason. I would really like to know what that is."

She wanted to tell him. It would explain everything. Why she was often distracted in public, why she wanted everyone to think she was a flake, why she carried those stupid spray bottles with her. Even the perfume bottle in her purse was just saltwater, for moments when she needed to disrupt a ghost without raising suspicions.

But more than anything, she wanted him to understand why she had turned him down every time he asked her out. Why she turned away every time he looked like he was about to kiss her.

Her vision blurred as tears filled her eyes again. She didn't let them fall.

"I am not your doctor," he said. "I'm your friend. I've always been crystal clear about that. But even still, I'm legally and morally bound to make sure you are safe, that you are healing properly—that you aren't a danger to yourself or others."

She nodded, sniffing as her nose started to run. "You need to protect yourself. I get that."

"I don't give a damn about that. I care about you. I have to be sure you're getting the help you need."

He let out another sigh, then leaned back in his chair and rubbed his eyes again. She hadn't noticed the deep circles underneath them or the layers of extra stubble on his jaw.

How much sleep had he managed in the last two months? Every time she'd woken up at the hospital, he had been at her bedside. And he always had news about Elsa and Dante, or Jazz. Rachel didn't know how he did it.

She leaned forward and grabbed the hand that was still resting on his knee. "You don't have to take care of us all. We're stronger than you think."

He looked more than a little bewildered when he lowered his hand from his face. "We?"

"Elsa and Dante. Jazz and me."

"You sure that's what you meant?"

"I don't understand."

He stared at her for a few moments in silence, then said, "When you met with your psychiatrists, did anybody mention DID?"

"Of course not." She laughed and shook her head. "The only acronym they threw around was PTSD."

"Did they talk about schizophrenia?"

"I know what's real and what's not, Garrett. And I only have one personality. Why are you even asking me this?"

"Because I've been wondering about you for a long time. When we were working on my house, you were like a completely different person. A person I've caught glimpses of from time to time, but seems buried under this —"

"Ditzy socialite?"

He snorted again, and his lips quirked up in a tiny smile. "You said it. Not me."

She let go of his hand as she debated how much to share with him. He couldn't truly understand her choices unless he knew what she was dealing with. But she couldn't bring herself to tell him. Not yet, anyway.

The only way to convince a skeptic was with proof. For that she needed a spirit who would talk to her and who knew things that would convince Garrett she was really speaking to a ghost.

As far as she could tell, he didn't have any spirits haunting him. And Rachel didn't have connections on the other side anymore. Not since she'd started to pretend her powers had vanished and that she was so hapless no spirit would turn to her for help. Not since she started hanging poppets in her windows and spraying everything with saltwater.

"The truth is I don't really know who I am."

The words slipped out before she could think them through. But they were honest words—ones she had longed to share with someone. With him.

"My parents didn't shelter me. They *sculpted* me. To be the perfect daughter. The perfect accessory to my father's political career and my mother's social aspirations."

She had never really let herself think about it before, let alone talk about it. Garrett didn't prompt her to go on, but let her take her time to formulate her thoughts.

"I tried to live up to what they wanted. Live down to it, really. My mother always told me not to sound too smart. She didn't want me offending people or scaring away suitors. 'A proper lady is neither smart nor...'" Rachel stopped herself from finishing her mother's standard statement—*nor psychic.*

Garrett took in a quick breath as if he was about to say something, but stopped, then let it out slowly. Rachel shook her head, laughing to try to cover her near mistake.

"Anyway, you know how boring those social events can be. I was always relieved when you were there. At least I would have someone to talk to without...pretending."

"You never have to pretend with me," he said.

If only... She took a deep breath as she figured out the best way to share her thoughts without giving away too much.

"I've always been different. Strange, even. I have what I like to call idiosyncrasies. Hanging poppets in the windows and using my spray bottle everywhere to sort of mark my space... The behavior isn't a warning sign that I'm heading for a psychotic break because of what happened to me. It started way before *this*."

She leaned back and straightened her arms a bit, which pulled her sleeves up far enough to reveal her scars. There were still pressure marks over the bands of pink and silver flesh from the stupid tennis outfit.

Garrett's gaze went to her wrists and seemed to get

caught there. His jaws clenched, muscles standing out along his cheeks.

She pulled down her sleeves, breaking the spell her scars had cast over him. His gaze shifted back to hers.

Sitting next to him, staring intently at his face, it was impossible to ignore how beautiful he was, the warmth that spread through her body from his closeness, the way her heart seemed to become as infinite as the sky when he looked at her.

"Right now, I am okay," she said. "Being here with you, I'm okay."

His eyes glistened. The sight nearly broke her, but she forced herself to be strong.

They were together. They were safe.

In that moment, nothing else mattered.

Chapter Five

"How many more of these do you intend to make?"

Garrett mentally counted the windows in his house. "Ten more. That'll make an even sixteen. One for every window."

They were sitting on barstools that lined the counter dividing his kitchen from his living room. Behind them, his couch, recliner, coffee table, and a big-screen TV filled the room. When he cooked for gatherings, his friends would hang out in the living room and they could all still talk. Well, if he ducked down lower than the cabinets that hung above the counter.

"You don't have to hang them in all the rooms. Mine would be enough."

"They make you feel better. We're putting them up everywhere."

He made another stitch in the tiny doll, pulling the thread tight, but not too tight. He tied it off, then started carefully turning the doll inside-out with the seams tucked away inside like she had taught him.

Rachel set to work cutting out more figures from some plain white cloth she'd brought along.

"Only in the windows," she said.

Poppets. He didn't know why the featureless things made her feel better. She called it an idiosyncrasy. He would call it a neurosis. There was more to it—he was sure. Until she was ready to tell him everything, he would play along.

Helping her make the dolls was an excuse to stay near her. He could observe her to make sure she wasn't having the relapse he feared. And he had to admit he just plain enjoyed being with her. She was tense, but he kept seeing glimmers of the way she had been when their relationship was just starting.

"Whatever you need." He lifted his latest poppet and wiggled it like it was dancing. "These things are kind of cute." Halfway between cute and creepy.

"Yours look better than mine ever did."

He grinned and said, "Never thought I'd use my medical school training like this."

She laughed—an honest-to-God laugh—and his stomach did a somersault.

"I'm sure the poppets are honored to have such a skilled physician working on them."

He snorted as he added the finished doll to the pile, then picked up another set of cloth and started to sew. For a while, they worked in silence, settling into an easy companionship.

"Why did you quit, anyway?"

Her question came out of the blue, and he almost answered it honestly.

"Because I wanted more of this—more time with you—and working crazy hours at the ER wasn't going to get me there."

Instead, he said, "Too stressful."

"Sure." She arched an eyebrow and cast him a wry grin. "It seems a waste to retire so early. Can't you start up a private practice or something?"

"I'd have to do another residency. I'm not up for that. Anyway, I keep myself busy."

"*We* keep you busy."

"I don't mind. It's nice having someone to take care of."

She looked up at him, her face curiously unreadable. "Who takes care of you?"

"I'm a big boy. I can take care of myself."

"Size is not commensurate with competence. Look at Elsa. She's tiny, but when she's around, she's in charge of us all."

"I can't argue with that."

After a moment, he laughed and shook his head.

"What's so funny?"

"You. 'Size is not commensurate...' Throwing around three-dollar words like that, you'll never get anyone to think you're a ditz again."

She smiled and said, "I never felt like I had to be a ditz

around you. Not when we were alone."

"I noticed." He set the latest finished doll on the stack, then started another. "Why is that?"

"Because when it was just you and me, I felt safe."

The floor seemed to drop out from under him. He wished he was sitting on something more substantial than a barstool.

He made her feel safe. Warmth spread through his chest.

He wanted her to feel safe with him. He wanted her to always feel safe.

"I kept trying to get them to let me sign papers that would enable you to make medical decisions for me, but they said you couldn't because you had privileges at the hospital. How does that make any sense?"

He remembered her doctors asking him about it—and the nature of their relationship.

"Friends," he'd kept saying. "We're just friends."

But he still wouldn't consult on her case.

"It's a good rule. It protects everybody from doctors working cases…" He stopped himself from saying *they're too close to*. Instead he finished with, "…they shouldn't."

She gave him a half-shrug, lifting one shoulder. It wasn't the flirty gesture he'd seen dozens of times before. More like she was tuning him out.

"It made sense to me. I mean, you're a doctor."

The warm feeling in his chest chilled.

He shouldn't push it. He knew he shouldn't. But he was afraid she was reeling him in again. Telling him she felt safe with him, sharing that, then turning around and focusing on his medical knowledge…

It reminded him of when she had lived there before. One minute she'd say things that seemed to bare her soul, the next she'd laugh coquettishly and joke that she could never get involved with a doctor because it would make her mother too happy. She'd shut down or flit away.

The worst was when they'd be sharing a moment, and she'd abruptly start telling him about the type of woman he should find and settle down with. He already knew the exact woman he wanted to settle down with. He was looking at her.

"Is that it, then? It was just because of the credentials?"

"Of course not."

She glanced up at him, but whatever she saw on his face must have been too much for her. She quickly turned back to her poppets, lips pressed tightly together.

"I'm sorry. I shouldn't have—"

She cut him off. "No. You have every right to…feel that way. I get it. I'm flaky and confusing." Almost under-her-breath she added, "Especially for you."

She lifted one of the dolls and started to gently fill it with cotton balls she had found in his bathroom and fluffed up to act as stuffing.

"A lot of things are going to need to change," she said.

"I realize that now. I don't think I can play the ditz anymore. It's outlived its usefulness."

"You ever going to tell me what the *use* was in the first place?"

She set down the doll and gave him a calm, level look. "I hope not."

"Why?"

"For a start, you wouldn't believe me." She picked up another poppet and stuffed it like the first.

Garrett smiled. He couldn't help it. He wouldn't believe her? That was rich. He shook his head and laughed.

"What?" she asked.

He tried to stop laughing. It was hard.

"I think I might surprise you there." He grinned. For once it seemed that he had confused her. "I'm very open-minded about all sorts of stuff."

"Really?" She arched an eyebrow. "How about Bigfoot?"

"Never met the fellow. Can't say one way or the other."

She snorted and rolled her eyes, turning back to her work. "See? I knew you wouldn't believe me."

"I didn't say I didn't believe. I just said I never met the guy. There could be a whole troop of Bigfoots running around in the Everglades for all I know."

"Don't make fun of me."

She glared at him for a moment, genuine hurt playing across her features.

Well, damn. She'd given him his first clue about what the hell was going on. And it was...Bigfoot?

"I'm not making fun," he said. He was sure to keep his tone serious. "As soon as you're both up for it, we're having Elsa over. Once you've had a chance to catch up, you tell me what I won't believe."

"Elsa? Come on. If there's one person in our group more grounded in reality than you, it's her." Rachel kept filling the little dolls, stacking them up like cordwood.

"My definition of reality expanded a while back. I get that there are things going on that we don't understand yet. That science can't explain."

"I'm not talking about things like the placebo effect."

"Neither am I."

Garrett's best friend had shifted his world view years ago. Finn's demonstration had knocked Garrett on his ass, as did the follow-up experiments Finn let Garrett run. It had taken a few weeks for the world to feel real again. Garrett was absolutely convinced that the world was full of mysteries well beyond what science could handle at the moment.

He was grateful Finn had shared his abilities with Garrett for many reasons, not the least of which being that Garrett hadn't flipped out when Elsa explained her own powers.

Time travel.

Once his mind wrapped around that whopper,

everything else seemed tame in comparison.

Maybe Rachel had something going on too. Garrett couldn't guess what, except that it might deal with the voices she kept screaming about during her psychotic break—if that was actually what it was.

He looked at the poppets she had finished, a chill sweeping over his skin. They reminded him of bodies in the morgue. White sheets and…

Ghosts.

That was it. Had to be. He almost stabbed himself in the thumb as things started to fall into place.

Rachel had been fine in the ambulance, coherent and taking everything remarkably well. Once she was settled in her hospital room, she went out of her mind with fear.

She didn't mention what had happened to her, didn't ask about her friends. She just kept screaming about voices, covering her ears and thrashing her head. She begged Garrett to make the voices stop, to sedate her. Eventually, her doctors had to knock her out just to treat her injuries.

At the time, he'd thought the trauma of what happened to her had fractured her psyche. He'd never considered that the voices she was talking about were real.

Relief flooded through him, washing away the worry he'd been carrying since that night. Garrett didn't know how it worked, but he was sure he was right.

People died in hospitals every day. If spirits tended to

linger, there had to be an abundance of them walking those halls. And if Rachel could hear them, that would have to be its own kind of hell.

He reached for her hand, brushing his thumb over the backs of her fingers. "You can tell me anything. You know that, don't you?"

"I know." She smiled at him faintly, then pulled her hand away.

Maybe she wasn't ready to talk about it. He didn't want to push, so he went back to his little pile of poppets, taking the matter quite a bit more seriously.

When they were finished, she had a stack of sixteen little dolls with loops of thick white string attached to their heads for hanging them in the windows. They still had openings in their sides where Rachel had added the cotton stuffing.

"Is it time to close them up?"

Rachel shook her head and said, "They aren't ready yet."

They looked exactly like the one that had been hanging in her bedroom window. Garrett set down his needle and thread.

"Okay. What's next?"

"Do you still do a lot of cooking?"

"Yeah." He'd picked up the hobby after he retired, imagining family dinners and special gatherings with friends—like the dinner parties she had helped him host.

She let out a little breath and smiled. "Great."

She slipped from her barstool and walked around the counter where they were working. She opened some cabinets and started pulling down spices.

"If you're hungry, I can make us something."

"I want to get this done first." She took out a bowl, then started sprinkling spices into it.

"Anything I can do to help?"

She paused, her gaze sliding to the nearly empty spray bottle she insisted on carrying around with her. He hadn't seen her use it since the car.

If she understood that he was open to helping her, she might decide to tell him about what she could do. And he wanted her to tell him. He didn't want to trick it out of her or confront her with it. He wanted her to want him to know—to trust him enough to share it with him.

Garrett slid from his stool and walked around the counter. He reached into the open spice cabinet and pulled out a big cylinder of iodized salt, then picked up the spray bottle.

"What's the ratio?"

She blinked a few times, like her brain was slipping gears trying to process his words. "What?"

"The ratio. Salt to water." He held her gaze, noted how her lips thinned, her throat worked to swallow. He had her thinking, and that was perfect.

"About an inch of salt at the bottom, then fill it with

cold water and shake it."

"Anything else go into the mix?" He had never seen such intensity in her eyes.

She stared at him for a long time before saying, "No."

"Should I dump it and rinse it first?"

"Yes, please." She turned back to her concoction, getting out a fork and stirring everything together.

After he rinsed out the bottle and added salt and water, Garrett showed it to her before shaking it. If this thing was as important as she acted, he wanted to get it right.

"This good?"

"Yes. Thanks."

He sealed it and shook it up, then walked back to his seat. He set the bottled saltwater on the counter within arm's reach.

Wasn't there some TV show where the people were always using salt against ghosts? But they used the actual crystals, not saltwater. There had to be some connection, though.

When she was finished, she put everything away except her bowl of spices, then joined him. She looked pensive.

"You're not going to ask?"

Garrett shook his head. "You'll tell me when you're ready. I can wait."

Her lips pulled into a frown and she fixed her gaze on the poppets. She picked up a pinch of the spice mix and put it inside the doll.

"You can seal it now. Just don't let anything spill out."

"We doctors generally don't like letting things spill out when we're closing up a patient." He was trying to lighten the mood, but all she gave him was a tiny smile.

He turned his attention to finishing the poppet, pinching the cloth together so the seams were inside. He kept his stiches as tiny and unnoticeable as possible while sealing it up.

Rachel handed him doll after doll until her stack was empty and his was full. She gathered them all up, then held them close to her chest, closing her eyes and whispering something. It was almost like she was praying over them.

She probably was.

"They're ready."

"Is that it? We just hang them up?"

That intense stare was boring through him again. "No. We have to do it in a special order. We'll start on one side of the house and work our way to the other. And there's a little more to it than hanging them in the windows."

"Lead on."

He smiled at her, but the lines of tension around her eyes only intensified. Her stare turned into a glare.

He cleared his throat and gestured toward the dolls. "I can hang them up for you."

She handed them over, then bent down to dig around in her backpack. When she stood, a small bronze cup suspended on three small chains dangled from her hand. Openings in decorative patterns covered the lid and sides.

"I've seen one of those before," he said.

"Priests sometimes use them during ceremonies. It's called a censer." She set it on the counter, then opened the lid.

She bent to her backpack again and this time came up with a box of matches and some cones of incense. She put the incense in the censer, then lit it. She extinguished the match and set it in the bowl that had held the poppets' spice mix.

Smoke from the incense pricked at Garrett's nose, the scent strong and not entirely pleasant. He was a fresh-air kind of guy. But if this would help Rachel, he didn't care how it smelled. She grabbed the spray bottle, then handed him a box of thumbtacks.

"We're going to have to put a hole above each window. I hope you don't mind."

Her voice was thin and low. She wasn't looking at him at all anymore.

He wanted to make a joke about her being the one who would have to fix it the next time he asked for help repainting, but thought better of it.

All he said was, "Not a problem."

They started in her room at the far end of the house. Rachel had him hang the poppet in the window, then she sprayed the window with saltwater.

She swung the censer through the whole room, in every corner—even in the closet. Especially in the closet. Then she sprayed the doors with saltwater as well.

"This one is done." Her voice was tight and she was still frowning.

Garrett kept his mouth shut and nodded. Better cut his losses and not dig himself in deeper. They treated the whole house in the same way, moving from one end to the other as if they were herding something, pushing it away. His confidence in his theory grew.

After reaching the far end of the house, they doubled back to the front door, which Rachel sprayed down liberally. She turned to the last space in his house and paused. This time, it only took Garrett a second to remember why.

The garage.

"You don't have to," he said. "I've seen enough. I can do it."

"No." She shook her head. "It has to be me."

Chapter Six

Rachel saturated the door that led to the garage with saltwater before opening it. Her heart was pounding in her chest. For a few moments, she stood in the doorway looking inside. The space was empty except for a washer and dryer with a counter built into the wall next to them.

When she'd worked on Garrett's house, he'd told her that he loved natural light and wanted it everywhere. She never thought it would be such a boon when she changed out his garage door for one that had windows in it.

This was the antithesis of Michael's garage. His had been packed with workbenches and shelves lined with mason jars full of bizarre and disturbing things—the space a labyrinth of the macabre.

In Michael's garage, her shackles had been mounted on the wall opposite the door. Even in the dim light filtering in from the windows in Garrett's garage door, she could see the beautifully blank wall right in front of her. She let out a sigh and stepped down into the room.

"Do we need to hang a poppet over the garage door?"

Rachel started at Garrett's voice, not quite as at-ease as she thought. She tried to laugh it off, one hand to her chest, a forced smile on her face.

"Sorry. I'm a little jumpy."

"You never need to apologize to me. And you don't need to do that either." He briefly bobbed his head up in a gesture he usually saved for greetings.

"Do what?"

"Pretend you're okay when you're not."

She stammered out, "I…I know. It's just habit."

"It's okay. I'll keep reminding you as often as you need me to."

He eyed the windows set in the garage door, then past her shoulder to the door that led to the side yard. It also had a window. The glass in all of them was lightly frosted, obscuring the view from both sides.

"Only one left." Garrett held up the last poppet. "Where do we put this guy?"

"I'm not sure what to do with this space."

"Why don't you explain to me what we're doing? Maybe I can help."

Sure. If she tried to explain, he'd *help* her by taking her straight back to the hospital. No matter what he said about being open-minded or believing things that might surprise her, she doubted he would accept that ghosts were real and she could communicate with them.

Still, she wanted to give him something. He deserved that much.

"They're sort of good luck charms. I hang them in the

windows to keep bad luck away."

"There are four windows in the garage door. Five counting the door to the yard. Should we make more poppets?"

"I don't think so. This space is challenging."

"Does the garage door really count as a window? The front door has glass in it, but you just sprayed it down. No poppet."

"That's a good point."

A really good point. Could he be grasping more of what was going on than she thought? She stared at him for a few moments trying to assess his expression, his body language, anything that might give her a clue. All she saw was a man desperate to help her.

She should have been more distant when they were working on his house together—refused the job outright. But she couldn't stay away. Like now. She wanted to be with him—no, *near* him. She could never be *with* him.

He deserved a normal partner, someone he didn't have to rescue constantly. Someone who didn't have trouble tracking a conversation with the living because of whispers from the dead.

She played into Garrett's weaknesses—his compulsion to help people. She knew it. And she still couldn't stop herself from calling. Because it meant another few hours —even minutes—in his company.

"The bottle's running low. Should we go make some

more?"

"I need to stay here with the incense."

The hair on her arms lifted at the thought of being alone in the garage. She pushed aside the terror that was leaping up from the pit of her stomach trying to find purchase on her thundering heart.

Of course he picked up on it.

"Can't I do that? Stay in your place?"

If only. But this was her ritual and she had to be the one to finish it. Backtracking into the house would weaken the work she had already done. She smiled at him and shook her head, then handed him the spray bottle.

"Just be quick, okay?"

"Can I at least turn on the light?"

"I prefer the sunlight."

He nodded, his mouth a tight line underscoring the tension in his face. She would make this up to him. She would find a way.

He handed her the last poppet, then ran from the room. Full-on ran. He would be back as fast as humanly possible.

Human speed couldn't match inhuman.

Seconds after he left, the light in the room dimmed. The afternoon's thunderstorm was rolling in early.

She wanted to walk to the garage windows and look at the clouds, but she couldn't will herself to move. She felt rooted in place, fear spreading through her muscles in an icy grip that paralyzed her.

Darker. Darker. The light in the garage faded, shadows deepening, lengthening, reaching for her.

She clutched the poppet in her hand, focused on the scent of the incense. The house was already cleansed and warded. All she had to do was make it across the threshold from the garage to the hallway and she would be safe.

She was already safe. She hadn't heard so much as a whisper.

"Rachel."

Closing her eyes, her entire body began to shake. Had they found her already? Even out here?

"Rachel?" A warm hand gripped her shoulder. She screamed.

"Rachel! It's me!"

There was no mistaking Garrett's silhouette against the light from the hallway. Why hadn't she let him turn on the light?

Because the artificial light reminded her of Michael's garage. His had no windows, no sunlight, only the cold, controlled buzzing of the fluorescents overhead. And that was when he decided he would spare her from utter darkness.

She shook her head, forcing the fear away. The adrenaline flooding her system was making her shake.

"Sorry, I guess I'm just…" *Hearing things.*

She should be able to say it without the risk of landing in a psych ward. But she couldn't. Because she wouldn't tell him the truth.

"I wish you'd stop apologizing to me. To anyone."

"Old habits."

"Yeah, well it's high time to make some new ones. Like instead of carrying around one spray bottle, let's make it two."

She laughed—a sound that bubbled up like the last breath when being held underwater. Her chest was too tight. The room was spinning.

"Come on." He handed her the full bottle. "Let's finish this and get out of here."

She nodded, focusing all her attention on that task.

Half the bottle was empty by the time she finished with the doors in the garage. She set the poppet on the counter next to the washer and dryer, positioned as if it was watching over the space, and set an intention to match.

It would have to do.

When they were back inside, Garrett shut the door behind them and locked it. His front door was a few feet away, connected to the same foyer. He checked that it was locked as well.

"I'm not worried about burglars or anything like that," Rachel said.

"Yeah, well you make yourself feel better in your way and I'll do it in mine." He grinned.

Garrett was being too supportive. Even for him. He wasn't asking questions about her odd behavior. The way he was acting, it was almost as if he understood what was going on.

Either that or he was humoring her for long enough to call in reinforcements. One way or another, she had to know.

"We need to talk," Rachel said.

"We need to eat."

He led her back to the kitchen. She set down her spray bottle on the counter and took out a trivet to place under the censer. The thick scent of the incense surrounded them.

Her body had gone numb while standing in the dark garage, but she knew she must be hungry. She wasn't sure she could keep anything down though.

"I'd just like some water."

Thunder clapped nearby and they both jumped. The sound of rain pelting the roof quickly followed.

"That was weird timing," he said. "Have any other wishes you want granted?"

She spoke before she could think better of it. "I want this all to have been a bad dream. I want to be normal."

"I'm with you on the first one a hundred percent. But I can't back the second."

"Why?"

"I want you just as you are."

Her mouth fell open at his honesty. She could read it a couple of ways, but she knew how he meant it. He accepted her, cared for her, as she was.

But he didn't know everything.

Maybe telling him would help. Maybe it would push him away.

He headed for the refrigerator. "I hope turkey sandwiches are okay. As I recall, you really like them."

"Garrett." She waited to speak till he was crouched in front of the fridge, the door blocking her view of him. Somehow, that made it easier.

"Yeah?"

"I'm clairsentient."

"Clair-what-now?"

"Clairsentient. It means I can perceive things using Extra Sensory Perception. ESP."

He kept rattling around in the fridge. "What kind of things?"

"Ghosts. Voices of the dead."

He stood up, mustard and mayo tucked under one arm and bags of turkey and cheese in his hand. "I think I saw that movie." His face was deadpan, but he had to be joking.

"I'm serious."

"So am I. I'm trying to get a common frame of reference. I want to understand what you're telling me."

She hadn't expected that. He was being rational about it. Hearing her out. Part of her was excited at the opportunity to explain herself. Maybe, just maybe, he would believe her.

But a bigger part was terrified. She wasn't sure which she dreaded more—him thinking she was crazy or... believing her. This was supposed to push him away, not open possibilities.

"I only hear them. I don't see them. Well, except in reflections."

"That's why you had me cover the mirror in your bathroom."

"Yes."

He nodded. "Okay. After lunch, we cover the rest of them. There aren't many, so it won't take long. And let's cut up a sheet or two instead of using towels. They'll stay put better."

"Are you listening to me? Ghosts are real. They're around us constantly. And I can hear them."

"Yeah. I get it." He set down the food on the counter, then closed the door to the fridge. He kept working on lunch as he talked. "And that's why you aren't taking your meds. There's no point in taking anti-hallucinogens when you aren't hallucinating."

It couldn't be this easy. He must be trying to keep her calm. As soon as he had a moment to himself, he would call someone to come get her or figure out a way to take her to the hospital himself. In the meantime, he was casually making them sandwiches.

"I'm not going back."

She bit out each word. She would run into the swamp

before going back to the hospital. At least there all she'd have to face were alligators. And snakes. And bugs.

Okay, maybe she wouldn't run into the swamp, but she sure as hell wasn't—

"I know."

He spoke so softly her furious thoughts almost drowned him out. His voice was tired, gentle, resigned. If he had said it any other way, she probably wouldn't have registered him speaking. But there was a power to his quiet.

"How can you know? How can you believe me?"

He handed her the sandwich. "First we eat. Then we talk."

She had seen that look before. He wasn't going to budge.

She took a tentative bite. Her stomach didn't balk at food as she had feared, and she was hungrier than she thought. She still glared at him the whole time she ate. He just smiled.

When she finished inhaling her sandwich, he handed her his own, then made another for himself and brought her some iced tea. How could he be so nonchalant about this?

When they were done she said, "You really believe me?"

He aimed a dazzling smile at her. "Being able to hear ghosts isn't the most outlandish thing I've heard *this month*. Your ability is kind of mainstream in comparison."

Garrett knew other psychics? She had trouble believing it, then realized the hypocrisy of her thought. Adrenaline fired through her system, this time tinged with excitement instead of fear.

He shook his head and said, "I'm starting to think you can't throw a rock in this town without hitting a psychic."

"Only the ones without precognition."

He laughed. It wasn't much of one, but it made her heart skip in her chest—which was a bit hard to notice, since it was already flipping out from the joy of knowing she wasn't the only one.

Well, aside from Lillian. And Lillian didn't count.

"Let's move to the couch," he said. "This might take a while."

He picked up the spray bottle, then pointed at the censer. "Do we need to bring that?"

"No, it just needs to burn itself out."

She followed him into the living room, then sat on the couch and curled her legs up under her. Instead of sitting in his recliner, Garrett joined her. He pulled out his phone and set it on the coffee table.

"How many do you know?"

She wanted names, phone numbers, ability descriptions. But if they were anything like her they would want their privacy. Maybe she would have Garrett give them her contact information and pray they were as curious about her as she was about them.

"With you, it's an even four."

"Seriously?" She leaned forward, rising up on her knees.

He laughed again. "Don't get too excited. There's only one that I know for sure wants to talk to you about it. The others... Well, their secrets aren't mine to share."

"Wait, why would they want to talk to me?" Unless they already knew about her. "Do they have precognition?"

"Not exactly." He picked up his phone, then pulled up a contact. "You need to talk to Elsa."

Icy dread threaded through Rachel. Her veins crackled with it. She hadn't spoken to Elsa or Dante since they'd been hurt.

"Elsa is busy taking care of Dante. And I don't want to wake them if they're sleeping."

"It's the middle of the day. They'll be awake. Plus, Dante is doing great. She'll be glad to hear from you, trust me."

Rachel shook her head, shrinking back on the couch. Her vision blurred with tears. "No. No, she won't."

"Why not?"

"Because I'm the reason that she and Dante were hurt. They were trying to save me. I'm the one who was stupid enough to get involved with Michael."

"Stop. Stop right there. I won't let anyone speak against

my friends like that. Even if it's them doing the talking. And if Elsa was here, you know she'd say the same."

He took Rachel's hand in his, letting his strength and warmth seep into her. "It isn't your fault that this happened. Michael fooled everyone. Even Jazz was clueless, and you know how good she is at reading people."

"He didn't fool Elsa. She knew something was wrong. She tried to warn me, but I wouldn't listen." A flash of insight hit Rachel. "It's not... It can't be Elsa, can it? Can she see the future?"

Garrett sighed, holding the phone out to Rachel. "You need to talk to her. I'll stay or go. Whatever you need."

"Stay. Please. I don't want to be alone."

"All right."

For this call, she wanted all the support she could get. As if he sensed her need, he draped his arm over her shoulder. She nestled against him before taking the phone.

Elsa's number was already displayed. Rachel took a deep breath and made the call.

Chapter Seven

This was a level of Hell. Pain and pleasure tore at Garrett's heart as Rachel snuggled next to him on the couch.

He'd dreamt of holding her like this. The circumstances were vastly different in his imagination.

Rachel put the phone on speaker and held it in front of them so he could share in the call. He felt a tremor run through her and pulled her closer.

"Garrett! How are you?" Elsa's voice was lighter than ever. He'd never seen or heard her as happy since she and Dante became a couple.

Rachel must have heard it too. She seemed stunned, staring at the phone with her mouth slightly open.

"Doing good. I'm here with Rachel."

"Rachel? Hi! How are you?"

"I'm…good, thanks. Thanks for asking." Rachel wiped her eyes and sniffed, then beamed at the phone. "I'm glad you guys are okay."

A peal of giggles drowned out the end of Rachel's sentence. She looked at Garrett, her eyes wide. She must feel like she'd slipped into *The Twilight Zone*. He was right there with her.

Normally, Elsa was the reserved one and Rachel was ebullient. Things changed.

"Stop that!" Elsa said. "You're supposed to be resting."

"Dante's with you?" Garrett asked.

"Yes. I'll put the phone on speaker."

"Only if Winston isn't around. This conversation is going to be a little bit sensitive."

There was a slight pause, as if Elsa was picking up on the tension on the other side of the line. Her voice was more subdued when she spoke again. "He's in his room listening to audiobooks with the door closed. You're on speaker now."

Elsa and Dante were staying in their loft in the city to be close to Dante's doctors. Garrett missed having them next door, but agreed with their logic.

It did make having private conversations like this one a bit more problematic, since Elsa's butler, Winston, was staying with them in the much smaller space. They had even moved their cat, Leonardo.

"Hey, Dante," Garrett said. "How are you feeling?"

"Marvelous. Modern medicine's modalities are mesmerizing," Dante said.

"He's been doing this for the last half-hour. Alliteration was not listed in the side effects of his medicines. Do you have anything to make him stop?"

There was laughter in Elsa's tone and Garrett chuckled.

"I think this conversation will put a stop to it," Garrett said.

Dante laughed. "Quell it quickly to quash any quarreling."

"Quiet," Elsa said.

Garrett waited for them to stop laughing before asking his question. "Dante, when were you born?"

"Quite a question."

"Dante!"

Dante's tone became a bit more serious. "The second of April."

"The year," Garrett said. "Rachel needs to know."

There was a long pause. When Dante spoke again, his voice was low and the playfulness was gone.

"Eighteen hundred and forty-five."

Rachel turned to Garrett, her eyebrows knitted. He nodded in what he hoped was a reassuring manner, then said, "And how did you get here?"

Elsa jumped in. "I brought him."

"How?" Rachel's voice was weak.

"According to Jazz, I used astral projection to travel back in time and brought him forward 'through sheer stubborn willpower'. I haven't had a chance to research it myself, but it's Jazz, so she's probably right."

Rachel was shaking her head, as if she couldn't believe what they were saying. "Wait, you didn't know what you were doing when it was happening?"

"I knew what I was doing, just not what it was called. I've always thought of it as 'traveling'. It's something I've been able to do since I was a child. I never researched it because I was afraid to be seen with books about paranormal phenomenon."

When Garrett had been helping Dante get settled in the loft a few weeks back, Elsa had explained her powers and that she had saved Dante's life by pulling him through time to the present.

Jazz had been there and had already been clued in. She seemed to know more about Elsa's powers than anybody. It had confused Garrett initially, but made more sense now that he knew Elsa hadn't researched her own abilities— which still struck him as odd. He hadn't said anything at the time because he had been too busy pretending to be surprised.

Finn had already been looking into Dante at Garrett's request, and straight-out told Garrett that Dante was from the 1800s and Elsa had teleported him to the present. That plus the pre-surgery blood work that showed Dante had never received any inoculations…

Yeah, Garrett had come to terms with the idea of time travel before Elsa had said a word.

Being friends with Finn had given Garrett plenty of practice wrapping his mind around serious weirdness. He wondered how Rachel would hold up to learning about what Elsa could do. At least she had personal experience with the paranormal to draw on. Garrett hoped it would help.

"Garrett, you know I trust you," Elsa said, "but some context would be nice."

Her trusting him—or anyone, really—was another amazing change. She hadn't hesitated to answer his questions. She had been the biggest control freak he'd ever met until she became involved with Dante. She took charge of every situation, never trusting anyone else to do anything for her.

Garrett still wasn't sure how Dante had helped Elsa let go and start enjoying her life. Garrett sure as hell appreciated it though. They all did.

Rachel had the opposite problem. She seemed to be enjoying life, flitting through it blithely, but deep down she had been suffering the whole time. She used her poppets to control her environment, but she was trapped in the space she created.

Garrett didn't know what to do about that. Yet. But he could help her now—take the pressure off so she wouldn't have to share her own ability until she was ready.

"It was time," he said. "That's all."

"Is that…" Rachel's voice crackled. It was low and raw. She cleared her throat and said, "Is that how you knew? About Michael?"

"Yes, my powers helped me find you."

"No, I mean… Is that how you knew he was

dangerous? You tried to warn me."

Rachel covered her mouth, her eyes clinched shut as tears streamed down her face. She was trying not to let Elsa and Dante hear the pain—shielding them from it.

Garrett wasn't so lucky. The cracks along his heart where it had broken time and again with Rachel started to bleed as she shuddered and silently cried in his arms. He pressed a kiss against the top of her head and helped hold the phone still. From the way her hand was shaking, she looked ready to drop it.

"No." Elsa's voice became cold. "My parents hurt each other. Sometimes they hurt me too. I can recognize the potential for violence."

Rachel's hand moved to her chest as her breathing became rapid. "What?" She choked back a sob. "I'm so sorry. I didn't know."

It was news to Garrett too. His grip on the phone tightened.

"Nobody did. And it almost cost me Dante. It almost cost you your life."

"I don't understand," Rachel said.

"If I had explained how I knew about him, maybe you would have listened. I'm so sorry, Rachel." Elsa sniffed.

This was not what Garrett had planned. He wanted Rachel to understand that he believed her, not to have both her and Elsa upset and crying.

Garrett pulled Rachel closer, gently running his hand up

and down her arm. He hoped Dante was comforting Elsa too.

"Please don't be sorry," Rachel said. "It's my fault, not yours. You were only hurt because you were trying to help me."

Dante spoke up, sounding much more focused and coherent. "The only involved party who bears responsibility is Michael."

Next time Garrett saw Dante, a manly hug was in order. Everybody was blaming themselves for what happened. Even Garrett, every time he thought of that damned voicemail from Finn. It needed to stop.

"I think we can all agree on that," Garrett said. "Can we also agree that we're done with the apologizing?"

"Absolutely," Elsa said.

Rachel nodded. "Yes. Of course."

"I can't believe you've been blaming yourself this whole time," Elsa said. "I hope we never go through anything like this again, but no matter what you're dealing with, if something's bothering you and we can fix it just by talking, please don't wait to call me."

Garrett suppressed a little laugh. That was the Elsa they all knew and loved. Telling people what to do. Order was restored to his universe.

"I won't. In fact that's why we called." Rachel looked at Garrett and smiled, eyes bright with tears.

His heart seemed to lurch toward her. He wanted to pull

her closer and kiss away her tears. She turned back to the phone before he could do anything so stupid.

"I have a gift too," Rachel said.

"A gift?" Elsa asked.

"A psychic ability."

"You're kidding!"

Rachel laughed. "I told Garrett about it, and when he believed me right away I thought he was humoring me."

"Yeah, he does that." An edge of playfulness had returned to Elsa's tone. "Can you travel too?"

"No, mine's more…mainstream."

She grinned at Garrett. He smiled back, trying to pretend that everything was okay, that his heart wasn't constricting in his chest, suffocating from having her so close and knowing he couldn't do a damn thing about it.

"I hear ghosts," Rachel said.

"Ghosts are real?"

"Yeah."

"And they talk to you?"

"It's more like they talk near me. I've been trying not to let them know I can hear them, but I think the cat's out of the bag. It tends to make them clingy when they find out. The whole thing is not as fun as it sounds."

"I can imagine. Can you turn it off?"

"Not really. But there are things I can do to keep them away."

"That sounds awful." There was a short pause, then

Elsa asked, "It isn't Michael, is it? You're not hearing him?"

Garrett's heart dropped through his stomach. He pulled Rachel closer against his chest, looking all around.

How the hell had he not thought of that immediately when Rachel told him about what she could do? His relief that she was confiding in him—that he finally had an explanation for her behavior—had clouded his mind.

"No, it's not Michael. His body was cremated—I checked. There have to be earthly remains for a spirit to linger."

Garrett lowered his head to Rachel's shoulder for a moment, willing his heart to slow down. She briefly leaned her head against his.

"That is still a very scary thought," Elsa said. "Being surrounded by people you can't see."

She wasn't kidding. Garrett would make a dozen more of those poppet things. Hell, he'd make Rachel a dress out of them.

"What can we do to help?" Elsa asked.

Garrett listened with keen interest.

Rachel wiped her face dry with the back of her hand and seemed to melt into Garrett's chest, her tension flowing out of her. He hoped she couldn't feel his heart beating, fast and urgent.

"Just knowing you believe me—knowing I'm not the only one with a gift—really helps. Thank you."

"Of course. I still wish there was more we could do."

"Don't worry about me."

"I do not wish to add to an already tense subject," Dante said, "but I must inquire... Is Elsa safe when she travels? If there are spirits about that she might encounter while outside her physical form, some of whom may be dangerous, I would rather we know and address the situation."

"I've never heard of people running into ghosts during astral journeys," Rachel said. "Maybe they're on a different wavelength or something. The bigger issue is protecting your body while you're journeying."

"I always make sure I'm in a locked room when I travel and I'm the only one with a key."

Rachel's brow knit together and she cast a glance at Garrett that was not reassuring. "I meant protect your body from possession. Florida is filled with spirits. An unoccupied body is easy pickings for any coherent ghost. They just step right in. If a spirit's personality is strong enough, they can even possess occupied bodies."

Garrett felt a chill shoot down his spine. How many times had Elsa left her body unattended, flirting with disaster without even realizing it?

"That is a most alarming bit of information," Dante said. "What can we do to protect her?"

"First you stay calm," Garrett said. "Stress won't help with your recovery."

"She just needs to refrain from traveling," Rachel said. "Until I can make a talisman to protect her."

"You know how to do that?" Elsa asked.

"I have a pretty good idea. I'll research it more to be sure. I'll need materials, but I'll take care of it. Don't worry. You just focus on taking care of Dante."

"Thank you," Dante said.

"Yes, thanks. And thank you for telling us, Rachel. I know how hard it can be to open up about these things. But secrets between friends aren't a good idea. Not like these."

Rachel nodded. "I'm starting to see that. You guys take care, okay?"

"You too."

Rachel disconnected the call and immediately dialed another number. She didn't put the phone on speaker, but lifted it to her ear instead.

"Hey, Jazz. Yeah. Yeah, I know. Yes, I should have called sooner. I've been distracted."

Rachel rose to her knees, which took her out of Garrett's arms. He tried to hide his disappointment. She was focused enough on her call that she didn't seem to notice.

"I need your help. I'm going to text you a list of things I need from Bookwyrm. Yes, the hippie bookstore you like. Yes, I've been there. Well, I never mentioned it because... Look, I'll explain when you bring me the things on the list." She rolled her eyes at Garrett and shook her head. "Can you bring it to Garrett's house this afternoon? I'm staying with him for a while. Yes, I left my mother's house."

Garrett could hear Jazz's enthusiastic response from two feet away. Rachel moved the phone from her ear. She sighed when she started listening to Jazz again.

"I know, I should have done it sooner. I'll explain everything when you get here. Okay. Thanks! Bye."

She disconnected the call, then set the phone on the coffee table. Her lips were pulled into a broad smile.

"Thank you for doing that for me," she said. "For believing me, for letting me stay here, for…everything!"

She threw herself forward, wrapping her arms around his neck. Garrett rested his hands on her back and closed his eyes, letting the feel of her soak in—warmth and joy and the brightest essence he'd ever felt. He took a deep breath, filling his lungs with her scent.

Something shifted in her embrace. For a moment, she softened against him. Her cheek grazed his, her breath tickled the fine hairs on his neck.

Warmth turned to heat and the thought of cradling her face in his hands and kissing her senseless became almost overwhelming. But then she stiffened and pulled away. Again.

It didn't surprise him anymore, but it still hurt like hell.

"I need to get my books," she said. "To research the

talisman for Elsa."

Garrett nodded. "I'll help. Any way I can."

She wouldn't meet his eyes and her cheeks were flushed. There was attraction between them. He knew she felt it too. But there was something else standing between them—something he couldn't see, couldn't touch, couldn't tear apart.

Damned if he knew what it was.

Chapter Eight

The coffee table was covered in open books when the doorbell rang. Rachel didn't jump at the sound. She let out a little sigh, realizing she was more relaxed than she'd been in months.

She felt safe. Safe enough to convince Garrett to take a shower and leave her on her own for a little while.

"Coming!"

She ran to the counter to grab the censer before heading for the door. She had already refilled it and lit fresh incense, knowing Jazz would arrive soon. Now Rachel had the fun of explaining why she needed to smudge Jazz when she came inside.

The windows along the side of the front door let Rachel see Jazz standing on the stoop, holding a bright green bag decorated with a picture of a dragon lying on its back and reading a book. Its tail wound around a crystal ball.

Rachel smiled as she opened the door. "Hi!"

Jazz hesitated before saying, "Hi."

Her dark eyes glittered strangely in the late-afternoon light and her long black hair hung around her shoulders as if she hadn't done more than brush it. She still wore her signature black leather pants, but instead of her usual white V-neck T-shirt, she had on a dark, oversized sweater that practically engulfed her slight frame.

Rachel panicked. Where was the cocky smile and knowing gaze? Aside from a few times when Jazz lost her temper, Rachel had never known Jazz to be genuinely upset.

"What's wrong? Did something happen?"

"Are you kidding me?" Jazz's voice was shrill instead of her normal rich tenor. "Yes, something happened. I haven't seen you since you left the hospital, and you've barely texted or called!"

She stepped over the threshold and swung the door shut, then grabbed Rachel in a crushing hug. Rachel wanted to make a joke to try to lighten the moment, but she couldn't. Jazz's affection was usually lots of light touches and quick hugs. She had never hugged Rachel like this before.

A tight ball of emotion filled Rachel's chest, making it hard to breathe, to think, to do anything but not cry. Careful of the censer, she hugged Jazz back.

"Are you okay?" Jazz asked. "You look better."

"I am better. Getting there, anyway."

"Why does it smell like a temple in here?"

Rachel laughed, finally pulling back from the hug. "That would be from this." She lifted the censer, streamers of smoke following its movements.

Jazz arched an eyebrow and waited patiently for an explanation. Much more normal for her.

"If you don't mind, I need to smudge you."

"You want to cleanse my aura?"

"That's the idea."

Jazz stepped away from Rachel and lifted both arms. Rachel moved the censer around Jazz's body, wafting the smoke closer with one hand. Knowing about auras—the energy field around people's bodies—was one thing. But understanding smudging? Compared to discussing her ability with Garrett, talking to Jazz would be a breeze.

"If you need me to open the bag to cleanse the stuff inside, let me know," she said.

Rachel finished her circuit, holding the censer under the bag for a few moments.

"That should be good enough." She let out a small laugh. "I know we've never discussed paranormal stuff before, but I have to say I'm very grateful you're into it and already know so much."

"I didn't know you were into it at all."

"It's kind of been a necessity for me. Let's sit down and talk." Rachel took the bag from Jazz, then led her into the living room. "Can I get you a drink or anything?"

"I'm good." Jazz walked around the coffee table to sit on the couch, looking over the books Rachel had been using for research. "I'm guessing this isn't a passing interest."

"No."

Jazz looked around the room and noticed the poppet hanging above the stationary side of the sliding glass doors that led to Garrett's back patio. "I see you're already redecorating."

A little surge of jealousy ran through Rachel. How often was Jazz a visitor that she noticed such a small change to Garrett's house so quickly?

Rachel shook it off. Jazz was super-observant. And Garrett could have over whomever he wanted. If he and Jazz hooked up, great. Great for both of them. Rachel wanted them to be happy, even though her heart sort of stuttered at the thought of Garrett with someone else. Anyone else.

"It's a poppet. They keep away spirits." Rachel cleared a small space on the coffee table, then sat on the floor in front of it.

She opened the bag from Bookwyrm and pulled out the supplies she had asked for. Some silver jewelry wire and a wire cutter, a silver chain in a velvet pouch, and a small clear plastic bag that held a few stones.

"Snowflake obsidian, fluorite, and opal, as requested," Jazz said. "I picked out three that looked like you could make them work in a necklace."

"These are perfect, thanks."

Rachel emptied the bag of stones onto her palm, then placed them on the table in front of her. The first, black with speckles of gray that looked like snow, the second a translucent mix of rich purple and blue, and the last a milky white with iridescent colors only visible when viewed from the right angles.

Jazz had managed to pick specimens that would work well together aesthetically. That was good, since Rachel hoped Elsa would wear it constantly as soon as it was hers.

Rachel set to work.

"I spoke with Elsa on the phone today," Rachel said. "She told me what she can do."

"Elsa can do a lot of things."

"So can I."

Rachel paused in her work. She looked up at Jazz, wanting to see the expression on her face when she heard about Rachel's abilities.

"I can hear spirits. Sometimes I see them in reflections. Especially mirrors."

Jazz was silent, her lips slightly pursed and one eyebrow arched on her forehead. She stared at Rachel for what felt like a long time.

"Aren't you going to say something?"

"I'm being inscrutable. It's an Asian thing."

Rachel laughed and Jazz finally smiled.

"Okay," Jazz said. "I need more information."

"You know how I sometimes get distracted? That's usually when I'm hearing spirits having a conversation. Florida is filled with ghosts. That's why I'm making this for Elsa."

"I don't see the connection."

"Elsa travels astrally. She leaves her body behind, ready to be occupied."

Rachel was still a little nervous talking openly about what she could do, but at least Jazz would understand the logistics of it. She had always been openly fascinated by the paranormal.

"Occupied?"

"It's easy for a spirit to enter an empty body."

"You're talking about possession."

Rachel nodded. "Some ghosts can even take over bodies that have souls in them. If they have a strong enough personality, they can overcome the existing consciousness. All they need is an opening or conduit. It would be easy for a spirit to take over Elsa's body while she's traveling."

Jazz's lips thinned. She gestured at the necklace that Rachel was wiring together.

"Are you sure this will protect her?"

"It should. She's been lucky."

"What about a salt circle? Would that help?"

"If she can control when she travels, yes, that would keep spirits away. I'm not sure how the circle would affect her, though. It might trap her inside or keep her from being able to get back. We can run some experiments and see."

"She's not going to want to try anything until Dante is

better. Since she can control her ability by not being around any art, it shouldn't be a problem."

"Art?"

"That's what triggers her ability. I guess it's like you only seeing spirits in reflections."

Rachel nodded. "That will buy us some time."

"What about you? Are these poppets enough to keep spirits from bothering you?"

"That plus spraying saltwater on all the doors and windows. Florida is so humid and there's already salt everywhere from the ocean being close. It doesn't take much extra to ward entryways."

"I'll keep that in mind. What do you do when you leave the house?"

Rachel was quiet for a moment. She wasn't sure how to respond. Elsa's warning about secrets resurfaced in Rachel's mind. The truth, then.

"I don't."

Jazz's eyebrows hiked up her forehead. "You can't stay here forever."

"I'll figure something out. If Dante and Elsa are staying in the city for a while, maybe I can stay at their place."

"That isn't what I meant. You can't let ghosts keep you imprisoned for the rest of your life. They can't hurt you, can they?"

"It's difficult for them to hurt people physically through direct contact. They're more likely to try to startle me so I jump out in front of a car or maybe impel an animal to bite me or something."

"That's not reassuring."

"It's hard for spirits to control animals. They'd have to be extremely willful and focused. Death tends to distract people and scatter their thoughts. It takes them a while to regroup and be able to think rationally."

Unless they had a single-minded focus in life. Like tormenting people. She wished that Michael was her only experience with that type of personality—on both sides of corporeal existence. She had done her best to convince spirits she couldn't hear them anymore with very good reason.

"What about—"

"Michael is dead and gone. His body was cremated. Without any remains, his spirit can't linger." Hopefully, that would be the last time she had to talk about the matter.

Jazz let out a huge breath and nodded. "Okay. What about these other yahoos? How do we get them to stop bugging you?"

"I'm still working on my long-term plan."

She could ward her mirrors—very carefully—and make herself a set of earrings like her mother wore to deafen herself to the voices. If Rachel had spent less time and energy on ignoring her abilities, she would have thought to do so years ago.

"There's more you're not telling me," Jazz said. "I want

to help."

"The best thing you can do is get this to Elsa."

Rachel held up the necklace for them both to see. It had actually turned out pretty well. The stones were balanced, and Rachel had positioned them to enhance the color and beauty of each component. The silver chain matched the jewelry wire she had used and would look gorgeous against Elsa's perpetual tan.

Jazz shook her head. "You are a miracle worker. I keep telling you I could sell your work in the gallery easily."

"I have a trust fund, remember?"

"Is that why you fought me so hard on getting a paycheck?" One corner of Jazz's mouth twitched in the barest hint of a smirk.

"The knowledge you've shared with me is worth more than any paycheck. You've given me a chance to do something meaningful that I love."

"How's that working out for you?" There was a bitter edge to Jazz's voice.

"Are you kidding? I've learned more from you than anyone."

Rachel looked up to Jazz for how she handled herself and others. Jazz didn't put up with crap from anyone. She didn't even put up with the crap Rachel piled on herself.

She had pushed Rachel to try new things and take on responsibility for projects that had intimidated her. Jazz refused to accept the limits Rachel had set on herself, and because of that, Rachel had become a stronger person. Strong enough to stand up to her mother. Strong enough to finally leave.

"If knowledge is all you wanted, you could have gone back to school," Jazz said.

"There are no schools that could give me the experience I've gained working with you."

Jazz opened her mouth, but shut it abruptly. It was unnerving to see her censoring herself. Not as unnerving as the way her eyes started to glisten again. She cleared her throat, but her voice was still gravelly when she spoke and even lower than usual.

"Is there anything special I need to do when I give the necklace to Elsa?"

"No, but I need to charge it with an intention first. If you give me a moment, I can do that now."

Jazz nodded, then leaned back against the couch. Setting the intention in front of someone was going to be a little weird. After cleansing the entire house with Garrett, Rachel was starting to get used to performing rituals around people, though.

Holding the necklace cupped between her hands—like it was a butterfly that might try to fly away—Rachel closed her eyes and cleared her mind. She shut out all her doubts and fears and focused on what she wanted.

Elsa safe and sound, authentically herself, no outside influences present or affecting her in a harmful manner.

Rachel held the thought for a few moments, then imagined the thought as energy and pushed it into the necklace.

She chose two runes to go along with it. For protection, Algiz—which looked like a vertical line with a capital "Y" superimposed over it. And Uruz—an upside-down, angular "U"—for strength. She focused on each symbol, merging them with the energy she visualized infusing the necklace.

When she was done, she opened her eyes. She set the necklace on the coffee table, then flicked her hands to release any residual energy.

"Seriously? That's it?"

"The simplest solutions are usually the most powerful."

"I might have taught you about running a gallery, but I'm guessing you had other mentors."

"I had two teachers," Rachel said. "One on each side."

"Each side of what?"

"One was a spirit. The other was a medium."

"I suppose that makes sense. Actually, a lot of things I wondered about you are making sense now. Like why you try to get people to think you're scatterbrained when you're actually brilliant."

Rachel felt her eyebrows leap up her forehead. She faked a laugh, trying to recover, but she was off her game.

"I don't know about that. But I appreciate the compliment."

"It wasn't a compliment. It was a statement of fact. And you're doing it right now." Jazz let out a long sigh. "I wish you would stop."

"I don't know what to say."

"Forget it. I'm just glad you're away from your mother. I've been trying to get you out of that pit since we met. Garrett's going to get a deep discount on his next piece for accomplishing that."

"A pit? I've been living in a mansion."

"That's putting lipstick on a pig. Your mom could suck the joy out of a sold-out opening show. I've seen her do it. Belittle your accomplishments and demean you in front of a room full of people."

It wasn't the worst thing her mother had ever done. Rachel forced a laugh again, but it was an uneasy sound, even to her ears.

"You're the one who makes the sales."

"Stop. Now you're doing it to yourself."

"You sound like Garrett."

"Good. If we all remind you to disregard the crap she's told you over the years, it might help you to stop telling yourself the same lies she taught you."

Rachel felt herself tear up. She always tried not to think about the things her mother said, pulling a comfortable numbness over her heart during the worst of it. That shield was cracking, along with all of Rachel's boundaries.

She shoved thoughts of her mother into a tiny box in the back of her mind. There were other things she needed to address. Friends to protect and spirits to help.

"Thanks," Rachel said.

Jazz nodded. "Will it disrupt the energy if I touch the necklace?"

"It's best if others handle it as little as possible." Rachel slid the necklace into the velvet bag that had held the silver chain, then handed the pouch to Jazz.

"I'll see that she gets it tonight," Jazz said. "But what about you? How do we get all these ghosts to leave you alone?"

"I can take care of myself."

Jazz reached across the table and grabbed Rachel's hand. She squeezed it hard.

"We take care of each other. Now more than ever."

Rachel couldn't speak. A few choking sounds came out of her throat, her eyes burning as she held back tears—tears she saw mirrored in Jazz's eyes.

Jazz dropped to her knees next to Rachel and hugged her again. Rachel buried her face in Jazz's hair and squeezed her just as hard.

When Jazz pulled back, her eyes were red. She actually sniffed. Rachel's stomach felt weightless, like she was on a rollercoaster just before a drop-off.

"You need me—you need *anything*—you call. Understand?"

Rachel nodded.

"Okay." Jazz put her hands on Rachel's cheeks and kissed her forehead as she rose. "Give Garrett my regards.

And be sure to lock the door after me."

Rachel nodded again. She couldn't do anything else in that moment, couldn't even will herself to move.

She was stunned. She stayed where she was on the floor as she watched Jazz leave.

Chapter Nine

Living in the subtropics, steaming up a bathroom wasn't hard. Water condensed on the cooler glass of the windows that lined the top of Garrett's open shower area. The whole room looked like it was part of a fog bank.

Garrett let the hot water pound on his shoulders for a while, trying to get rid of some of his tension. When he'd worked the ER, he was used to long stints of light sleep and heavy activity. Too much time had passed since he left —he was out of practice. The last few weeks had drained him.

Heck, the last few *hours* had drained him. He couldn't believe so much had happened in such a short amount of time. He'd thought he was already emotionally exhausted, but facing off against Mrs. Montgomery, that talk with Elsa, Rachel's ghost issue, and having her living with him again... It was a lot.

At least he knew Rachel wasn't as bad off as he thought. What she was dealing with sounded pretty terrible, but she was being open about it. Garrett would make sure that she had the help and support she needed.

Dante and Elsa were doing well and Michael was gone.

Garrett let out a sigh. Things were finally looking up.

Then he heard the scream.

He bolted out of the shower space, barely aware of opening the bathroom door before running through his bedroom and down the short hall that led to the kitchen.

Rachel had her back to him as she grabbed a glass from the cabinet. She was holding a spatula in her other hand.

"What the hell happened?" All the fine hairs on his body were standing on end, the cold air on his wet skin mixing with an adrenaline rush strong enough to make him lightheaded.

Rachel laughed, but it turned into a choking sound when she turned toward him. It took him a moment to realize why.

Her eyes widened and her cheeks flushed scarlet. That plus her gaze locking on to his privates helped to clue him in. He grabbed the hand towel from the handle on the oven door and used it to cover as much of himself as he could.

"Why'd you scream?"

"Um," she cleared her throat, her gaze stuck to the towel. "There's a scorpion in the dishwasher. It startled me."

"A what?"

"A scorpion."

"Did it sting you?" He barely recognized his own voice, high and tight. His heart pounded.

The few scorpion species in Florida weren't considered

that dangerous, but they all had venom. Everyone reacted to venom differently.

"Relax. It's just a common striped scorpion."

He would hyperventilate if he wasn't careful. He took a deep breath and let it out slow. His voice lowered to a register he was more used to.

"Did it sting you?"

"No. I was going to catch it in this glass and use the spatula to keep it trapped, then take it out back and let it go."

He felt bile rise up in the back of his throat. No way was he letting her near it.

"Give me the glass."

She laughed, tossing her head so that her hair fell past her shoulder. Such a casual gesture. She really wasn't afraid at all.

He was scared enough for both of them.

"I can catch the little guy and take him outside. I'm not afraid of scorpions."

Her words sent a chill down his spine. Garrett had heard a similar sentiment plenty of times when he was a kid. Dylan had always been overconfident when it came to wildlife. Reckless.

"Relax, little bro. I've got this."

Garrett held out his hand, forcing it not to shake. "Give me the glass."

"It's going to take two hands to get him and you're a

little…busy." She let her gaze return to his towel, then looked back to him and laughed. "I can handle it, really."

No. Way.

He tossed the towel onto the counter and held out his empty hands. "Hand them over."

Rachel's gaze shot back to his privates, her eyes seeming ready to pop out of her head. She extended her arms slowly.

As a doctor, he was used to viewing the human body with clinical detachment. He wasn't used to being the one under inspection. And she was examining him thoroughly. He didn't know if he was more flattered or chagrined.

She snapped her gaze back to his at last and did one of her fake laughs. "I guess now we're even after what happened earlier."

Earlier? Right. When he'd helped her out of the tub.

That was just a day in the office, though. She needed help, he gave it. He had done his best not to look.

This was different. The way she stared with that unfocused look, as if she wasn't just seeing him but was thinking about things she'd like to do with what she saw—that was different.

She was ogling him. No doubt about it. And if he kept thinking about that, there was going to be more to see.

Garrett took the glass and spatula from her, then knelt on one knee next to the dishwasher. The scorpion was near the drain. How had it managed to squeeze through the drain cover?

Its tail was curled over its back and its pincers extended. An aggressive stance.

"Did you poke it?"

"Poke..."

Sweet Lord, have mercy. He cocked his head to the side and gave her a look that said, *really?*

Apparently it was enough to get her mind back on task. There was a potentially dangerous animal right next to them. Now wasn't the time for flirting or games.

She cleared her throat and said, "Of course not."

He reached into the dishwasher—grateful for his long arms—and quickly dropped the glass over the scorpion. It immediately lashed out, its tail and pinchers bouncing off the glass with a *tink-tink-tink*.

"Are these things always this cranky?" he asked.

"It could have come across some soap or something that set it off."

He lifted the glass just enough to slide the spatula beneath it. Rachel had picked one out that didn't have any slats. There was no chance for it to escape. When the scorpion was secured, he flipped the glass over, keeping the spatula flush with the top.

"Nice form," she said. "I mean, with the trap. Not that the rest isn't nice as well." She gestured to him, then looked away, her cheeks reddening further. "I'm going to stop talking now."

He tried to give her a smile, but what he managed felt more like a grimace. He stood, and this time she kept her face pointing at the ceiling.

"I'm going to take it outside." He headed through the living room to the sliding glass door that led to his backyard and she followed.

"I'll get the door for you."

He slipped into the shoes he kept by the back door, feeling absolutely ridiculous. Six-foot seven, dripping wet, and carting around a pissed off scorpion while wearing nothing but a pair of sandals.

Rachel slid open the door and Garrett stepped into the brutal late-afternoon heat. The air was humid enough that the water on his skin didn't even feel like it was going to evaporate.

He crossed his backyard, glad for the privacy provided by living away from the city. The canal was a good thirty yards from his back door, but he didn't want to chance the scorpion finding its way back into the house.

There was a sheer drop-off to the water on both sides of the canal and it wasn't more than six or seven feet across. The occasional gator passed by, so even though they didn't have a slope to get onto Garrett's lawn, he carefully scanned the area for any visitors.

He paused by the edge of the water, then removed the spatula and swung the glass so that the scorpion flew across the canal and landed in the grass on the other side.

There was his good deed for the day.

Garrett shivered, even though the heat had killed the last of the chill from the AC on his wet skin. Buttonbush and saw palmettos grew thick among the yellow pines and palms on the other side of the water. There were probably hundreds of scorpions out there. Snakes, spiders, all kinds of things that could hurt Rachel.

If he thought about it too much, he'd never sleep again. And those were just the threats he could see. Living in the country gave him privacy from the living, but who knew what wandering ghosts might happen by.

He headed back to the house at a brisk pace, eager to put on some clothes. Rachel was staring at him through the kitchen window.

He slowed, unnerved by the intensity of her stare. He glanced over his shoulder, wondering if she was seeing something he couldn't. She didn't look scared though. Maybe she was checking him for tan lines.

When he reached the house, he scraped the bottoms of his sandals against one of the landscaping rocks next to the patio to knock loose the few sandspurs he'd picked up. Cold air hit him as Rachel slid the door open again. He stepped inside and kicked off his shoes.

She was waiting for him with two big towels from her bathroom. She handed one to him as soon as he set the glass and spatula on the counter that ran between the kitchen and living room.

"Thanks," she said.

"What for?"

"For not killing it. The poor thing was probably lost and confused."

She handed him the second towel once he had secured the first around his waist. Garrett wiped his chest and arms dry, then started on his hair. He didn't miss the way she kept staring at his chest and arms while he worked—lips slightly open, eyes heavy-lidded.

He was grateful for the towel, but he needed more to keep himself from getting into an even more embarrassing predicament. Diverting her attention would help.

"Only you would call a scorpion *poor thing*. That was a slick containment system you came up with on the fly."

"I just used what was available."

He shook his head and laughed. "Well, it worked pretty well. Remind me to call the lawn service later. That grass is too long."

Rachel peered out the window, then looked back at him, one eyebrow arched. "Your yard has a buzz cut. I can see patches of sand everywhere."

"I'm more concerned with the things we can't see. Cutting the grass shorter might not help much with scorpions, but it'll give us a better chance at spotting snakes."

"We could go out with a black light at night some time to see how many scorpions are out there."

"What, they'll all come out for a rave?"

She laughed, her broad smile soothing his frayed nerves. "Scorpions phosphoresce in black light. They should light up with a pretty blue glow."

Pretty wasn't a word he would use to describe a bunch of scorpions. He was certain there'd be plenty if they checked—that was a downside of being out from the city.

"How do you know this stuff?" he asked.

"I read a lot."

"I'd rather not know how many are out there. I like to spend time on the patio and I don't want to be worrying about how many scorpions are in my yard. Unless those citronella candles and box fans you started me using will take care of them too?"

"Sadly, that's only for repelling mosquitoes. How are they working for you anyway?"

"Haven't been bit for a while, thanks."

"Do you still take out the telescope?"

"Sometimes." Every chance he had.

He would crack open a beer and spend hours looking at the stars and planets, thinking about Rachel and her astronomy lessons.

"We should take it out tonight. I can test you on your constellations and see if you remember what I taught you. It'll be just like old times."

"That sounds like a great idea."

Primarily because she wouldn't be able to see how he

was blushing if they were hanging around in the dark. He wasn't sure he'd ever stop with how she kept looking at him.

He'd imagined her seeing him naked many times. His daydreams were a far cry from the reality. For one, they were usually both naked in his fantasies. And he had never dreamed she'd have such a…hungry look to her. It was hard to ignore and even harder not to do something about.

He cleared his throat, then asked, "Do we need to do anything to keep ghosts away while we're out back?"

She shook her head. "It would be a huge undertaking and I doubt it's necessary. I've never detected a ghost out here. That's one of the reasons I loved staying with you during the renovations. It was peaceful."

His heart sank. Those months with her had been the best of his life. The way she'd opened up to him—the person she had revealed herself to be—had made him feel special.

But what if all her talk of feeling safe with him had more to do with an absence of ghosts rather than his presence? Thinking about it was too depressing.

"Well, I better get dressed. Be careful around that dishwasher and make sure it's shut tight. We don't want any more unexpected guests showing up."

"Right."

He felt her gaze on him as he retreated to lick his wounds.

Chapter Ten

Dinner had been quiet. After gawking at Garrett, Rachel could barely work up the courage to try to make eye contact. When she managed to glance at him, he was always looking away. Now he had her off prepping the telescope while he did the dishes.

He'd blushed all through the meal—unless his tan had managed to turn to a burn in the few minutes he was out back. Her face was probably red too. Her cheeks—among other parts of her anatomy—hadn't stopped tingling since he appeared in his kitchen absolutely naked. She tried not to think about it. And failed.

She had known he was built from the way his clothes hugged his frame. She'd used her imagination countless times to fill in what was hidden underneath. Imagining was very different from seeing with her own eyes.

He wasn't totally ripped with hard angles and rock-hard planes, though he obviously had plenty of muscle. The lines of his body were smooth, inviting her to explore them. That touch of softness amid his masculine lines did way more for her than abs that looked like rows of rumble strips.

Six-foot-seven and he was proportional. Everywhere.

The tingling in her cheeks intensified till they almost stung. Her bra started to chafe.

The things she could do to that body of his.

She shook her head, and whispered, "Not now." Not ever, in fact.

Everyone came with baggage. Hers extended to include the unresolved business of any ghost around that knew she was psychic. She wasn't dumping that on Garrett.

The telescope was in the hall closet, a six-foot long refractor she had picked out for him. The shorter optical tube of a reflector would have been much more practical for Garrett's use, but he had insisted on a refractor when she said that was her preference.

She liked the old-fashioned look of refractors—and that they used lenses instead of mirrors for magnification. If a spirit happened by the aperture of a reflector telescope while she was viewing the sky with such a powerful mirror... She had no idea what would happen.

The thought gave her a chill. His refractor might be more cumbersome, but she was grateful for his choice.

As she pulled the telescope from the closet off the foyer, she noticed there wasn't a speck of dust on the case. The huge tripod was also easily accessible—a good sign he was using it often. She was glad the scope wasn't languishing. It took several trips to cart everything outside and set up in the center of the patio.

Garrett joined her. He lit a couple of citronella candles and set up box fans for the mosquitoes. It didn't take much of a breeze to keep them at bay. The candles might not be as effective, but their dim light wouldn't interfere too much with stargazing and would help keep them from stubbing their toes.

He turned off the outside lights when everything was ready. The lights inside the house were already off. He walked to the patio table and set down an open bottle of beer—presumably for her since he held another in his hand.

Her heart gave a little tug as she remembered the first time he'd given her one and the many they had shared on this very patio while looking at the stars. It would be so easy to pretend that nothing had happened—nothing had changed—and fall back into that comfort zone. But it wasn't really comfortable. For either of them.

While waiting for their eyes to adjust, Rachel said, "I can't believe you wanted to cover your patio." She tilted her head back, following the thick cluster of stars that made up the Milky Way. "You have the most amazing view of the sky. Can we start with Lyra?"

He leaned against the back of one of his wrought-iron chairs, his empty hand in the front pocket of his jeans. At least, she presumed it was empty.

"Whatever you want."

Whatever she wanted? She imagined walking up behind

him and sliding her hands into his pockets, seeing what all she could reach. Or she could approach him head-on, unzip his pants, and let her fingers follow the dark path that led to his manhood.

She bent over the telescope, working to bring Lyra into view. If she could draw him into a conversation, maybe that would distract her from her thoughts.

"I can barely see Lyra's Alpha star in the city, let alone the rest of the constellation. The light pollution in Summer Park becomes worse every year." He didn't say anything, so she tried harder. "Do you remember the name of the star I'm looking for?"

"It's probably rattling around in here somewhere." He pointed to his head with the hand holding the bottle.

"What about what I taught you about Alpha and Beta stars in constellations and asterisms?"

He took a deep breath and said, "If you don't mind, could we maybe skip the astronomy lesson this time?"

"Absolutely." She tried to sound upbeat and hoped the dim light hid her disappointment.

No astronomy lessons. Okay.

She started to wonder if he'd actually enjoyed her teaching him about the sky when she was staying with him or if he was just being polite. The possibility was crushing. He had always seemed eager to learn. It had reminded her of how excited she was to receive astronomy lessons from Hiram when she was a child.

Rachel lined up the scope with Vega, pushing away the doubtful thoughts. She let her mind fill with the wonder of seeing something that was so far away, imagining the vast distance between her and the star—the dark space between them.

The light she saw from Vega was actually cast by the star twenty-five years ago. She had always thought of stargazing as the closest she could come to time travel. Now she knew that wasn't the case. She had met Dante, held his hand, even hugged him. She never imagined she might meet someone from another time. It was incredible.

Starlight from twenty-five years in the past paled next to a human traveling over a hundred years through time. What must that have been like? She couldn't wait to talk to Elsa and Dante and learn more.

Except Rachel *would* wait. She would force herself to be patient. They had other priorities—and so did she. As soon as she found her footing, she would figure out a way to help the ghosts of Michael's victims.

But not tonight.

Stepping back from the scope, she said, "I have Vega lined up for you. Take a look."

Garrett nodded, then set his bottle on the table. He wiped his hands on his jeans as he approached her, walking slowly as if he was nervous. He bent to the scope, candlelight catching in his hair. Rachel wanted to reach out and run her fingers through the pale brown strands.

His hair was as soft as silk. She knew, because once she had lost control and let herself do the very thing that tempted her. The memory came back, sharp and full of pain and longing.

They had been laughing about something while working on his house. Reaching for him had been instinct, the pull she felt toward him irresistible. He'd responded immediately, leaning in to kiss her.

It had been the most abrupt dodge she had ever done. She'd felt his breath ruffling her hair as she stepped away. The awkwardness of the following moments had been brutal—she still hated herself for letting it happen and putting him through that.

"Lyra is filled with double stars." She started to talk just to hear something other than her own thoughts. "It's really a fascinating constellation. If I'm remembering correctly, Vega is the third brightest star visible from the Northern Hemisphere."

He stood up straight, but didn't move away from the telescope. And he still didn't say anything back.

"But you didn't want an astronomy lesson. Right." She fished around for anything to say instead. "Have you ever heard of Tanabata?"

"Can't say I have."

"It's a celebration in Japan that involves Lyra. There are a bunch of myths about the stars Vega and Altair being lovers separated by the Milky Way. My favorite version portrays Vega as a Celestial Maiden who fell in love with a human. When her father found out, he forbade them from being together and put the Milky Way between them to keep them apart."

Even in the near-darkness, she could feel the tension build in him. A warning sounded in the back of her mind, but her momentum carried her forward. It was a beautiful, sad story.

"On the seventh day of the seventh lunar month, the Sky Gods take pity on them and create a bridge of magpies so that they can be together. I guess technically that would make it take place in August, but if you go by the Gregorian calendar and wanted to celebrate it here, Tanabata would have been yesterday."

"It sounds like a sad thing to be celebrating."

"They're focusing on the time the lovers can be together. You can look at the bitter or look at the sweet."

"Take what you can get, huh?" He snorted and shook his head, then walked back to the table. He picked up his beer and held it for a while before taking a drink.

The idea of a star-party for two had been impulsive, like almost everything Rachel did. Instead of making Garrett feel better and easing any embarrassment or tension between them, she had only made it worse.

"I'm guessing you aren't interested in lessons on Japanese culture and religious festivals either," she said.

"I was actually thinking we could just enjoy the view."

"Sure."

Like she had enjoyed the view earlier—especially watching him walk to the canal. She doubted she would find any dust on his exercise equipment, either. Judging by his backside, he must do a few dozen squats every day.

The assessment of her plan to ease the awkwardness between them with some stargazing shifted from failure to dismal failure. It wasn't even keeping her mind off his body. And the more she thought about his body, the harder it was to resist him.

The last thing Garrett needed was to get involved with her. It would condemn him to a life filled with the dead. He deserved better.

Rachel was skirting the issue, trying to avoid or deny what had happened and hope it would go away on its own. It was how she dealt with everything in her life—her powers, her family issues, even her feelings for him. For once, she wanted to face something head on and just deal with it.

"Listen," she said. "We should probably talk about what happened earlier."

"It's been a full day. You'll have to be a bit more specific."

"The thing with the scorpion. How I behaved." She wasn't surprised when he stayed silent. "I'm sorry I kept staring. I didn't mean to. It's been a really long time since I've seen a naked man and well, you're just…"

She lifted her hands toward him and waved them up and down like she was showcasing his physique. "It was difficult to look away. But I should have. And I'm sorry."

She forced herself to pause so that he could respond. Silent moments dragged on, time seeming to dilate as she shifted from one foot to another. Finally, she couldn't take it.

"Aren't you going to say something?"

"That's a lot to process. How could you have not seen a guy naked when—" He shook his head. "I'm sorry. I shouldn't go there."

"When what?"

"Well, you were pretty serious with…"

The hair on her arms stood on end. Her stomach cramped, the pasta from dinner feeling like a lead weight.

"Michael."

She didn't blame Garrett for not wanting to say the name. She didn't want to say it, either. But she refused to let Michael have power over her anymore.

Garrett let out a huge breath of air and ran his fingers through his hair, holding it back from his face. "I don't want to bring up bad memories."

"No, it's all right. Talking about it is supposed to be healing."

He shrugged and let his hand drop to his side. "But you don't have to push yourself. You can take your time. As long as you need."

"I don't *want* to take my time. I don't want to still be talking about this a year or even a month from now. I want to move on with my life."

He nodded and simply said, "Okay."

Rachel walked over to him and sat in one of the patio chairs. He sat next to her. She picked up her beer and took a long drink before she began.

"Michael told me he wanted to take things slow. That was fine with me. I didn't want... Well, I haven't done more than kiss a guy for a couple of years now."

Garrett sat back, his eyes wide and glittering in the light from the candle on the table. He let out another huge breath that he must have been holding, and shook his head.

"I'm glad you didn't..." He shook his head. "I'm glad you don't have that to work through on top of everything else."

"Me too."

Her chest felt tight, but the dread in the pit of her stomach was lessening. Talking to Garrett was lightening the burden she carried. And it seemed to be doing the same for him.

"I know I've been dating a lot, but none of those relationships were serious at all. I was trying to distract myself more than anything."

"From the ghosts?"

She felt her eyebrows rise, the warm citronella-laced air tickled her tongue as her mouth dropped open. The candlelight couldn't be covering her reaction. He had to see it too.

"Among other things."

He had asked for her honesty, but telling him how she felt about him would ruin their friendship. Worse, it would make him even more impossible to resist because he would want to take action based on that knowledge.

Then he'd be stuck with a weirdo who could see spirits and constantly spouted awkward factoids. When she wasn't pretending to be a socialite at the beck and call of her somewhat—totally—evil mother.

"I'm dealing with a lot," she said. "I understand that. But it isn't as much as you think. I had already broken up with him."

"What?"

She shivered at the memory. Michael had been calm when she told him. He said he understood and wished her the best. He only had one request—that she sit for him so he could make a portrait to remember her by.

At the time, she'd thought of the paintings in his gallery room. His opening show consisted of a dozen portraits of women in painterly style. The portraits evoked despair, with the women having distorted bodies and either hiding their faces or keeping themselves turned away from the viewer.

As grim as they appeared, the dark red and gray paint he used hid a more disturbing secret—he had mixed the paint with the blood of his victims, the subjects of each painting.

He had started Rachel's portrait before she was rescued.

She'd ignored her own misgivings when he asked her to sit for him, like she ignored the voices of the dead around her. She was too practiced at ignoring things. She had agreed and gone with him to his house.

"It might have accelerated things," she said. "After I told him."

Garrett looked like he was going to snap his beer bottle in half. She reached over and took it from him, then set it on the table.

"I'm sorry," he said. "I'm having trouble with my poker face. I don't want to make this harder. I want you to be able to talk to me."

"You don't have to put on a face for me. I guess that's what makes our friendship so special. We can both let our guards down."

"I suppose. I still appreciate you sharing this with me."

"I want you to know that I'm doing better than you think."

"Yeah. I kind of noticed when you lit into your mom." He smiled, one side of his mouth curving up and a deep dimple appearing in his cheek.

Oh she had missed that dimple. She wondered if she could bring out the other one. But that would be a bad idea. His smile was devastating. It made her want to crawl into his lap and kiss him.

"That kind of surprised me too," she said.

"It was a long time coming."

"Jazz says she's going to give you a big discount on the next piece you buy for getting me out of my mother's house."

"That was all you. I only gave you a lift."

"And a place to stay and the motivation to finally do something." She couldn't believe how much her life had changed just since that morning.

"Yeah, but you're still the one who did the work. It took courage to walk out of that house—way more than I understood at the time."

"I feel like I had help. Watching Jazz over the years and how she doesn't take crap from anybody has been very educational. It was like I was channeling her or something."

"Not literally, right?"

She knew he was joking by the way his smile deepened. *Dimples...* Keeping her focus on the conversation was difficult, but she managed.

"No. That would require training to be a medium. I'm just psychic." A thrill went down her spine and she shivered. "It's strange to say it out loud. But it feels good."

"I'm glad." He leaned closer and asked, "What's it like? If it's uncomfortable to talk about, you don't have to answer."

"I don't think you could ever make me feel uncomfortable." Her voice had a bit of breathiness to it she hadn't intended. Consciously, anyway. She laughed and looked away.

"Give him a kiss."

Rachel was so caught up in the moment, the quiet voice caught her off-guard.

"It's obvious you want to. Him too, from the looks of it."

Rachel leapt to her feet.

"What is it? What's wrong?" Garrett rose right after her.

"Someone is here."

"Who?"

"I didn't mean to ruin your moment." The voice was male. He sounded older, genial.

She didn't care if he sounded like a super-friendly grandpa. Rachel shook her head, then ran to the house. She kept her eyes shut tight as she approached the glass doors. Whoever it was, she didn't want to see him in the reflection from the candlelight.

Seeing always made it worse.

Scrabbling for the handle, she managed to slide the door open and jump inside. She still couldn't bring herself to open her eyes and bounced off something—probably Garrett's recliner. As upset as she was, she couldn't remember the room's layout.

She dropped to her knees and wrapped her arms around her middle, waiting for Garrett to come to her rescue—again.

Chapter Eleven

Garrett ran after Rachel and shut the door behind them. When he turned back around, she was huddled in a ball on the floor.

"It isn't Michael, is it?" he asked.

She had said Michael was gone, but with the way she reacted, Garrett had to wonder. His hands kept flexing into fists. If it was…

If it was, he couldn't do a damned thing about it. His insides boiled at the thought.

"The water bottle," she said. "Spray down the door."

He grabbed it and did as she asked, then knelt at her side. "It's done."

She was trembling, shaking her head. She started to rock back and forth, like she had at the hospital. He did not want to go down that road again.

"I'm going to touch your back," he said. He gently placed his hand on her back and let out a little breath when she didn't scream or jerk away. "Do you still hear the voice?"

"No. I don't." She shook her head again and her rocking slowed.

Garrett rubbed her back, trying to soothe her.

"All right, then. Rachel-1, ghost-0."

She stopped rocking, but the trembling increased. At first he worried he had made things worse, but then he realized she was laughing. She leaned toward him. As soon as her shoulder touched his chest, she reached up to wrap her arms around his neck. Her eyes were still pinched shut.

He sat and pulled her into his lap.

"What can I do?"

"I'm just trying to build up my nerve to open my eyes again."

Garrett glanced around the room. "I don't see any reflections."

She pressed herself closer to his chest and opened first one eye, then the other, looking around carefully. She let out a huge breath and leaned her head on his shoulder.

"Thank you."

"No problem."

But it was a problem. Rachel curled up in his lap with her arms around him, her face nestled close enough that her warm breath fanned his neck... Biology took over. He had never held her so close, felt her press herself against him this way.

He shifted beneath her, trying to get more comfortable and keep her from noticing his predicament. The citrus scent of her shampoo was driving him crazy. He could tilt his head a few inches and kiss her if he wanted to. And he did want to.

Trouble was—he wanted a whole lot more than kisses from Rachel.

Desperate to distract himself, he asked, "Do you know who it was?"

"No. I didn't recognize the voice."

That was a relief.

She shook her head. "I don't understand how he found me so fast."

"I still don't know how it works. Do ghosts have to… walk to where you are? How do they even get around?"

"They sort of will themselves to go places—if they aren't tied to a person or place. If the ghost is haunting a location, they're usually stuck in one spot. But if they're haunting a person, they can follow them around. If the person dies or somehow severs their connection, the ghost is free to roam."

The thought of people being haunted… And the voice was male. Garrett's stomach tightened. Maybe the ghost wasn't tied to Rachel at all. Maybe it was him.

"Were there any other distinguishing characteristics?"

She shook her head. "He sounded older. With a bit of an accent."

Garrett felt some of the tension ease from between his shoulders. If the ghost sounded older, it wasn't Dylan. The thought of his brother's spirit lingering for so many years was more than Garrett could deal with on a good day. It had been a long time since Garrett had experienced a good day.

"What did he say?"

"Nothing scary." Her face reddened and she looked away. "He didn't even ask me for anything, which is kind of strange. Ghosts usually are pretty fixated on getting what they want. He actually reminded me of Hiram."

"Hiram?"

"He was the only ghost I ever became friends with. He watched over me. In life, he had been an astronomer. He's the one who taught me the constellations." She smiled, her eyes getting a faraway look. "We would sit out back and look at the stars and talk for hours sometimes."

No wonder she loved the scope so much. Garrett doubted her mom had been more loving when Rachel was younger. At least Hiram had been there.

How messed up was it that the most supportive adult in her childhood had been a ghost?

"Could it be him?" Garrett asked.

She shook her head. "No. Hiram crossed over decades ago."

"You sure about that?"

Her eyes filled with tears that immediately spilled over.

Dammit. He wished he would stop stumbling into topics that obviously caused her so much grief.

"I was there," she said. "He did it to protect me. He was

always protecting me. He's the one who told me to act like I couldn't hear spirits anymore and helped to convince the others to leave me alone."

"Why do I have a feeling there's a lot more to that story and I'm not going to like it?"

She laughed and leaned against his chest again. "Because you know me better than anyone."

Sometimes he felt that way. Sometimes he felt he didn't know her at all.

"Could Hiram have come back?"

"I don't think so."

Garrett let out a sigh. "I have a lot to learn."

"You can borrow some of my books if you want. I've managed to collect a few good resources over the years."

"Thanks."

"I'll go get you some. Could you bring in the telescope? I can help put it away after we spray the door again."

"Don't worry about any of that," Garrett said. "I'll take care of it."

"You're really good at taking care of people." She lifted her hand to his face, resting it along his jaw.

He tried to stop himself from sucking in a fast breath— and failed. Her smile faltered and she shifted away.

She braced herself on his shoulders as she rose. It was all he could do not to reach for her and pull her back. She didn't say anything else as she walked away.

Garrett sat on the floor for a few minutes, trying to find a sense of equilibrium. A frantic night at the ER was nothing compared to the emotional toll of being this close to Rachel.

He needed to get up and move around. Shake it off.

Bringing in the scope would help. And maybe he'd have a word with whoever was out there. Bolstered at the thought, he jumped up and headed for the patio.

Outside, insects were droning loud. Garrett glanced up at Lyra, remembering Rachel's story of the star-crossed lovers.

He blew out a breath and shook his head. Best not to go there.

He carried in the scope and packed everything up, then went back for the tripod and fans. When he was done inside, he grabbed the spray bottle and stepped back into the muggy summer night. The candles were still flickering, putting off a sharp scent. It was eerie—knowing there was a ghost hanging around—a stranger he couldn't see.

Garrett wondered why Rachel didn't use mirrors more often. If he could, he'd be checking his surroundings constantly to be sure he was alone.

Then again, maybe it was better not to know.

Rachel said Florida was filled with spirits. He imagined what it must be like walking past a mirror in a busy store and not knowing if the people he saw were dead or alive. He wondered if the ghosts showed signs of how they had died…

Garrett was more grateful than ever that he lived out in the country. Only one ghost to deal with—at least, for the time being. But how the hell did you start a conversation with a dead person?

He glanced at the spray bottle in his hand. It felt like a weapon. That wasn't him. He set it on the table, then ran his fingers through his hair.

Best to focus on the *person* part. Garrett decided to talk to him as such.

"I don't know who you are or what you need, but Rachel's been through a lot. Give her some time. Please."

He blew out the candles and grabbed the spray bottle before heading back inside. He closed the door, then sprayed it down twice.

"You're starting to be paranoid, like me."

Garrett jumped at Rachel's voice. The creepy atmosphere outside must have hit him harder than he thought.

"Sorry," she said. She was holding a small stack of books, hugging them to her chest.

Garrett shook his head. "No need to apologize. Guess I'm just feeling a little high-strung after today."

"I feel like I should apologize for that too. You wouldn't have had such a stressful day if you hadn't come to my rescue."

He couldn't have slept another night without knowing

she was okay. Not that he'd been sleeping much lately anyway.

"Friends help each other out."

"Yeah."

Her voice was small, like the fake smile pasted on her face. It couldn't break through the tension around her eyes. All he saw there was sorrow.

She walked to the kitchen counter and set the books down. "Here are the books you wanted to borrow."

"Thanks."

"Could I have the spray bottle?"

He nodded and handed it over. "Rachel—"

"It's late. We should try to get some sleep."

"Yeah. I guess we should."

"Well...good night."

"Night."

She turned and walked away without another word. Something was obviously upsetting her. Beyond what she'd been through and knowing that there was a ghost close by. For once, she didn't seem to want to talk.

Garrett didn't know how to help her. Yet.

He picked up the books and headed to his room. Once there, he closed his blinds before stripping and pulling on his pajama pants. The thought of someone lurking outside —watching them, listening... It was freaking him out. And Rachel lived with that every single day.

He couldn't imagine how awful that must be. Surely

there was a way to keep the ghosts away. He was even interested in the solution for himself. It was creepy as hell to think about walking around not knowing how many ghosts he might be brushing elbows with.

He made sure the bedside lamp was on before turning off the overhead lights. At this rate, he would probably sleep that way. He slid into bed with Rachel's books, but didn't open them immediately. His thoughts were spinning too much to concentrate.

She'd dropped several information bombs on him. Of all the ones to fixate on, he kept thinking about her saying that she hadn't been with a man in years. She had dated at least a dozen guys in that time span. Garrett hated every single one of them.

They disrespected her, talked over her, didn't seem to pay attention or listen when she spoke.

He wanted to think that he would have been happy for her if she settled down with a decent person, but couldn't be sure. It didn't matter, because she had seemed to seek out the worst example of a human being to date. If Rachel brought any of them home, her mother must have been mortified. But then, that might have been part of the allure.

Garrett wondered again if her mother had something to do with why Rachel kept shutting him out. It was obvious she felt the chemistry between them. She seemed to enjoy his company. But damned if her mother wasn't practically trying to arrange a marriage between the two.

His own mom had repeatedly mentioned that she was surprised to receive so many invitations to events hosted by the Montgomerys. Rachel's mother had even openly talked to his mom about what an attractive pair they would make.

His mom would never push the matter. She just wanted Garrett to be happy and could tell there was something not quite right with the dynamic. When he said Rachel wasn't interested, his mom dropped it.

Then Jazz had decided to try to match him up with Elsa. It hadn't worked out, but at least he and Elsa had managed to build a strong friendship. She came to him when she needed help, big or small, and he appreciated that probably more than she knew. He was well aware of how much he needed to feel...needed.

Now that he thought about it, Rachel hadn't actually asked him for help at all. Sure, she took him up on his offer of a place to stay, but she had other options. She could stay at Elsa's house.

If she did, he knew he'd lie awake wondering if she was okay the whole night. Sharing a roof helped him as much as her. He needed to know she was safe, even if he had no clue how to protect her himself.

He had the books to read—a way to learn more about how he *could* help her. He needed to get to it. If things did blow up eventually, he wanted to be useful.

He cracked the first book open. It landed on an etching

of a man holding his hands over his head as a seriously creepy ghost flew at him.

Garrett heard a soft rapping sound. The hair on his arms stood on end. The sound came again—from his bedroom door. His heart was hammering in his chest. It had to be Rachel… Didn't it?

"Come in," he said.

She opened the door slowly and stepped inside. Garrett's pulse jumped for a different reason, scenarios playing through his head about why she might be coming to see him in the middle of the night.

Because we're both awake, jackass.

"I forgot to bring—"

Her eyes grew wider as she looked at him, her gaze slowly trailing down his chest and over the sheet that covered his hips and legs.

He forced a smile, trying to get her to laugh off some of the tension between them. "Don't worry. I'm not naked under here."

She gave a quick laugh—a bit too high to be real. He'd take it.

"What do you need?" he asked.

"I…forgot to bring pajamas. None of my clothes are comfortable for sleeping, and being naked in the dark is not high on my list of things I'd like to do right now."

Her mouth dropped open for a second, but then she clacked it shut, cheeks glowing scarlet—betraying her thoughts. He was thinking the same thing.

Being naked in the dark with Rachel was about at the top of Garrett's list of things he'd like to do any time, any day. Increasing the awkwardness between them by letting her see just how much that idea appealed to him was close to the bottom.

He tried to look casual as he strategically placed his book over his lap, then nodded toward his closet. "Help yourself."

"Thanks."

She didn't waste any time, quickly walking to the closet and pulling out a couple of T-shirts. She was tall, but his shirts would still be huge on her.

The thought of his shirt dusting across her long, slender legs, her breasts brushing the fabric…didn't help his predicament. He shook his head and picked up another book, burying his nose in it as if it held all of his attention.

He couldn't let himself look up at her. No way could he hide how much he wanted her. He wouldn't burden her with that knowledge.

Clearing his throat, he said, "If you need anything else, don't hesitate to come get me. Okay?"

"Yeah. Thanks again."

He didn't set down the book till after she had gone and shut the door behind her. He closed his eyes and leaned his head against the headboard.

This was torture.

If she wanted him, she could have had him at any time in the past couple of years. Garrett made no secret of that. Hell, she could have him right now.

No matter her reasons, she *didn't* want him. Not really. He had to keep reminding himself of that. And maybe that emotional pain would help him keep his physical reactions to her under control.

He wouldn't hold his breath.

Chapter Twelve

There was a ghost right outside the house. A stranger.

If the voice had been one of Michael's victims, menacing as they were, Rachel would have understood their presence. With that understanding, there would have been some twisted form of comfort. But this ghost was a complete unknown.

She sat on the edge of her bed, staring at the window. The blinds were closed, but even still there were little cracks around the edges that would allow glimpses into the room from outside. Why hadn't she put in curtains?

Because Garrett loved natural light—and she didn't want to deny him even a particle of it.

Every room in his house only had blinds to cover the windows. Well, except for her bathroom, which had no windows at all. She considered sleeping in the bathtub, but that wasn't an option. As much as the windows bothered her, the mirror in that room—even covered—scared her more. The living room had the sliding glass door, so that nixed the couch.

There was always Garrett's room, with only one clear-glass window that would have a limited view from the backyard. A narrow row of frosted windows lined the wall that faced the front of his house, high up and running parallel to the ceiling. His bed was huge and looked very comfortable—especially with him in it.

Her mind immediately pulled up an image of him walking back to the house after the scorpion incident. That memory was burned into every synapse. His confident stride, the determined set to his features, his strong chest, his muscled legs, a certain other part of his anatomy…

The things she wanted to do to that man.

She knew he was thinking about it too—acting on their mutual attraction. But he was most concerned with protecting her. He wouldn't even let her get close to a tiny scorpion. It was sweet, but unnecessary.

She went through her list of all the reasons that she shouldn't be with him in the first place. At the top was how being involved with her would affect his peace of mind.

Learning about her powers—and that ghosts were real—had already impacted him negatively. When she went to borrow a shirt to sleep in, she noticed the blinds in his room were closed. He had always kept them open before. Always. He must be freaking out, trying to protect her yet again by shielding her from how much his new awareness disturbed him.

At least Rachel was used to dealing with this kind of thing. Now that Garrett knew ghosts were real and how prevalent they were, he might never be able to truly relax again.

She didn't want that for him. For any of her friends. Having Rachel around was a constant reminder of death. It robbed them of even the small comfort of thinking that death held finality.

Jazz wanted to help. So did Elsa. But Rachel wanted to preserve their peace of mind—just like she wanted to preserve Garrett's. She needed to figure this out on her own, to keep them out of it as much as she could.

The more they tried to help, the more they would internalize that none of them were ever really alone. It didn't make for a happy life.

She leapt up from the bed and started pacing. The soft fabric of Garrett's T-shirt brushed against her legs as she walked, distracting her from her anxious thoughts. It carried a hint of his scent. She paused and took a deep breath to saturate her senses with him.

She wrapped her arms around herself and closed her eyes, imagining that Garrett was holding her. He'd been doing a lot of that lately. It was taking a toll on both of them.

She was having trouble resisting the pull she felt toward him. The desire to be with him was stronger than ever. The more time they spent together, the worse it became.

But she was weird. He deserved normal. A happy,

loving family to join with his, a partner who didn't get distracted by—

Something tapped on her window. Rachel's eyes snapped open. She backed toward the bed.

It happened again—a fluttering thump.

She took a deep breath, then slowly approached the window. At least it was shut. She was certain of that. Still, the persistent flutter-thump was making her heart beat in her throat. When she was close enough, she pulled on the cord that raised the pleated blinds.

Outside the window, all she saw was inky darkness. The light cast by the bedside lamp was strong enough that she could see the reflection of the room around her in the glass.

And of the pale, blonde ghost staring back at her—*from inside the room.*

Rachel's heart beat even faster. There couldn't be a ghost in the house. She had cleansed and warded the whole thing.

She took a deep breath and let it out. So did the woman in the window.

Her heart seemed to stop. It wasn't a ghost at all. It was her own reflection.

Rachel avoided any mirror bigger than a compact. She couldn't remember the last time she'd actually seen so much of herself at once. Her eyes were wide and there were dark circles beneath them. Her hair was a tousled mess.

No wonder everyone was worried. Especially with the obvious fear on her face, the lines of stress etched around her eyes. In the dark glass of the window, her reflection was translucent. It was as if she was the ghost, haunting her own life—a living shadow.

Rachel leaned closer to the window just as something huge and bright yellow whacked into the glass. She yelped and jumped back. She was still holding onto the cord for the blinds and it tangled around her arm. As she tried to free herself, her movements caused the blinds to bang against the window with an awful racket. She quickly grabbed at them, pushing them against the glass to stop the noise.

Still holding the blinds, she looked at the windowsill. Two lubber grasshoppers stared back at her. Each was at least three inches long, with bright yellow and orange carapaces. Lubbers were everywhere in Florida, but she'd never noticed them being active at night. One crawled a few inches toward her while she watched.

"Rachel?"

She jumped again, jostling the blinds and getting her wrist tangled in the cord even more. Garrett ran forward before she could extricate herself. He was just wearing pajama bottoms.

She was staring again, but she couldn't bring herself to care. His chest was covered in fine dark hair that flowed together and cascaded down his stomach, all the way to—

"I didn't mean to startle you," he said.

"It's okay." She laughed and shook her head, trying to force the image of Garrett naked out of her mind with limited success. She tried to lighten the mood, wiggling the cord as he helped free her hand. "I guess I'm a little high-strung too."

Apparently, he wasn't in a laughing mood. He didn't say anything until he had lowered the blinds.

"Was that ghost bothering you again? I thought the poppets were supposed to keep them away."

"It's not always ghosts." She wanted to help him normalize what he'd learned. Maybe he wouldn't fixate on the idea of ghosts if she gave him another explanation. "There were some grasshoppers flying against the window. They must have been drawn to the light coming out from around the edges of the blinds."

"Grasshoppers at night?"

She shrugged. "I didn't mean to disturb you."

Again.

"I was already up."

"You can't sleep either?"

He shook his head. His gaze kept flicking to her wrists, his eyes getting an angry, haunted look.

She was tired of it. She was tired of people—especially Garrett—asking her if she was okay and looking at her like she might shatter at any moment. He had done enough for her. Maybe she could do something for him.

"Do you need me to tell you about it?" she asked.

"What, the bugs? I was born here too. I know all about the pesky things."

"About what happened with Michael."

He looked away and shook his head. "You don't have to tell me."

"I think I do. I need to tell someone what really happened."

"I thought you talked it all through with your doctors and the police."

A lump was forming in her throat. She shook her head.

"Only part of it. What they could believe."

His mouth opened and shut. His chest stilled as he held his breath, waiting for her. Always waiting. She walked to the bed and sat, then patted the spot next to her.

"Sit with me?"

Garrett hesitated for a moment, but then joined her.

How to begin?

Not with the feeling of dread when she entered Michael's house—yet another warning sign she had ignored. Not with the chloroform or waking up in darkness chained to a wall.

As bad as that was, she wasn't haunted by what Michael did to her. She was haunted by the voices of the other women. The ones he had killed.

The voices had started before she woke. She was

dropped into the middle of a conversation between half a dozen ghosts sharing the room with her. Sharing their darkness.

They spoke in whispers, even knowing Michael couldn't hear them. They were that afraid.

How could Rachel help Garrett understand? Hearing those spirits, she could almost feel their pain—pain strong enough to keep them chained to this world even after death.

"What you're imagining is… It's not what happened," she said. "It's not what anyone thinks."

He was quiet for a moment, then said, "I'm listening."

She took a deep breath and blew it out to steady her nerves before she began.

"I had been avoiding Michael all week. I would tell him I was busy setting up Dante's loft after work at the gallery —which was true. But I went out of my way to make sure I didn't have any spare time. When opening night for Michael's show was close, I realized I couldn't avoid him any longer. We met for lunch and I told him we were done."

"I can't imagine that went over well."

"That's the thing—it did. He said he was proud of me for figuring out what I wanted and saying something about it. That it was high time I took a stand for myself." Her stomach churned at the memory. "I ate it all up. Every word. When he asked me for one last favor, it seemed such a small thing. He seemed reasonable."

"What did he want?"

"He wanted me to sit for him. To pose for a final portrait so that he could *keep a piece of me near him forever*." She let out a tinny laugh. "Little did I know."

She shivered. Garrett scooted closer to her, but she didn't let herself lean into him for comfort. The whole point was to let him know that she was stronger than he thought—that this hadn't broken her.

"Rachel, you don't have to tell me this if it's too hard."

"What's hard is the way you've been looking at me. How worried you are about what Michael did."

"How could I not worry?" he asked.

"I won't lie. It was terrible and sickening and for a while I didn't know if I would make it through with my sanity intact. But there were other things going on. Things that made what he did to me more bearable—less awful in comparison with what he had done to others. Because I escaped. Do you understand, Garrett? *I escaped*."

Garrett looked perplexed. His brow furrowed and he shook his head. "I don't understand."

She didn't want to come out and say it. Saying it made it more real. But she had to. She had to help him understand.

"The others didn't."

Her eyes burned with tears, but she held them back. Understanding flowed over his features as he sucked in a breath.

"There were ghosts with you? People he had…"

"Killed. Yes. Half a dozen that I could distinguish. I heard whispers as soon as I arrived at his house. They were so quiet, I could barely hear them. But I didn't even try. I tuned them out, like usual. If I had only tried to listen to them, maybe I could have escaped. Prevented what happened to Elsa and Dante."

Garrett shook his head. "No. You can't let yourself go down that road again. Remember what Dante had to say on that. None of this is your fault. You can't keep beating yourself up over what Michael did."

She closed her eyes and the tears she had been fighting spilled over. The lump in her throat grew. She forced out the words anyway, her voice raw with guilt and fear.

"I can't keep hiding my head in the sand, either."

She had to start helping people—the living and the dead. She was sick of always being the one who needed to be rescued.

"After I woke up, the women kept talking about what happened to them. About what was going to happen to me, in graphic detail. They said I was lucky because…"

"Rachel—"

He started to put his arm around her, but she needed space to get through telling him. She shook her head and put her hand on his chest, which was…probably the best possible thing she could have done.

The sadness and fear dispersed as she took in the feel of him. The soft texture of the hair on his chest. The heat of his skin and the strength of the muscle beneath.

Warmth flooded her—not the fiery chemistry she was used to fighting with him, but soft waves of well-being and safety. She felt his desire to comfort her and drew on that strength to go on, her voice much stronger than before.

"They said the women he had killed more recently were lucky because he had more practice. He was better at taking blood and knocking us out when needed—even at using the blood for his paintings. He had it down. They said I was lucky because it would be over quicker."

She could feel each deep breath he took, her hand rising and falling with the movements of his chest. Focusing on the rhythmic motion helped her go on.

"Thanks to Dante and Elsa, I was only there for one day. The other women were held for days or even weeks. And the ones that couldn't move on after... The ones haunting him were with him for *years*."

"God, Rachel. That's awful."

"Do you see now? Those women—they were alone when this happened to them. They couldn't hear the voices of the others hovering near them."

She shook her head. "What happened was terrible. But I didn't go through it alone. They were with me. Knowing what they went through forced me to make peace with whatever was going to happen to me. To accept my fate. If I didn't, I knew my spirit would linger."

She wiped the tears from her cheeks. She never wanted to lead the existence of the ghosts she heard. Whatever was on the other side, she wanted to be willing and able to cast herself into it instead of clinging to a shadow of her life.

"And it's terrible and yes I have nightmares about it still, but I can handle all that. What I can't handle is knowing that those women are *still* out there. Still suffering. And I don't know how to help them."

"Why didn't they move on when he died?"

Rachel's heart gave a little sideways-leap, like it was trying to escape her chest. She was about to chisel away another bit of his peace of mind.

"I'm sure some did. But not all of them. Some were too hurt, too angry."

"How can you be sure?"

"Because they're directing that rage at me. That's why I freaked out when we left my mother's house. I saw them in the reflection in your car window."

"That doesn't make any sense. You didn't have anything to do with what happened to them."

"Toward the end, some of them figured out that I could hear them. They begged me not to kill Michael. They were afraid he'd be able to hurt them on the other side—to pick up where he left off."

Garrett hissed in a breath. "But they were wrong. You said Michael is gone."

"He is now. Now that his body has been cremated. For those few days after his death and before that, I…I don't know for sure what happened."

Garrett's voice lowered to a growl. "Did you ever hear him?"

"No. Usually it takes a while for a spirit to collect itself enough to figure out what they are and remember who they were. He might have been able to manifest more quickly."

The guilt from her choice was still crushing her. She didn't want Michael to inflict even a moment's more suffering on those women. But she also couldn't let him hurt anyone else. He had to be stopped.

"For whatever reason, some of his victims are still lingering. They need help to move on and I don't know what to do for them."

"We'll figure it out," he said.

"No. *I* will. You've done enough already."

He shook his head and let out a deep sigh. She could sense his disappointment, sharp and bitter through her chest.

"I don't understand what happened," he said. "What made you stop letting me help you?"

"You help me all the time."

"No, I rescue you when you've gotten yourself in so

deep you can't see a way out. You call me in as a last resort."

"I wouldn't say that."

She would just think it.

She started to pull away, but he covered her hand with his, pressing it firmly against his chest.

"Listen to me. I know you're dealing with a lot. And I know you're trying to handle it on your own. You said those ghosts helped you through your ordeal. That it was easier for you because you weren't alone. You aren't alone now. You haven't been for a while."

She knew her friends would help. But she didn't deserve it, didn't want her own drama to impact people she loved so dearly.

"Garrett—"

"You're not an echo of your mom," he said. "You're not set-dressing for her life—something to be seen and not heard. You don't have to figure out all your problems on your own."

It came out of left field, but it was exactly what she needed to hear. How did he always know just what to say? She felt enveloped in his warmth and compassion. Accepted. And he wasn't done.

"You're a vibrant, brilliant, kind-hearted person, and you deserve to be surrounded by people who appreciate you and are happy to help you. Like I am."

She let out a little laugh and said, "Are you trying to

make me cry again?"

"Never." He put his hand on the back of her neck and drew her forward, placing a gentle kiss on her forehead.

God, she wanted so much more than that. She wanted to plant her hands on his shoulders and push him back on the bed. She wanted to put all this talk about ghosts and death far behind her and just sink into him.

She wanted so much—too much from him. She was already tilting her head up, staring at his lips. Their faces were close enough that her nose grazed his cheek. His stubble tickled her skin.

He smelled like the ocean. Salt-tang and open spaces.

Flutter-thump.

They both jumped. Garrett muttered something under his breath that sounded like, "Damn grasshoppers."

But it was a good thing. A strong reminder of what it meant for someone like Garrett to be with her. Someone who didn't know what he was signing up for.

Lubbers weren't active at night. She was sure of it. Which meant something was influencing them to fly against her window. Something or someone.

She remembered the ghosts at her mother's house. The anger in their eyes as they lifted their arms to show Rachel the bloody wounds they had once all shared.

The accusation.

If Michael's victims had found out where Rachel was staying, going outside might become outright dangerous—

for her and the people around her. The people who dared to help her.

Even the genial ghost who had talked to her on Garrett's patio was at risk. If they thought he was standing in their way… She almost felt bad for him.

She felt bad for everyone at the moment.

"They seem to like this window. I think I'll sleep on the couch tonight," Rachel said.

"You can have my bed. I'll take the couch."

"I wouldn't hear of it."

He shook his head. "If you think I can't be as stubborn as you, you're wrong. I'm taking the couch. Come on."

She didn't have it in her to fight him on it or resist as he stood and pulled her up after him.

Chapter Thirteen

Garrett's couch was not meant for someone his size. He sat against the cushions, another of Rachel's books open in his lap.

The things he was reading about made his skin crawl. Bad enough to know that ghosts could be walking around him all the time, but learning that they could actually affect the physical world? He shuddered at the thought.

The chapter on poltergeists had been a particularly rough read. He'd seen enough movies to know about them throwing around stuff. He didn't know about the scratches, scrapes, bruises, and *bite marks* that sometimes came along with it.

How did Rachel do it? How did she walk around with a smile and pretend that everything was normal when she knew about all this—when she heard them all the time?

His appreciation for her grew. Along with his desire to help her. To support her any way he could.

The book also explained how salt helped to neutralize ghosts. It was all about energy. Salt could disrupt them. What he was still struggling with was how intention factored in. He was having trouble wrapping his mind around…the mind being able to influence the spiritual world.

According to the books, some clairsentients—people like Rachel who could perceive ghosts—weren't just receivers but could transmit energy into the ghostly realm as well. He wondered if there were any spectral objects on the other side that could be thrown around by psychics. Give the poltergeists a taste of their own medicine.

He snorted and turned the page. The next chapter was all about possession. Great.

He skimmed the introduction, but stopped cold at the first section header. In bold print, it read, "Spectral Influence on Animals." Attention caught, he read each word with care.

No. Freaking. Way. Ghosts could control animals?

The text used words like *impel* and *motivate*, but it boiled down to the same thing. Some ghosts could get animals to do what they wanted. If the ghost was powerful enough, they could even control several animals at a time.

Shit.

Garrett thought back to the scorpion in the dishwasher. To the lubbers bouncing off the windows. The possibilities were chilling.

What if the ghosts who were ticked at Rachel were *impelling* animals to try to get into the house? To get to Rachel. What if they were pissing the animals off in the process?

Grasshoppers were no big deal, but that scorpion could have been a problem. Florida had any number of dangerous and mobile species running around. An angry ghost could find a sick bat and get it to fly at Rachel, or send wasps her way, pathogen-carrying mosquitoes, snakes…

His mind reared back from that concept like a startled horse. He set aside the book and leapt up from the couch, then paced back and forth in his living room.

If there was more than one ghost after her, and they figured out how to send more than one animal at a time… Things could get hairy fast. How could he possibly keep Rachel safe at this rate? The poppets and saltwater kept the ghosts outside, but they hadn't been effective against that scorpion.

He had to deal with this. To address the issue at the source—the ghosts. Maybe there was some way he and Rachel could help them to move on. Resolve their issues, like the books talked about.

That seemed the best solution. The permanent solution.

But once they had dealt with these ghosts, what about the next batch? Rachel hadn't hedged around the fact that Florida was filled with lingering spirits. If they all came for her, wanting closure or resolution or whatever, how could she handle that?

He wouldn't let her do it on her own. That was for damned sure.

If she wouldn't let Garrett help her, he'd recruit Elsa and Jazz. Rachel couldn't stand against that pair. And if they all worked together, they could find a way to make sure that Rachel could lead whatever kind of life she wanted. He was certain of it.

Too bad that life didn't include him.

She had been opening up with him about so many things. He hoped she would explain her mixed messages at some point. The way she kept touching him, nestling close, then pulling away…it was driving him crazy.

When she'd patted the bed next to her, part of him had wondered if it was a different kind of invitation. Then she had put her hand on his chest and left it there for what felt like forever. His heart had pounded the whole time—from what she was saying and her touch.

Nuzzling his neck, his cheek… Her breath warming his skin.

He had nearly lost it before that lubber went and broke the moment. Damn bugs. He couldn't help but wonder what would've happened if they hadn't been interrupted. Scenarios danced in front of his mind, an array of possibilities he had longed for.

There was no time to feel sorry for himself. He had too much to do. Too much to learn.

He picked up the book again and opened it, then flopped down on the couch. The topic he happened across was psychometry—the psychic ability to read the history of objects through touch. Finally, something he knew about. He shook his head and started to read, just in case the book had more to teach him.

Chapter Fourteen

Sleep had eluded Rachel until light was just starting to peer around the edges of the blinds in Garrett's room. His sheets, his pillow, everything smelled like him. That alone would have been enough to keep Rachel awake in his huge bed.

His huge empty bed.

Everything else going on—the spirits outside, Garrett on the couch, her with no ideas about where to go or what was going to happen next—that didn't help either. It also didn't help that her resolve to stay away from him was breaking apart after only one day.

Instead of thinking about why they shouldn't be together, her mind kept conjuring up possibilities that just might work. What if she could shield him from the spirits in her life?

Her parents seemed happy together, though Rachel doubted her father was in on the secret Rachel and her mother shared. If Rachel could block the voices, she might be able to lead a normal life with Garrett.

A fake normal life.

No. She was tired of pretending. She wanted to be real,

to feel real.

She was different. It was time to admit it. Embrace it. *Do something with it.* Like help the women that Michael had killed.

Rachel checked the clock when she woke up after a fitful few hours of rest. Ten in the morning. She had slept late.

She slid from the bed quietly and made her way to the kitchen. The living room came into view as she approached the counter that separated the rooms. Garrett was sprawled on his couch on his stomach, one arm under his chest and the other above his head.

He didn't even have a pillow, poor guy. He must be exhausted.

His chest rose and fell with his breath and his hair was splayed over his cheek. Rachel was tempted to dust his bangs away from his face, but she didn't want to risk waking him. Making breakfast was out, since the noise would certainly disturb his sleep.

She decided to start in on her plan to help Michael's victims. And she was going to listen—in part—to Garrett's advice.

She would ask for help, but from the ghosts themselves. They were the ones who knew what they needed. She just had to find a way to get through to them, to get them to understand that she wanted to help.

The first thing she needed was more information. She

didn't know why they were lingering when Michael was gone. Did they want Rachel to tell their families what had happened to them? Was there something the police had missed? What could help them let go and move on? She headed for the sliding glass door.

Opening it slowly and quietly, she glanced back over her shoulder at Garrett. Still asleep. She slipped outside into the muggy morning air, then slid the door shut behind her.

Initiating a conversation with a ghost wasn't something she had done before. Even with Hiram, he had been the one to introduce himself.

Sweat was beading on her chest before she finally said, "Hello?"

"Good morning, my pet." The voice was male—the older ghost from last night. *"Did you sleep well?"*

"Well enough, thank you."

Her heart was beating fast and she had the urge to run back into the house. But that would wake up Garrett and then he'd insist on helping her—rescuing her again. She watched for possible threats to keep herself safe. Flying insects, birds, even fire ants.

"You don't need to be concerned, my dear. It's just the two of us."

The thought was mildly comforting. She glanced around at the palms swaying in the breeze and took a deep breath, trying to calm herself.

After all the hours of social etiquette classes her mother had sent her to and all her practice, she was having trouble making small talk. The ghost bailed her out.

"Where is your gentleman friend?"

"He's still asleep. Just inside." She corrected herself quickly. No sense in letting the ghost think she didn't have backup, even if she didn't want to call on Garrett.

"Goodness. Well… I remember those days." The ghost gave a chuckle that made her blush.

"He's not… We didn't…"

"My dear, I didn't mean to embarrass you. It's nature, regardless. I thought your generation was less stogy about such things."

"We are. I just don't want you to get the wrong idea about Garrett and me."

There was a pause, as if the ghost was considering her words. *"How on earth could that idea be wrong? A beautiful woman, a handsome man. You're obviously attracted to each other."*

"That doesn't mean we should do something about it."

The ghost chuckled again. *"My dear, when you cross over to this side, do you think you'll regret a night with that handsome man or all the nights you spent alone because you never dared to reach for him."*

His words struck her soul like a tuning fork, chills flowing over her skin. He was right. He was absolutely right. Rachel would go to her own grave regretting never having the chance to be with Garrett. But she had reasons. Good reasons.

The irony that a ghost was giving her tips on how to live… Her irritation was tempered by how much he reminded her of Hiram.

"Who are you?"

"My name is Misha. I think you knew a late colleague of mine."

"You knew Hiram?" Her voice rose to a squeak. She coughed to clear her throat.

"Yes, pet. We weren't much more than acquaintances in life, but grew a bit closer afterwards. He was always so fond of you. He asked me to keep an eye on you after he moved on. I've done my best, but you didn't make it easy."

"I didn't know."

Hiram hadn't mentioned anything to her. But it did seem like something he would do. He was always looking out for her. Protecting her.

"Well, I'm glad to finally get a chance to talk. I've been watching you with the good doctor and I haven't been able to figure out for the afterlife of me why you aren't together. It's obvious you care deeply for each other."

"Garrett deserves a better life than I can give him."

"Has he said that? He strikes me as a man who would rather have a choice."

"He can't make an informed decision. What I'm offering is too…alien."

Misha scoffed. *"So you string along other men who don't really have a chance with you? How is that fair to anyone?"*

Advice was one thing. Criticism was another. She didn't like his tone or what he was saying, even if there was truth to what he said.

She hadn't thought about her dating distractions in those terms at the time. She hadn't thought at all. Thinking made things harder.

Most of the men she'd dated seemed self-absorbed. She joked with Jazz that they didn't even notice when Rachel broke up with them. Maybe Misha had seen things she hadn't.

"I didn't mean to hurt anyone," she said.

Misha was quiet for a long time. Long enough that Rachel wondered if he had left.

"Misha? Are you still there?"

"Yes, pet."

His voice was a bit thinner. Sharper. The hairs along her arms stood on end.

"You sound angry."

"I apologize, my dear." His tone was genial again. *"I'm a bit distracted keeping the others from speaking with you."*

"Others? What others?"

"Those bothersome women who have been troubling you."

Her stomach lurched. Michael's victims *were* there.

"How are you keeping them from talking to me?"

"I can be persuasive." He laughed shortly.

"I need to talk to them."

"That's not a good idea. They're quite angry with you."

"I want to help them. Can you tell them that for me?"

"Help them how?"

"If they tell me what they need to be able to move on, I might be able to do something for them."

"Oh, pet," he said. *"I don't think you'll like their answer. The afterlife has not been kind to these women. They're focusing all that rage on you."*

"But I want to help."

"It's kind of you, but they've made their choice."

"No. I'm not going to let them keep suffering. I'm not going to give up. Let them talk to me."

He was quiet for a moment, then said, *"I'm afraid they've gone away for a bit. As I said, I was keeping them from you. But now that I know your wishes, I won't do that again."*

"Can you tell them I want to help? Try to get through to them?"

"I shall do my very best. But in the meantime, perhaps I *can help* you.*"*

"I don't need any help."

"Oh but you do. My sweet pet, you are wasting your life by focusing on the dead. You fear us so much that you

haven't really even started living."

She didn't like hearing it from him, but couldn't argue his point. "What do you suggest?"

"I think you should walk right into that house and kiss the good doctor."

"You seem keen on us getting together."

"What can I say? I'm a romantic. I'm also keen on seeing you happy. And I think you two can make each other happy—unlike your other misadventures in romance."

"I know he would make me happy, but all I would bring him is…strangeness and anxiety. He was happier before he knew that ghosts were real and everywhere. Having me around is a constant reminder."

"I hardly think his mind is occupied with thoughts of death when you're standing close." He paused for a moment while she digested his words. *"Have you talked to him about it? Asked him what he thinks? What he wants?"*

"No…"

"Maybe you should. You of all people know how terrible it feels when others make decisions for you."

Another good point. "I guess you've sat in on some family dinners."

"A few. Your mother is a most intriguing woman."

"That's one word for it."

He chuckled again. *"Pet, I know that you are lonely. It's difficult to watch you prolong your suffering—and that of the good doctor."*

"I don't mind suffering if it gives him a chance at a normal life."

"He doesn't want normal. He wants you."

Rachel snorted and shook her head. "You have a weird way of giving pep-talks."

"Forgive me. My manners are a bit skewed from dealing with the dead for so long. But please believe me that my sole purpose is to make you happy."

Strangely, she did believe him. She wasn't sure she trusted him yet, but he seemed sincere in this at least. He had been watching her—and Garrett. And whatever Misha had seen convinced him that they were right for each other.

If she could admit it to herself, she already knew they *felt* right together. Being with Garrett felt like home—like...forever.

She didn't want to have regret at the end of her life. She wanted memories. Wonderful memories. She didn't want to deny either of them that potential.

Rachel smiled at the thought, excitement bubbling up through her. Maybe it was time that she started focusing on living her life instead of avoiding the dead.

Chapter Fifteen

Too many nights of not enough rest were taking their toll on Garrett. He woke up to the groggy state of half-sleep, disoriented and stiff. His left arm was numb from being pinned under his torso and he had drooled on his couch.

Light was filtering into the room from the blinds that covered the sliding glass door. They had shifted a bit, enough to let the morning sun stretch across the bamboo floor.

Something was wrong. Why were the blinds open at all?

He jumped up, nearly cracking his shins on his coffee table, then ran to the door. Rachel was sitting on one of the chairs outside. She was still wearing his T-shirt. She hugged her knees to her chest and had her feet resting on the chair. And she was laughing.

Garrett paused, trying to triage the situation. She looked relaxed. Comfortable. She wasn't scared. But she was talking to someone. Her voice was too low for him to make out what she was saying through the glass.

Had she already made contact with one of the ghosts

they had talked about helping? It seemed quick work to win them over so fast, even for someone as charming as Rachel. If anyone could do it though, she could.

The thought of her outside alone with a ghost was unsettling. Especially now that he knew there was more danger involved than she had let on.

He opened the door, the heat from the stone of his patio blasting him. Rachel turned at the sound, her smile stopping him in his tracks.

How long had it been since he had seen that smile? He felt an odd sense of loss that someone else had brought it out of her. He had been trying so hard to be supportive. Whatever ghost she was talking to had done a better job lifting the weights from her spirit.

"Hi Garrett. I was just talking to Misha."

"Misha? Who's that?"

"He was a friend of Hiram's. It turns out he's been hanging around me for a long time." She paused as if listening to something, then laughed again.

Garrett bristled. He wasn't sure why.

Whoever this Misha was, he was helping Rachel feel better. Shouldn't that make Garrett happy too? Instead, his stomach coiled up like a rattler. He wanted to get her back inside the house, safe behind the wards.

"Have you had breakfast yet?"

"No, I was waiting for you to wake up. Do you think I should take down some wards so he can join us?"

Chh-chh-chh-chh. The hair on his arms stood on end. Who the hell was this guy that Rachel was talking about letting her guard down? Letting him into Garrett's house?

"I don't think that's a good idea. Misha isn't the only one hanging around."

"Right." She shook her head. "Sorry, I guess I wasn't thinking. Misha, I hope you don't mind. Would you excuse me?"

She was quiet again, her head cocked to the side, then she laughed. She stretched out her legs and put her feet on the ground, then yelped and pulled them right back up. They must have been talking for a long time, since she hadn't realized the stones had heated up.

"Hold on." Garrett slipped on his sandals, then stepped into the sun. At least Rachel had been sitting in the shade of the umbrella attached to his patio table.

"Garrett, you don't have to—"

He picked her up before she could finish her sentence. She smiled at him and wrapped her arms around his neck, but he couldn't bring himself to smile back. Even feeling the soft skin of her bare thighs resting on his arm couldn't quell his misgivings.

When he stepped inside, his top priority was to grab the spray bottle and make sure the door was secure. Rachel leaned into him, breaking his concentration.

Holding her close against his chest felt too good. His mind was already coming up with excuses to keep holding her. He pushed the thoughts away.

When he started to set her down, she left her arms around his neck and slid down his torso. He could feel the T-shirt she was wearing bunch up against him, moving up past her hips as he lowered her. Her legs had to be completely bare—at the very least. Her T-shirt felt like it was bunched above her waist.

She was probably wearing panties. No, she was definitely wearing panties. He had to believe that. If he envisioned anything else, things would get embarrassing fast. Even that brief thought was enough to set things stirring down below.

He cleared his throat and locked his gaze on the spray bottle, stepping away from her. "I'll take care of the door."

He slid it shut as he stepped to the counter. Then he sprayed the whole thing down and pulled the blinds shut. Rachel was heading for the kitchen when he dared to look at her again.

Those long legs stretching out past the hem of the T-shirt she was wearing caught his attention. The way she swished her hips wasn't helping, the fabric rippling against her backside. She paused by the barstools, resting one hand on the counter as she looked back at him over her shoulder and smiled.

It wasn't exactly a fake smile, but it wasn't a real one, either. It was flirty. Coquettish.

He'd seen her use that walk—that smile—before. He

always felt sorry for the poor saps blasted by it. And now, he was in the line of fire.

Holy shit.

"What would you like for breakfast?" she asked.

He took a step toward her, felt his hands flex like they wanted to reach for her. But he stopped himself.

She caught every nuance. Her smile turned to a smirk, her gaze softening as it flowed over his body then back to his face. She knew she was pushing his buttons, and she was doing it on purpose. Garrett just couldn't figure out why. Why now, of all times?

She'd had years to make a move. Why do it during the storm of chaos surrounding them?

Unless that was exactly why she was doing it. Because she needed to feel in control of something when her life seemed to be in a tailspin. And she knew she could control Garrett, if she really wanted to.

God help him, it looked like she did.

"I could make French toast," she said. "Or pancakes and eggs."

She turned toward him, giving him a new view. He let out a little grunt, but wasn't sure she heard it. He stifled it as best he could. His chest felt constricted.

The soft fabric of his T-shirt clung to her full breasts, faint outlines showing him where her nipples had stiffened beneath. She leaned forward on the nearest barstool, both hands planted firmly on its surface so that her arms pushed her breasts together and exaggerated the effect.

Dammit, that was not okay. He could feel himself starting to get hard.

If she needed to feel in control of something, this was not the way to do it. He pulled on the anger rising up in him to help calm his body down as he kicked off his sandals.

"Cereal is fine."

"Are you sure? You've done so much for me. I'd like to do something nice for you in return."

He could think of a slew of nice things they could do together. None of them involved food. Wait, no there was a can of whipped cream in the fridge.

He needed to rein this in.

"I'll take care of breakfast. Maybe you should go get dressed."

She looked confused, the seductress façade slipping. The tightness in his chest eased up enough that he could breathe again.

"You seem upset," she said.

He could hardly deny it. But voicing his immediate concerns didn't seem like a good idea. He chose some from earlier instead.

"What were you doing out there by yourself?"

"Talking to Misha."

"But you didn't know it would be Misha," he said. "It could have been one of Michael's victims. The ghosts that are pissed off at you."

"They can't hurt me."

"Not directly. But those grasshoppers weren't having a mosh party against your window last night for no reason. And don't think I haven't figured out that's why the scorpion was in the dishwasher."

His anger spiked as he remembered the jolt of fear brought on from that knowledge. The ghosts were already sending insects after Rachel—even venomous ones. What if they started sending something worse?

No way he was letting her go outside alone again, especially barely dressed as she was. Too much unprotected skin waiting to be bitten or stung. His stomach clenched at the thought.

"I was being careful. Besides, Misha told me the ghosts who are mad at me aren't here right now. He scared them away."

"Did he?" Garrett didn't buy it. Something about this Misha character was off.

"I told him my plan—that I'm going to try to help them. He thinks it's worth a shot and is going to let them know the next time he sees them. If they even come back." She shrugged as if it was no big deal.

"You seemed pretty determined to help them last night."

"I was. *I am.*" She sighed, then walked back to him, stopping so close he could almost feel her body heat. "Do we have to talk about this now?"

Leaning forward even an inch would bring their bodies together. He clenched his hands into fists to keep from touching her.

"I'm worried," he said. "You wanted to let this guy into the house. That doesn't seem safe."

"That was a mistake—I admit it. But lucky for me, I have you looking out for me."

The playful teasing was coming back to her voice again. Garrett wouldn't mind it a bit if the circumstances were different. But they weren't.

Of all the messed up twists of fate, having Rachel come on to him now... He steeled his resolve, doing his best to ignore the way she stared at his lips, the way she radiated desire.

It wasn't happening. Not like this.

Chapter Sixteen

"Rachel, this is serious. You wanted to let a ghost into the house."

The conversation was not going the way Rachel had expected. The fact that they were still talking at all baffled her. She'd expected them to be naked by now.

She let out a sigh and said, "Misha isn't just a ghost. He's a friend."

"Really? You just met the guy last night. And you couldn't get away from him fast enough then."

"I was wrong. Last night I was afraid of every ghost. But I'm seeing things differently now. You even said you wanted to help me with them."

"That's exactly my point. You should have waited for me to come with you."

"You were sleeping."

"You could have woken me up." He shook his head. "I know you're...spontaneous, but there's too much at stake for you to not be more careful."

"*I'm* the one in danger."

"And do you think the rest of us wouldn't be hurt if something happened to you?"

His words felt like a slap. She amended his sentence in her head. If something *else* happened to her.

Everyone in their circle of friends had been hurt. Some physically. Horribly. And it was her fault—no matter what they said.

What had she been thinking, trying to start something with Garrett? Even if he could handle her ghost issue, which he clearly couldn't, Rachel still had too much baggage.

Her eyes filled with tears and she crossed her arms. "Right. Because I'm such a terrible judge of character. That's how we all landed in this mess in the first place."

"Rachel…" He reached toward her, but she threw her hands up and backed away.

"I'm sorry I'm not perfect like Elsa or Jazz. I don't always know what to do next. I screw up."

And that was probably what Garrett saw in Rachel in the first place. He was a classic rescuer. An ex-ER doctor, for crying out loud.

Rachel's string of mistakes and failures gave him something to focus on. No wonder things hadn't worked out between him and Elsa. Elsa was always on top of everything.

"That isn't what I meant at all. And everybody makes mistakes," he said.

She snorted and shook her head. "Not like this."

She sniffed to keep her nose from running and wiped

the back of her hand across her eyes. "Listen, I said I was going to handle this myself. And I will. I'll get on your computer and find a place and be out right away."

"No. Hell no."

Garrett let out a huge sigh and ran his hands through his hair. Instead of leaving them there and staring at her like he usually did, he dropped his arms to his sides. He walked over to his recliner and sat, then rested his elbows on his knees.

"This is exactly why doctors aren't allowed to work on people they're involved with." He glanced at her quickly and said, "I mean care about."

He shook his head and laughed, then ran his hand over his face. With another sigh, he leaned back in his chair. He looked exhausted.

"I'm messing this all up," he said. "Nothing I say is coming out right. Please let me try again. Can I start over?"

Her anger fizzled. Garrett asking for a second chance… How could she say no to that? Even if they didn't have the huge mass of things he had done for her—second, third, fifth, eleventy-ith chances he'd given her—she would have melted at the request.

He was hurting. It was probably the clearest thing they'd communicated to each other yet, etched in the lines around his eyes, the furrows between his brows.

She sat on the edge of his coffee table in front of him.

"I'm listening."

He leaned forward in the chair again, which brought him close. Really close.

His jaw was coated in dark stubble that accentuated his strong cheekbones. She wanted to run her fingertips across the coarse surface, but shook herself internally and brought herself back to task. He deserved her full attention.

"I'm just going to lay it all out there," he said. "You've always been the first to admit that you're impulsive."

She opened her mouth to argue with him, but realized that was true. It stung, but she kept her silence and heard him out.

"I don't know if that's your nature or how you've been dealing with these voices your whole life or a little of both. But it's who you are and I—"

He lowered his head for a moment and took a deep breath, then let it out slow. When he looked up at her again, his expression was shielded.

"I care about you. I don't want you to have to change because of this. Because of what Michael did to you or being born psychic or anything."

"I appreciate that."

He nodded. "What I do want is for you to be safe. I've seen your other side—the reflective, detail-oriented person who pauses and thinks things through before acting."

"In other words, you want me to be more like Elsa." It

felt like he was using her heart as a punching bag.

"Not at all. If you'll recall, I met you first. If anyone's the baseline, it's you."

Rachel had forgotten that she had worked on Garrett's house before he and Elsa met. It helped. A little.

"I want you to be more like *you*. I think if you let yourself stop playing the socialite and take some time to figure out who you really want to be, you'll be a lot happier. And I want you to be happy. You can stay here as long as you need while you sort it out."

"I don't want to impose."

"It's not an imposition. I love…hanging out with you."

He winced as he obviously changed the direction of his sentence. She didn't dare let herself think of what he might have been about to say.

"I know I had a great time during those months when you stayed here before," he said. "I thought you did too."

Her throat felt thick again. "It was wonderful."

"I'm glad." He smiled at her, so sad it broke her heart. "I think I'm the one messing things up now and I promise I'll work on that. I just have a lot of anger when I think of what happened to you. It's hard for me to hide it and it's making everything become exaggerated. I'm sorry."

"You don't have to be sorry."

She lifted her hands to his face, cradling his cheeks. The prickling of his hair against her palms made her shiver. He closed his eyes and lifted his hands to her arms, taking more slow, deep breaths.

When he opened his eyes again, Rachel couldn't look away. They stared at each other, gazed into each other's eyes. It was incredibly intimate. She felt exposed, vulnerable, but he was right there with her. As always.

He was so beautiful.

She wanted to kiss him, but if she did, their friendship would be over. She couldn't fool herself into thinking that they could go back to the status quo after that.

And if they did become involved, she'd have to stay in constant crisis to keep him interested, to keep giving the rescuer part of him that hit. That wasn't any better than the way she'd been living up to this point.

She wanted to be partners with him. She wanted to take turns shopping and paying the bills and doing laundry. She wanted to live as they had when she'd been working on his house.

Wait… That was when their relationship started—when she had been basically living with him over those months.

At first he'd been at work most of the time, but it hadn't been long before he was coming home earlier and taking more vacation days. They had spent tons of time together, talking, laughing, taking care of themselves and each other.

They had been partners then, and she had never felt more at ease in her own skin. She hadn't needed any rescuing. Her life had been calm. And he had been interested in her. Obviously, deeply interested.

Rachel had run away because she thought he couldn't handle her ability to see ghosts. Now she knew that wasn't a valid fear. He could handle it. In spades.

He could even handle her mom—who already loved him and had been pushing Rachel to try to seduce him into a marriage. Which had only inspired Rachel to run away more.

Reacting. Always reacting.

That was the impulsiveness that Garrett was talking about. It had grown the more she pinballed her way through life, bouncing off of whatever obstacles rose before her. Calling Garrett for help because she couldn't stay away from him.

She sat up straighter as another thought rocketed through her mind. Garrett might be a bit of a rescuer, but she was the one who kept initiating the problems by making ridiculously bad choices. Every time she dug herself in too deep, she had an excuse to call him. And every time, he came to help her out.

He wasn't a rescuer. She was a rescue-ee.

She had a list. Didn't she have a list? Reasons she shouldn't pursue a relationship with Garrett.

She played into his weaknesses as a rescuer. No, she was artificially creating crises to give herself an excuse to call him.

She could hear ghosts, and that would be too weird for

him to handle. Well, that was impacting him, but he didn't seem too put off by it. He just wanted her to be safe and use caution when dealing with them. That was fair enough.

Her mother was…her mother. Garrett had already stood up to Mrs. Montgomery when he helped Rachel leave her house. He could handle that matter.

Didn't she have a longer list than that? She couldn't remember anything else.

Like a lightning strike, she realized there were no actual reasons for them to not be together. Nothing but the shadows she had conjured up from her own mind.

She looked at him again, sitting patiently right in front of her. Waiting.

He had been waiting long enough.

Chapter Seventeen

Something shifted in Rachel's expression. Garrett couldn't miss it. He watched closely as she thought over what he said. Thought long and hard, from the looks of things.

She started off looking troubled, then shifted through perplexed and concerned before…relieved? Hopeful?

He didn't know how it was going to land.

Would she be mad? Hurt? Would she get up and walk out like she always did, leaving him to patch up his heart as best he could?

All he could do was wait. He held her arms lightly, let her stare into his soul, her hands gentle on his face.

She leaned in and kissed him.

He felt the shock of it in every cell of his body. Her lips —velvet soft—played across his mouth. A few tentative preludes before she became more aggressive. Her tongue found his, their breath mingling, her grip tightening to hold him right where she wanted him.

Was this still playing out from before? Was it about control or something else? Something deeper?

After everything he'd laid down on her, this wasn't at

all what he expected. But he couldn't bring himself to stop her.

She pushed him farther onto his recliner and molded her body against his in a graceful lunge. The force of her movement made the chair kick back and flatten. She brought her knees up on either side of him, pressing their hips together.

He groaned as he felt her heat through her panties and his thin pajama bottoms. When had he grown rock-hard?

Damn, she knew how to kiss. He had imagined this so many times, but it was never this intense. There was always a slow build. He should have known better with Rachel.

She raked her teeth along his jaw. He felt it echo in every nerve ending in his body. She started rubbing against his erection as she lightly bit down on his neck.

Garrett sucked in a breath, trying to form a coherent thought. All he could do was groan and rock against her.

So many years full of *want*. And now he had her. Finally.

He let his hands glide down her back, past her waist, and cupped the fullness of her backside. She let out a little grunt, then moved her kisses up along his neck so she could suck and nip his earlobe. His fingers clenched against her flesh as electric pleasure crackled through him.

This was happening too fast. He needed a moment to catch his breath, to make sure they were on the same page.

If she was just doing this to say thanks or to give herself comfort... Well, he could comfort her in other ways. But not like this. This was too important.

She ran her nails over his chest, letting her fingertips burrow through his chest hair as she explored his torso.

"Rachel..."

She lifted herself from him a bit. He thought maybe she was going to stop so they could talk, but instead she pressed her hand against his abdomen, sliding it all the way down, right past the waist of his pajamas so she could grip his erection tight.

His head hit the back of his—thankfully—cushioned chair as his back arched. She didn't waste any time before starting to work him, pumping her hand up and down.

Her skin was soft as silk. His body must be glowing white-hot from how his nerves were firing off. They wouldn't be the only thing firing off any second now if she kept that up.

"Rachel—"

He grabbed her hand to stop its movement, but she didn't let go. Apparently she wasn't nearly done with him yet.

She nuzzled his cheek as she brought her lips back to his. The kiss was slow and deep. It gave him time to enjoy the taste of her, the warmth of her skin.

He had a chance to kiss her back. Really kiss her. Maybe it wasn't all about control after all.

He indulged himself, holding the kiss for long enough to saturate his senses with her before moving his mouth across hers, pulling first one lip then the other between his.

Her hair fell across his face and neck, feather-light. He let go of her arm to tuck it back behind her ear, then slowly slid his tongue into her mouth.

This was more the give-and-take he had imagined.

She didn't start up her hand again, and he couldn't say that he minded. He was way too close to the edge. Even holding still, her hand wrapped around him was sending lightning arcs of stimuli through him.

He needed to get her to let go—to give him a chance to cool down. There were still things he needed to talk to her about before this went any further.

As if she sensed his need, she finally let him go. She kept her hand down the front of his pants, though—playing with the sensitive skin above his hip and along his lower abdomen.

She shifted above him, kissing his cheek and jaw, then down along his neck. His eyes rolled shut as her gentle touches relaxed him.

Still, he managed to say, "We need to talk."

She nuzzled his earlobe, and whispered, "There are much better things I can do with my mouth."

He didn't doubt that one bit after what they'd just done. He groaned at the thought of doing more, but it wasn't the time. There were things they needed to work through.

She started to slide down toward the edge of the chair. Garrett kept his eyes closed for a minute and took a deep breath to help himself focus.

He needed to calm his body down, but he was wound up too tight. And she still had her hand down his pants. It was planted on his thigh for some reason. Probably so she could sit up.

The cool air of the AC hit his erection. That was the only warning he had before she wrapped her lips around him and sucked him deep into her mouth.

He let out a guttural cry as his body rocketed back up, his nerves singing in ecstasy. Her tongue flicked along his length, swirled around in circles that stoked him even higher. And all the while, she kept pumping him, lips wrapped around him tight.

He wanted to grab her and move her away. Part of him really did. But a stronger part, a more primal part, couldn't resist this pleasure. He looked down at her, watched as her golden hair slid across his stomach, and he came.

It was harder and faster than any climax he had ever experienced. His fingers dug into the arms of the chair, he couldn't catch his breath or stop the low grunts that escaped him.

And she never once stopped. She never slowed down. Even when his hips bucked up against her, she just rode him until he was spent, taking everything he was giving her, till the edges of his vision seemed to darken as the sensory overload threatened to make him pass out.

When she finally had mercy on him and let him slide from her mouth, she gently released the waistband of his pajama bottoms, then glanced up at him and gave him a wicked smile. She had just taken him down to the most primal level a man could reach, and she knew it.

And he wasn't sure why.

She slid back up his body, kissing a path to his mouth. He was still thrumming from what they had shared—physically more relaxed, but more on edge in every other way.

He tried to form his thoughts while she kissed him, but they all blurred together. When she was done, she leapt up from the chair.

"Why don't we skip breakfast altogether," she said. "It's late enough that we can just have lunch."

What. The. Hell.

Chapter Eighteen

Rachel had never felt more energized. She and Garrett were together. *Finally!* She couldn't wait for things to get back to how they had been when she lived with him before. Only this time it would be even better.

There were no more secrets between them. No more reasons to stay apart.

They were already living together again. It was amazing. The house was cleared and warded, and as soon as they solved the problems of the ghosts that were unhappy with her, they could focus on each other fully.

She was absolutely going to start taking care of him now. That little episode in the recliner was just the appetizer. They would need their strength for the next things she had in mind.

As he rose from the recliner, she said, "Is there still lunchmeat in the fridge? I can make us more sandwiches."

Garrett was staring at her with his mouth slightly open. Oh yeah. He had enjoyed himself. She felt her smile broaden.

"Rachel, what the hell was that?" he asked.

She wanted to say *foreplay* but something in the way he

was looking at her made her stop. He ran his hands through his hair, resting them on top of his head and holding his bangs away from his face. The supermodel pose accentuated his broad chest and narrow hips.

He was unbelievably beautiful. With his hair out of the way, she had a clear view of his strong cheekbones and jaw—those rich blue eyes.

She wanted to push him right back down on the recliner. Except his eyes were pinched around the edges. And he was frowning—not what she expected after what they had shared.

"I don't understand," she said.

"*You* don't understand?" He let his arms drop to his sides. Even under all that stubble she could see a muscle in his cheek twitching.

He shook his head and said, "I can't keep up. One minute you're happy to be here, the next you're out the door any second. You ask for my help, but you don't listen to what I say, then you do a one-eighty and are going to do everything on your own. You're terrified of ghosts, then you're inviting one to breakfast."

"If this is about Misha—"

"This isn't about Misha! It's about *us*. It's always been about us. How you look at me like…something's there, then laugh it off and flit away." He pointed at the recliner and said, "And then you do *that* and immediately jump to lunch like nothing happened?"

"I—"

"You can't blow me just to let off steam! It has to mean something."

"Of course it means something." Her heart felt like it had stopped beating, like it was curled up in her chest.

"What? 'Thanks for letting me crash here'?"

"How can you say that? I would never—"

Anger and disappointment clawed at her throat, cutting off her words. She would never be so casual about what she'd just done. Especially with him. How could he think that of her?

He put his hands over his face for a moment, then slid them along his cheeks till they were held in front of his lips as if he was praying. He dropped his arms to his sides again, letting out a deep breath. Somehow, it seemed to diminish him, like more than air was escaping. He looked crushed.

"I'm sorry. I said I would get a handle on myself, and I…messed it up again." He bowed his head and murmured, "Shit. There's no going back now anyway."

When he looked up at her, his eyes were blazing. It wasn't anger or frustration. It warmed her—made heat pool deep in her belly—even in the midst of this awful conversation.

"I love you, Rachel. I have since the night we met."

The room started to spin around her. No matter how confident she was about his feelings for her, there was always room for doubt. Until this moment. Hearing the words was so much better than making assumptions about how he felt. And he had more to say.

"When you were staying here working on the house… I've never been happier in my life. It felt like how forever should be. I thought we had both found *the one*. Then it was gone—you were gone—and I didn't know why. Still don't."

He shook his head and went on. "But I still want it. What we had, whatever it was. I want it so much it eats me up inside. I've tried to get over it. To get over you. But every time I started to give up on the dream of us being together, you'd throw me a crumb and I'd think maybe we still had a shot."

Rachel's heart was pounding so much she was lightheaded. She knew she had hurt him in the past and wanted to make up for that. She thought that was what she had been doing. That she was starting something beautiful with him. But she had only managed to make things worse —to hurt him more.

"I can't keep doing this. I can't—" His voice broke. It actually broke. Rachel's heart cracked along with it.

He cleared his throat. When he spoke again, his voice was low and quiet—so gentle it made her ache.

"You can stay here as long as you need. I will help you any way I can, except…" He angled his head slightly toward the recliner. "Except that. But I need to know where I stand with you. Once and for all."

Rachel couldn't speak. Her chest was so tight, she could barely breathe. She felt the tears on her cheeks but didn't move to wipe them away.

All she could do was nod.

"Take some time," his voice was still painfully gentle. "I'm going to go cool off."

She closed her eyes so she wouldn't have to watch him walk away, but she felt him passing. She wanted to reach for him, to tell him he had it all wrong. But that would be reacting again. She couldn't risk hurting him any more than she already had.

She still didn't understand what had happened. She replayed that last few minutes in her mind, picking everything apart for clues.

They were talking... He wanted her to be more authentically herself. She thought that was what she was doing. Showing him how she really felt, letting herself be free to express who she was, passionate and adventurous and energetic.

And he couldn't keep up.

She was mercurial. She couldn't change that. She didn't want to have to change to be with someone. With Garrett, she never felt that she had to. Until now.

He kept going on about how she could be practical and focused. It was true. When she was working on a project, she did feel different. Confident... In charge. She didn't need to jump from one topic or activity to another just to keep her mind occupied.

Which was the real her?

Both. She couldn't deny it. And because of that, for the first time she truly wasn't sure if she and Garrett should be together. Not for any of the paranormal reasons or issues with her dysfunctional family. But because of who she was.

The hopelessness of that thought weighed her down. She felt like she would sink through the floor at any moment.

She wasn't right for him after all. He wouldn't be happy with her.

Something thumped against the sliding glass doors. And again and again. More freaking lubbers.

Dammit! She had enough problems in her *own* life. She didn't need to be distracted by other peoples' afterlives.

She wasn't going to feel guilty that she was the only person to escape from Michael. Those other women needed to know that she was going to help them, but on *her* terms.

Going outside wasn't safe. She couldn't control the environment well enough. Plan B, then.

Rachel went to the kitchen and grabbed the container of salt, then stalked to her room. She trailed a thick line of the crystals across the entire threshold of her doorway, but left the door open. The barrier she'd made could be disturbed too easily. Besides, she wanted to be able to leap over it if she needed to. No ghosts would be able to cross that line.

They'd definitely need to get more salt soon. Rather, Garrett would. There was no *they* involved.

Wiping the back of her hand across her eyes and nose, she stood, then went to the bathroom. She grabbed a washcloth and wet it.

For a moment, she thought about tearing the sheet away from the mirror so she could face the women when she confronted them. Remembering their expressions, their wounds... Not a good idea.

She went back to her room and opened her blinds all the way. She wiped down the window, getting all the saltwater off the glass, then pulled her reading chair closer to it.

With a deep breath, she climbed up on it and took down her witch's ball and the poppet.

Nothing happened at first. That wasn't too much of a surprise. She climbed back down and tucked the poppet and glass ball under the sheet on her bed.

Turning the chair to face the window, she sat and waited.

Moments ticked by. She was getting restless. Her thoughts went back to Garrett and her stomach clenched.

"You look unhappy."

The voice whispering close to her ear made her jerk away. It was male, but didn't sound like Misha. A chill swept over her skin.

"I didn't mean to startle you, pet." The genial tone returned. *"Is everything all right with your doctor friend?"*

"I don't want to talk about that. Were you able to find the women I'm looking for?"

"Goodness but you sound serious. No, I'm afraid I didn't have much luck there."

"I know they're close. They keep sending grasshoppers to bounce off the windows and they impelled a scorpion to crawl through the drain in the dishwasher."

"That sounds unlikely. Impelling animals takes skill and a certain mindset. I doubt those women have enough self-control to do so."

Rachel bristled on their behalf. "Excuse me?"

"Because they're upset, of course. They would need to focus their emotions to channel them properly to get an animal to do what they want."

What he said made sense, even though she didn't like how he said it. What didn't make sense was the grasshoppers' behavior. One isolated incident wasn't suspicious. Three? That couldn't be a coincidence.

"Something is making them act strangely," she said.

"Does the doctor have a lawn service? Perhaps a chemical sprayed in the yard recently upset them."

"I suppose it's possible…"

"What's truly troubling you, pet?"

"I'm not a pet. Stop calling me that."

"Of course. My apologies."

She shouldn't have snapped at him, but the level of despair she felt was reminding her of her time in Michael's garage. Her hopes had risen higher than ever in her life, and then been dashed. Even the dream of being with Garrett was gone.

If she thought about it more she would start crying again. And she was sick of crying.

She stood and started pacing the room. "There has to be something else going on. Those women I saw at my mother's house must be around here somewhere."

Rachel remembered how angry they had been, how terrified. Both at her mother's and in Michael's garage. They weren't walking away from this—from her.

"My dear, if you would tell me what is wrong, perhaps I could help you."

"Find me those ghosts. That's how you can help."

"Patience is required in this case."

Rachel snorted. Misha wanted her to slow down too. More waiting. If she hadn't delayed so long with Garrett, things might have worked out differently. But could they have lasted as a couple, knowing the issues he was having now?

"I'm beginning to grow worried. Is Dr. Wolfstrom all right? I would check myself, but you've warded the house quite effectively."

"This isn't my first rodeo. I doubt it will be my last."

Her voice had a growl to it that even surprised her. Misha was quiet for a while. Good. Let him know—let them all know—she was done being messed with. She was done having people tell her who to be or how to act.

She was psychic. She was smart. She was weird. And most of all, she was tired of hiding it all. Hiding who she was and how she felt.

And how she felt…

She loved Garrett.

"Does he know you took the wards down?" Misha asked.

"Of course not," she said. "He would never have let me."

"He has good reason for his concern."

"I get it! He only sees me at my worst! When he's picking up the pieces after I make bad decisions. But this is the last time. After this, he won't be seeing me at all. He's done with me."

The words—the thought of it—tore at her heart. No more Garrett. He was out of her life forever. She had ruined everything.

"I highly doubt that."

She sat heavily on her bed, shoulders slumping. "He'll be better off. He as much as said so."

"There is no way he said such a thing."

"He can't keep up. That's what he said."

Misha chuckled. *"No one can keep up with you, my dear! I don't have a body to exhaust, and I still get tired following you around. That doesn't mean he doesn't want to be with you. Accept who you are and believe that he does the same and you'll both be happier."*

"No. I've put him through enough."

There was a long pause, then Misha said. *"If you walk away now, you'll destroy him."*

Misha's voice was somber and low. The hair on Rachel's arms stood on end. Ghosts only spoke like that if they had an ace up their sleeve.

"How can you be so certain?"

"Because I understand why he's so overprotective. Why the tiny scorpion brought out such a huge reaction."

She had thought it was weird at the time, but was distracted by Garrett naked in his kitchen. Even now, the memory of seeing him in all his glory—and nothing else— made her body tingle.

"He has a brother," Misha said.

"No he doesn't."

Garrett had never mentioned a sibling of any sort. Rachel knew his parents, had seen them at tons of social events. Garrett was the only person they ever brought along or talked about.

"Forgive me, I misspoke. He had *a brother."*

Had... Her heart sank at the thought, weighed down by countless tragic scenarios that played through her head.

It must have happened years ago—decades, even. She had never heard anyone, living or dead, speak of Garrett's brother.

"Garrett was with him when it happened," Misha said.

Rachel jumped up and shook her head. "No. You can't tell me this. If Garrett wants me to know, he'll tell me himself."

Why hadn't he told her? It must have been terrible for him. She wanted to know more, wanted to run to Garrett and hold him and for once be the one to comfort him.

"He won't have a chance if you run away after this. I know you, Rachel. It's what you do."

Misha's voice took on that strange cast again toward the end of his sentence. He sounded angry. She wasn't having it.

"Why does it matter to you? You already had your shot at life. This is mine. I can mess it up if I want to."

"Forgive me. It's just painful to watch someone I care about throwing away their best chance at happiness."

"Maybe I don't get to be happy."

The words escaped before she had a chance to think about them. Saying them hollowed her out, made her feel empty.

She had always considered happiness a choice. It was about choosing the way she thought about events, even when life rose up again and again to knock her down. Now, she wasn't so sure.

"What about Garrett? Does he deserve to suffer too?"
The ghost let out a derisive snort. *"You two are perfect for each other. Punishing yourselves for imagined errors and perceived imperfections. I truly hope you work this out if only so you won't inflict yourself on other unfortunates who are blinded by your charms."*

"Excuse me?" Rachel practically shouted the words.

What the hell was this guy's deal? He said he wanted to help her, then insulted her? His voice had changed again too. He sounded younger.

Why was he so angry? It was her life that she was messing up. Well, Garrett's too, according to Misha. She didn't understand why he cared.

Unless...

Unless he wasn't who he said he was. A chill shot down her spine as she thought of Michael. But no—it couldn't be him. Who did that leave? Who might be lingering around one or both of them, mad about choices they were making?

Whoever this was, he seemed to really want them to be together and to believe that was best for them both. Especially for Garrett.

She thought back over what Misha had said, about Garrett having a brother. Garrett's brother had to have been gone for a long time for Rachel not to have heard of him. Young children didn't linger, but if his brother had been older than Garrett by several years...

His spirit might have stayed. He might have watched as Rachel flirted and flitted away, over and over again. He might have seen Garrett fall in deeper, loving Rachel, wanting to be with her. He might have seen how happy she made Garrett once upon a time.

He might be pissed as hell that she was planning to run away again.

"Misha, I don't think Garrett and I will work out in the long term." She kept her voice as gentle as she could manage. "He deserves a woman who won't put him through so much."

"He wants you."

"That doesn't mean he should be with me. You've probably noticed how upset he's been since I came here. I want him to have a peaceful life. A chance at a normal family."

Misha let out another snort. He sounded much younger now, even the cadence to his speech changing. *"There are no normal families."*

"There are always challenges, but if he can't love me as I am, I can't be with him."

"You think you're so special that you're unlovable?"

Rachel was taken aback. She didn't know what Misha had been like when he was alive, but he sure was a jerk in the afterlife. And he wasn't done with her yet.

"All you have to do is say the word and Garrett would be yours. You're the one keeping the two of you apart.

Don't lay this on him."

"He can't keep up with me."

"Then slow down!"

"It's not that simple."

"Excuses. It's always excuses with you."

Brother or not, Rachel was reaching her limit with this guy. "You don't know me."

"Do you? Does anyone?"

Rachel opened her mouth to argue, but couldn't think of a response. Of everyone on the planet, Garrett understood her best. If she couldn't make it work with him, she knew in her heart she would be alone for the rest of her life. Except for the ghosts.

A life filled with spirits seemed easy compared to a life without Garrett.

Misha had regained some of his composure when he spoke again. He still sounded different, but the anger was contained.

"All you have to do is tell him how you feel. That's all he needs. Please, at least try."

Chapter Nineteen

Garrett didn't look up when Rachel walked into his bedroom. He sat at the foot of his bed, elbows on his knees and hands clasped together. His eyes were burning. She could probably see how damp they were. He was past caring.

"Hi." She hovered just inside the doorway.

He parroted back, "Hi."

"Can we talk?"

"You sure I'm the one you want to talk to?"

"I don't understand."

"I heard you," he whispered.

"Heard me what?"

He cleared his throat. "I came out to talk things through, but you weren't in the living room. I heard you talking to someone in your room. I'm guessing it was Misha."

After a short pause she said, "Yes."

He nodded, her confirmation hollowing him out.

"I made a salt barrier at the door," she said. "He can't come in further than the guest room and bathroom."

"Great."

Like that made it okay.

Yet again, she had turned to someone else—let someone else in—while she kept Garrett at arm's length. She was moving away from him already. He wanted to follow after her, but he didn't think he had it in him anymore. At least he knew she'd be back next time something blew up.

Was that all he had to look forward to?

He felt the bed move as she knelt next to him. He could see from the corner of his eye.

Please, Lord, don't let her try to start anything again.

He wouldn't be able to handle it if something happened between them before he had the answers he needed. If she so much as touched him, he would probably leap across the room like he was snakebit.

His stomach churned as he remembered Dylan again.

"I'm in a difficult situation here," she said. "And you are too. Because of me."

"I knew what I was signing up for."

Partly, anyway.

He knew she was going through a lot—it just turned out to be a different kind of hurting, from a source he would never have guessed. Being surrounded by ghosts... What she was dealing with was awful. He didn't mean to be putting more on her.

"But you didn't," she said. "Not really. You thought you were helping out a friend who had been through a traumatic event. You didn't know you were getting all of this. I did."

Her voice crackled for a moment, but she cleared her throat and went on in a strong tone.

"I knew how you felt. I knew you loved me. And I let you help me even though I knew it was hurting you. And I am so, so sorry for that. But I didn't do it to use you or lead you on. I did it because I couldn't stay away. I knew I was all wrong for you, but I just…wanted you so much. I hope you can forgive me. I know I never will."

"Rachel—" He glanced up.

Looking at her was a mistake. When their gazes met, it was like being struck by lightning. His heart seemed to want to break out of his chest to get to her.

Whenever they were close he felt it—electric energy, pulsing just beneath his skin. Never this strong before, though. His entire body was charged and ready to do whatever she needed, wanting just a little more time with her any way he could get it.

The pull toward her was like gravity—or a black hole.

Her lips parted and she leaned toward him. She felt it too. He was sure of it. What he wasn't sure of was whether it was love or lust on her part. And the ever-present question with her remained—when would she run away again?

"You asked me to think," she said. "But that's part of my problem. I think too much about some things, but not enough about others. I can be focused and calm or full of frenetic energy. I'm a person of extremes."

She shook her head and leaned back on her heels. "I'm passionate. I feel everything deeply and I process things so fast. It can come out...intense. I know it can be off-putting. Even *I* want to run away from me sometimes. Maybe that's what I've been doing. Running away from everything."

Garrett had never thought that Rachel might be exhausted by her own contradictions. "That doesn't seem like a good way to live."

"It isn't. I don't want to live that way anymore. I don't want to run away from you, Garrett."

His heartbeat instantly picked up. He could feel the blood rushing in his ears.

He tried to stay calm. She didn't want to run away. Okay. But what *did* she want? A casual fling? Or something more?

"I've never seen you yell or get as worked up with anyone else as you do with me," she said. "I don't know that it's a good thing I bring that out of you."

"I have a temper. That's not your doing."

"I know. I'm trying to explain why I act this way with you." She let out a breath and said, "Do you remember the night we met?"

"Of course. It was one of your mom's fundraisers."

"I'm not talking about seeing each other across a room.

I mean the first time we talked."

He had seen her half a dozen times before they ever spoke. They had exchanged glances across rooms, even sometimes grinned and raised their eyebrows or nodded their heads, sharing a joke that no one else seemed to get.

But the first time they talked... That was something he would never forget. It had put his life on a different trajectory.

He cleared his throat and said, "Jazz had that Halloween party at the Orange Grove Inn."

"And we both stepped outside to get some fresh air because there were too many people. You said you had already used up your quota for crowds with an event we both attended earlier that week. I told you I'd had my fill of crowds too. But it wasn't the kind you were thinking of. I couldn't tell you then, but I was freaking out from seeing so many people in costumes."

It only took him a second to figure out the issue this time. Everybody had shown up as monsters. The room was full of people dressed as the dead. That night must have been an ordeal for her.

"Why did you go?"

"The idea was hers, but Jazz had me do all the planning. It was the first big event she let me handle on my own. I couldn't not show up. When you and I were talking, I kept thinking she might fire me for being gone so long, but I didn't want to go back inside. Not because I wanted to avoid the costumes but because I wanted more time with you. There was something about you. Even then, I could feel it."

"It was probably the beer."

She laughed, and the sound tugged at his chest.

He wanted to make her feel better. If jokes would work, great. But the more they talked—with her kneeling next to him on his bed—the more he wondered if it would be so bad to have a one-night stand. If that was what she needed...

"That was the first beer I ever drank from a bottle," she said. "You had nabbed it from behind the bar and shared it with me. You've always shared whatever you had with me."

It didn't feel like sharing. After that night, everything he had—everything he was—was hers.

"You talked to me and I felt calm," she said. "Centered. I felt like I could finally let go of my socialite veneer, at least for a little while. I felt like I could be myself. We were out there for hours."

She had a soft smile on her face. She laughed again as she went on. "When you first ran into me on the balcony, you offered to leave. You said I was there first and you didn't want to trouble me."

Garrett nodded. "I remember."

"And I asked you to stay. I'm always asking you to stay. I can't say I'll always be right at your side. That isn't who I am. I'm flighty and full of energy and movement and I need you to be okay with that. But I ask you to stay because I want to be with you."

Yeah. He got that. She wanted to be with him on her terms. When, where, and how she wanted. He needed more.

"There are lots of ways to be with someone," he said. "Different relationship dynamics. This is all really... nostalgic, but it doesn't let me know where I stand. I don't get why you can't just come out and say—"

"I love you."

He blinked. He felt his eyelids close and open like shutters.

Love? His mouth went dry and his heart seemed to stop.

"Love means different things to different people..." he said.

She sighed and inched closer.

"I love how gentle you are and how passionate you can be. I love your intelligence and generosity. I love how you take care of everyone. I love how you can charm people without letting them past your guard. I love that you give me glimpses of who you really are and share sides of yourself with me that no one else gets to see."

Was she talking about how she felt about him or the other way around? He had thought these same things about her more times than he could count.

She paused for a moment, then said, "I love that you let me get away with just enough that I feel free to take risks and be myself, but not so much that you don't let me know when I've crossed a line, like I did earlier."

"Rachel—"

"I'm not finished."

She inched closer, resting her hand on his thigh for balance. He remembered the softness of her skin and felt himself start to get hard again. This time, it didn't bother him.

"Your house is the only place that ever really felt like a home to me. I thought at first it was because it's out in the country and so it's more peaceful for a clairsentient. But it was because of you."

She squeezed his thigh, sending a jolt of pleasure through him. He wanted to grab her and kiss her, to wrap his arms around her and never let her go. But even more, he wanted to hear what she had to say. He wanted to understand her—who she was and what she was offering him.

"I loved going to bed in your house every night and waking up knowing that you were going to be the first person I would see. I loved cooking for you and laughing with you. And I wanted to stay so much that it terrified me. Because then, I didn't think I could do that to you. It felt like it would be a punishment, and you deserved better."

"How could living with you ever be a punishment?"

"Because I'm weird and I see ghosts and I go off on tangents constantly and my mother is actually kind of evil and I say things without thinking them through, like that part about my mom."

He laughed and shook his head. "You don't see me arguing the point."

She smiled, shifting closer. He could lean forward and kiss her if he wanted, and he really wanted to. But damn, if he wasn't shaking inside. She was dangling everything he wanted right in front of him. If he reached for it, she might jerk it away.

Yeah, that killed the moment. He looked down, but she lifted her hands to his face and turned his head back toward her.

"You said you laid it all out for me before. Let me do the same now. What I want? I want you. Not just your truly exquisite body, but all of you. I want to see you every day. I want to go to sleep in this huge bed with you and wake up in your arms. I want—"

She locked her gaze with his, more serious than he'd ever seen her. Warmth flooded him from her hands on his face, her knees pressing against his thigh.

"I want the white-picket fence," she said. "To be your wife—your partner. With three kids and a dog and two cats. I want to go to family cookouts with you and make jokes that only we get. I want you to bring me breakfast in bed on mother's day and to send the kids to a friend's house on father's day so I can give you better memories in that ugly recliner that I know you'll never let me get rid of."

That one memory in his favorite chair was being painted in a whole new light with every word she said. She was still holding on to his face, as if she was the one afraid he was going to bolt for a change.

"What I want," she whispered, leaning in so close that her breath warmed his lips. "Is you. Forever."

Chapter Twenty

If she didn't kiss Garrett immediately, she was going to spontaneously combust. His lips were slightly parted as if waiting for her—welcoming her.

She hoped she was reading him right this time. She couldn't bear to bring him more pain. She also couldn't bear to not touch more of him.

His stubble prickled against her hands, strong muscles tensed beneath. She didn't dare let go. She would never let him go again. He had to understand that she was done running. This was it.

Gently, she pressed her lips against his. He wanted slow. She could do slow.

She let the feel of him soak in—his breath light on her face, the warmth of his lips and softness of his mouth. And for once, she waited for him. Waited for him to make some sign that this was okay. That it was what he wanted.

She didn't have to wait long.

He lifted his hands to her back, running them up along her spine and over her shoulder blades, then pulled her closer. His lips started to move in a slow, sensual caress that made heat pool between her legs. When he slid his tongue into her mouth, it felt like the most natural thing in the world.

No wonder the episode in the recliner had gone so wrong. She gave him a flash-fire when he was after a slow burn. The heat of his kiss spread through her body, resonating, echoing deep within her. She had never felt anything like it.

Primal energy uncoiling in waves that rolled through her instead of crashing around. His lips gripped hers, sucked and nipped. The sensation spread along her nerve endings as if they were each getting a massage.

Her muscles relaxed into him, tension dropping away even while a throbbing ache built in her core. He held her against his chest with one arm while he reached down with his other hand and pulled her thigh across his lap so she was straddling him on the edge of the bed.

A sharp spike of nerves rippled through her. Perched on the edge of the bed, she could easily fall off. But he was holding her up, keeping her safe—as always.

She pressed her hips down to feel his erection. She wanted more.

He thrust up against her, tantalizing her through the thin cotton of her panties. She was so wet. She could feel it. Aching and hollow and longing for him to fill her.

She wrapped her arms around his shoulders as he moved his kisses down her neck and over her collarbone, making a steady trail to her breasts. He nuzzled her through the soft fabric of her T-shirt till her nipples were so tight they almost hurt.

She was very glad she hadn't worn a bra.

He ran his nose over the point jutting toward him, then clasped his mouth around her, laving it with his tongue. She groaned low, not recognizing the sounds she was making. Her T-shirt was damp and clinging to her skin when he moved to her other breast.

No one had ever done anything like this to her before. Sex was always over quickly and then she was on to the next thing. She could tell with Garrett this *was* the next thing. And the next, and the next. She wasn't sure they would ever leave his bed again.

He ran his teeth over the inner side of her breast, then trailed his nose up along her cleavage.

"Stand up." His voice was rough—lower than usual.

At this point, she would do anything he said. She slid to her feet, standing between his knees.

His shaft was sticking out from the top of his pajama pants. Even after what they had done in the recliner, she felt like she was seeing him for the first time. Thick and glistening and ready for her.

She wanted to drop to her knees and take him again, but resisted the urge. Things would be over too fast. She wanted to keep savoring him, keep basking in this incredibly erotic experience.

"Look at me."

Her gaze flicked to his. The intensity of his stare sent another wave of electric sparks through her. Not in little trails or isolated parts of her anatomy. Everywhere.

There was really something to be said for taking their time. Every touch was magnified, the connection more intimate. She was saturated with him. From the way his blue eyes burned, he was only getting started.

He ran his hands up her sides underneath her shirt, cupping her breasts and kneading them. She gasped as he flicked his thumbs across her nipples, the jolt of pleasure echoing in her core.

She put her hands on his broad shoulders, wanting to knock him back onto his bed, but resisting. She could have him inside her in seconds. This was torture. The most exquisite, erotic, pleasurable torture she had ever endured.

"Look at me," he said again.

She didn't know when her eyes had rolled shut or her head had listed against her shoulder, but she snapped herself back to attention. She didn't want to miss a single nuance of what he was doing to her.

She shifted her weight and let out a moan. Even that small movement sent shivers up from between her legs to her breasts, intensifying the effect of his touch. With his right hand, he dusted the backs of his knuckles along her stomach. His left lovingly traced the curves of her backside before he rested his forearm firmly against it.

She wasn't sure what he had in mind until he slid his

right hand past the waistband of her panties, his wrist stretching the elastic down to give him access. His fingers raked through her curls, finding her core and sliding in effortlessly.

She had known she was ready for him, but not how ready. She could only imagine what it would feel like for him to bury himself deep inside of her, to feel her body expand to welcome his shaft.

She groaned as her body clenched around him instinctively, her grip on his shoulders tightening as well. His hands were so large he was able to press the heel of his hand against her most sensitive spot, rubbing it in slow circles while his fingers stayed buried deep.

Her knees weakened as the pleasure he had been building in her burst into a bright flame. He was already helping to hold her up, pulling her closer as he scooted to the very edge of the bed.

Her body was on fire, sparking, more alive than she had ever felt. Her nerve endings sang his praises with every languid thrust and pull of his fingers.

He brought his mouth to her breasts again, his kisses more aggressive, demanding. She lifted one knee to rest on the bed, bringing herself closer to him. She wanted him buried inside of her—as deep as he could go. She had never wanted anything or anyone with such intensity.

"Garrett, please," she moaned. "I need you. I want you."

"Look at me." His voice had devolved practically to a growl.

She blinked her eyes, staring down at him as if becoming aware she was dreaming while it was still going on. His fingers kept moving, palm pressed firmly against her.

Watching his face while he was pleasuring her made it even more intimate. Her quim was already starting to pulse around him, the sensations building to a tipping point.

"Come for me."

"I…thought we would do that together."

"Please, Rachel. I need this."

He increased the speed of his fingers, arcing his hand away from her so he could press his thumb against her sweet spot, gently circling it. He stared into her eyes the whole time.

She held his gaze as long as she could, letting him see how his touch affected her, hoping that sharing this intimate moment would help him believe.

She was done running. This was the life she wanted. In his arms, in his bed, in his life. She rocked her body against him, letting the sensations flow through her, push the pressure building between her legs and deep in her abdomen higher than ever before.

On a gentle breath he said, "I love you."

Her body seemed to collapse in on itself and then explode with infinite energy. She threw her head back and screamed as the release tore through her body, a shockwave of ecstasy that left her panting and writhing in his hands.

He finally stopped thrusting, but left his fingers buried within her, his chest heaving in time with her own. She felt her body continue to clench around him, sending aftershocks rippling through her.

He pulled her closer and she draped herself across his chest. She nuzzled his ear, then ran her tongue along its edge and nibbled his earlobe. As amazing as that orgasm had been, she still wanted more. Wanted to be closer, to feel him inside her. She wanted to share the deepest intimacy with him that she could.

When she thought she could speak again, she whispered, "I love you too."

Chapter Twenty-One

The relief Garrett felt made his heart pound. That and watching Rachel's uninhibited, absolutely open responses to his touch. There was no faking what she had felt, what *he* felt from her body through his hands.

The look in her eyes… He had almost lost control so many times, wanting to slide his shaft into her.

There was no need to rein himself in anymore.

He slid his fingers from her and pulled down her panties in one stroke. Most of her weight was already on his chest, and his arms were long enough that he only had to bend sideways a little to get the thin cotton fabric out of the way.

He stood, bringing her with him. The soft cotton of his waistband held his erection tight against his stomach. When her feet were firmly planted on the floor, he lifted her shirt over her head and tossed it aside.

He went to pull off his pants, but she was already there. She tore them off about as eagerly as he had stripped her, barely waiting for him to step out of them before leaping up and wrapping her arms around his shoulders.

Pulling him down a bit, she crashed her lips against his,

tongue hungrily seeking his out. He met every thrust, savoring the velvet feel of her mouth.

He loved that she was tall. He still had over half a foot on her, but he didn't loom over her like he did most women. She had to be pushing six-feet. He cupped her backside, squeezing and kneading the firmness of it.

She pressed herself against him, rubbing her stomach against his shaft. Her skin was so soft. She worked one arm between them to grip him, wrapping her fingers around his erection and starting to work her magic. Then she stopped abruptly and pulled away.

This was not happening. No way after everything they had just done was she stopping this. He couldn't believe it.

"I'm not going too fast am I? Do you want me to go slower?"

He let out a laugh that took the tense energy with it. That had scared the crap out of him.

"I want you to do whatever the hell you want."

Her lips pulled into a smile that was pure sex. His breath rushed out as if he'd been kicked in the chest. She let go of his shaft, then put her hands on his shoulders and pushed him down so he was sitting close to the edge of the bed.

As much as he wanted to feel her lips on him again, nothing could compare to being inside of her. And he wanted that so bad he was bursting at the seams.

She must have felt the same, because she put her knees

on either side of him, using her grip on his shoulders to keep her balance. He grabbed her backside to help.

"You should know I was always smart with the few guys I slept with," she said. "We used protection and I get tested regularly."

"Okay." Of all the times to bring that up. Yeah, he supposed this was a pretty good one. "Well, my experience is the same."

"I just want you to know because I was serious with that talk about kids. I want them. Tons of them. I don't want to wait."

He swallowed hard. What she was suggesting…

It was fast and sudden, like everything with Rachel. He started to do the math, calculating their ages and thinking about genetic risk factors, how many years they had left and how long they should wait between each child. Then there was the danger the ghosts presented.

No. He wouldn't let fear make up his mind. He thought about what he wanted instead. The decision was obvious.

A house *full* of children, a life full of love. With Rachel.

They would always face challenges—ghostly and otherwise. But they would figure them out together.

He couldn't force words around the lump in his throat so he nodded.

Without any more of a prelude, she lined herself up on him and slowly inched down. Bliss cascaded through him, a buzz of pleasure cantering along every nerve fiber.

Her flesh parted around him, unbelievably soft and slick. And the heat… It soaked into him, flooding his body as she pushed him deeper, taking all of him in.

For a moment, she stayed still, her hands gripping the back of his neck, gazes locked. His heart was pounding, his blood rushing through his body. His hands were trembling.

She loved him. This was what the rest of his life looked like.

He let his gaze slide down her body, lingering on the fullness of her breasts before grazing her flat stomach and finally resting on where they were joined. He took a deep breath to keep himself from getting too worked up. He wanted it to last—this first time of complete intimacy.

She started to move again, slower than he'd expected after the way she mounted him. She lifted herself up onto her knees, sliding along his length as far as she could, then lowered herself back down. He brushed his thumbs along her hips and squeezed her backside as he watched.

So. Fucking. Erotic.

She clenched her sheath around him, as if asking for his attention elsewhere. He was more than happy to oblige.

He let his gaze climb again, lingering only for a moment on her breasts as they swayed with her movement. He swallowed hard and kept going.

Her cheeks were flushed, her lips bright pink and full. Her eyes were open wide, like she was as moved by the experience as he was and didn't want to miss a thing.

She leaned forward to kiss him. Slow and deep, same as her hips. She was savoring him—giving him the chance to savor her. This was night and day from the recliner. Not that there wasn't a time and place for quickies.

His imagination went crazy with possible scenarios. The kitchen counter, the shower, the couch... Any horizontal surface was fair game. Hell, the vertical ones, too. He wanted her anywhere he could have her. He knew she could satisfy him, but he'd never get enough. He wanted her—forever. Just like she'd said.

He broke off the kiss and said, "There's a Justice of the Peace I know. He could hitch us this afternoon."

She laughed, the vibration traveling through her body and into his. His fingers tightened on her backside reflexively and he took another deep breath to calm himself.

"I want a big wedding, *Doctor* Wolfstrom."

"That is the first time I've ever liked being called that."

She bent down and nibbled along the length of his ear. Goose bumps scattered over his skin, heightening the sensations everywhere they touched. Especially where they were joined.

She whispered into his ear, "I promise I'm not going anywhere."

Rising back on her knees, she wrapped her arms around his neck again and quickened her pace. "Lean back on your arms. I won't fall."

"Yes ma'am," he drawled.

She grinned—her nose crinkling up the way he liked. When he placed his palms on the mattress, she gripped his shoulders for balance and upped her pace again.

The view was unbelievable. With the better leverage, he thrust up into her, meeting her hips with his own. It deepened each stroke, amped up the friction. His skin was thrumming with sensation, nerves lighting up everywhere.

The pleasure coaxed him to move faster, land harder. She matched him perfectly, taking everything he had to give her. He bent his head forward far enough to kiss her breast and she gasped, arcing her back so he could reach her nipple.

He ran his tongue around the tight circle, then sucked it deep into his mouth till she groaned. He had no idea she was so flexible. He was definitely going to have to work on his core strength after this.

He released her breast as she increased her pace again, focusing on matching every movement. She held on tight, eyes clenched shut as she pumped him even faster.

His hips rose to meet her, crashing into her as more sparks ran through his body, pressure building until he felt her spasm around him. She threw her head back and screamed his name.

The pressure within him exploded and he rammed his shaft into her as fast and hard as he could, spilling himself deep inside of her. Her muscles pulsed around him, coaxing everything out of him, everything he had to give.

It was hers. He would always give her everything he could.

She let out a moan and her breath hitched. She was still writhing on him. He kept on thrusting, even as he felt himself growing soft.

She dug her nails into his shoulders, eyes shut tight, head back. Another climax?

She let out a huge breath and finally sagged against him. He could still feel her pulsing around him.

Good Lord. And he thought he had trouble keeping up with her before…

Chapter Twenty-Two

After the incredible afternoon she had spent in bed with Garrett, Rachel didn't expect to wake up from a nightmare. She shot up in bed, glancing around the room frantically. For a few moments, she was disoriented, trying to figure out where she was and what was going on.

Garrett sat up and wrapped his arms around her. "What's wrong?"

"Nothing." She shook her head. "Just another nightmare."

"Do you want to talk about it?"

"I don't know. It felt so real."

He shrugged. "It might help."

What a novel concept. Talking openly about something she had been keeping secret for decades. The chill of the dream receded at the thought of sharing this with Garrett —something she hadn't told anyone about.

"It isn't just from recent events. I've had nightmares for about as long as I can remember. Not every night, but more often than I'd like."

"That sounds awful."

"It used to be standard ghost stuff. I had actually

acclimated to it. But since what happened with Michael, they've changed. Now there are two men reaching for me. One of them feels cold and…twisted. Like Michael. But the other one is warm and loving."

"Maybe that one's me." Garrett nuzzled her neck and she leaned into him.

"No. There's definitely a different feel to this one. More…familial." She shook her head. "It's strange, even for me. It felt like the warm energy was trying to find me, but couldn't because of Michael. Like Michael was keeping the other one away."

"Is it possible your powers are trying to tell you something?"

"I hope not."

Garrett leaned far enough to the side that she could see his quizzical expression.

"There's an urgency to the dreams that has been building. And this last one…" She shivered at the memory. "Whoever was trying to find me, the warm energy, it was grabbed by Michael's energy and…absorbed or something. It was awful."

She leaned into Garrett's chest to calm herself down. The fear from her nightmares usually faded quickly. This one left her with a lingering sense of anxiety.

"I hate to keep asking this, but—"

"Michael is gone. He has to be. Spirits need a corporeal connection. I have it from people in-the-know."

"Don't ghosts ever lie?"

"Of course they do." She thought of Misha and her suspicions. This didn't seem the best time to bring up the topic. "Hiram isn't the only one I talked to about it."

"Another ghost?"

"I keep telling you, it isn't always about ghosts."

"Who then?"

"The woman who owns Bookwyrm is a medium named Chloe. She does readings in the store sometimes. She's into the showmanship of the whole divination thing and really dresses for the part." Rachel laughed and said, "You should have seen my mother's face when Chloe showed up at the house the first time."

"Sounds like you should have sold tickets."

"Yeah. Chloe's the one who taught me about poppets and how to use a witch's ball. She still sometimes sends me books, but we have to be careful."

"Why?"

"For one, my mother threatened to sue her. I didn't take that threat lightly. Lillian would have found a way to ruin Chloe. And Chloe and I were trying to keep the ghosts from figuring out I could hear them so they would stop bothering me. Hanging out with her would raise their suspicions."

"She doesn't have your problem with ghosts?"

"Chloe isn't clairsentient. Not like me, anyway. She has to do all sorts of ritual preparations to contact the other side."

Chloe had always told Rachel what a gift her powers were. Now that things had changed, maybe Rachel could go to Chloe and learn more. For the first time since Rachel was a child, she was actually excited about what she could do.

"Can she help us with Michael's victims?" Garrett asked.

"I was just thinking something along those lines. I think she can. She'll be very happy I'm away from my mom."

"We're all happy about that. Especially me." He kissed the side of her neck—a small nip, but then he nuzzled her ear and moved to her lips.

This was much better than talk of nightmares and dysfunctional families. Rachel wrapped her arms around Garrett's neck and kissed him back. She was about to push him flat on the bed when her stomach growled loudly.

Garrett broke off the kiss.

"Sorry," she said. "I think we forgot to eat."

"We should take care of that."

He slid to the edge of the bed, holding on to her hand as she followed. He didn't let go while they walked to the kitchen. She stood on her tiptoes to kiss him, and finally dropped his hand so she could open the fridge.

"Sandwiches?"

He laughed and retrieved some plates from the cabinets. "What is it with you and turkey sandwiches?"

"They're nature's perfect food."

Rachel rooted around in the fridge for what she needed, then set everything on the counter. They worked in silence, exchanging a few sidelong glances and smiles. Garrett filled a pair of glasses with a sports drink and his grin turned wicked.

"We need to keep ourselves hydrated after that afternoon," Garrett said.

"And for tonight."

Rachel ran her hand down his chest, trailing her fingers almost all the way down the dark river of hair that bisected his torso. If she went too far, it would be a while before they ate.

"Maybe we should have put some clothes on…"

She hadn't even thought about the fact that they were standing naked in his kitchen. She was that comfortable with him. And he must be that comfortable with her. The thought delighted her and she giggled.

"When a man's body starts to get ready to please his woman, he's not looking for giggles."

Her gaze dropped past his waist and a different kind of hunger altogether stirred in her.

"Stop. Stop looking at me like that." He turned her around and playfully swatted her backside as she walked toward the living room. Then he slid the plates and glasses across the counter.

"Hand me a couple of towels, will you?"

He didn't ask why she wanted them—just opened a drawer and grabbed a pair, then handed them to her. She draped them over the barstools.

"They look cold," she said.

"Good thinking."

He joined her on the other side of the counter and they started eating, sitting so their knees touched.

When they were about done, Garrett said, "I have to ask. Did you ever tell your parents about what you can do?"

Rachel snorted. "My dad—no. And I didn't have to tell my mom. She already knew."

"How?"

"Because she can do the same thing."

Garrett choked on his last bite of sandwich. Rachel reached out and patted him on the back. He took a long sip from his glass when he'd cleared his throat.

"Lillian Montgomery is psychic?" he asked.

Rachel laughed again. "Please do not ever tell her that you know."

"I wouldn't dare. She'd probably have me killed."

Fear clawed at Rachel's heart suddenly. Her mother was capable of much more than hearing ghosts. Terrible things.

"Garrett, you really need to be careful with my mother. She's much more dangerous than you think."

He laughed. "I think I can take her."

"No," Rachel shook her head. "You don't know what

she's capable of."

"You mean aside from hearing ghosts?"

"Listen to me. I told you that Hiram crossed over to protect me. Something happened… Something terrible."

"This is that story you mentioned earlier. The one I won't like."

She didn't want to have to tell him this, but it was a vital part of her past. He needed to know, both understand the regular nightmares when they returned and so he knew the true horror that was Mrs. Lillian Montgomery.

"I talked about Hiram all the time when I was a kid. Even in front of strangers," Rachel said. "When I was younger, my mother could explain it away as an imaginary friend. But when I grew older, people started giving me strange looks. Then they started giving *her* strange looks."

Lillian Montgomery had found that unacceptable. Rachel felt her cheeks tingle with rage over what her mother had done to control her disobedient daughter.

"What did she do?" Garrett's voice was a low rumble. This wasn't going to go over well.

"My mother took me to a town a few hours away. She never paid much attention to me before that day. She had nannies for that. I was so excited." Rachel shook her head. She refused to cry over this. Not anymore.

"We walked into this abandoned building on the outskirts of the town. It had burned down years before. I was scared, but she was with me and I thought she would keep me safe, because that's what mothers are supposed to do. We walked to this huge empty room and she said, 'Playing with ghosts isn't all fun and games.' Then she stood there and smiled while they came for me."

Rachel was shaking. *Dammit!* She shouldn't be shaking. She dared to look at Garrett. His jaw was working again, his lips so tight they were bloodless.

"It had been a maximum security prison before a riot that killed dozens of prisoners in addition to several of the guards. I was eight."

"Jesus!" Garrett grabbed her hands and squeezed them.

She didn't let him pull her close. Didn't dare rest against his chest and cry. This was an old pain. She wanted him to know she could deal with it.

"After that, word spread about what I could do among ghosts that were not as kind as Hiram. That's why he brought Chloe to me. He contacted her during one of her rituals. He's the one who came up with the plan to pretend that I lost the ability after..."

Rachel shook her head, trying to turn her mind away from those horrible memories.

"Chloe taught me about poppets and helped me learn, and Hiram..." Rachel couldn't stop a few tears from rolling down her cheek at the thought of losing him. "Hiram crossed over as part of a ritual Chloe designed. He was able to grab a couple of the ghosts who had been especially…unpleasant…and take them with him."

Garrett didn't need to know just how bad those spirits had been. Judging from his reaction so far, Rachel had better not tell him about the ones who were able to affect the physical plane. About the scratches and shoving and the light touches to her hair she could almost convince herself she imagined.

Chloe had assured Rachel that Hiram wouldn't be dragged to the same place as those spirits. Rachel wouldn't have let them try the ritual otherwise. She was sure those ghosts were headed for suffering.

"How could your mother just stand by and listen to that?" Garrett asked. "How could she subject you to it?"

"She wanted me to stop talking about ghosts. Her plan worked. And she didn't know exactly what they said. Have you ever noticed that she wears two sets of earrings?"

"That's kind of a non sequitur. You're going to have to build me a bridge."

He would get it in a moment. "One set is always the same. Understated little moonstone studs. They block the voices. Apparently, they were passed down from generation to generation in my family. Hiram asked around and told me. All the women are clairsentient."

"That is…a lot to process. I mean, I would never guess in a million years that your mom knew a thing about any of this, let alone that she could do something so awful to her own daughter."

"She always told me, 'Watch what you say—a proper lady is neither smart nor psychic.'"

Rachel felt her grimace as she said her mother's favorite bit of advice. How many thousands of times had Mrs. Montgomery whispered those words in Rachel's ear to keep her daughter in check?

The set line to Garrett's jaw made Rachel uncomfortable. He was planning something and she doubted she would like it.

"I'm getting you those earrings. One way or another."

"You don't have to—"

"No, I *shouldn't* have to. She should have given them to you already."

Rachel let out another scoff. Her mother doing something supportive like that was such an alien thought.

Chloe had said that families with powers like Rachel's usually gave the children whatever tools were available to help them until they could control their powers. Lillian must have skipped that lesson from the grandmother Rachel had never met.

"It's okay."

"No, it's not okay! She's waltzing around like the Queen Bee while you're trapped in here behind poppets. She's your mother. She should have taken care of you, not..." He snapped his mouth shut, fuming.

Lillian had never taken care of Rachel. That was what the nannies were for.

Rachel kept the comment to herself. Garrett seemed ready to explode already.

"I'm okay," Rachel said. "I'll figure something out."

"What about our kids?"

Rachel's breath caught in her chest. Even though she had mentioned kids and he seemed on board, they hadn't actually talked about it. She had always wanted a big family, but didn't think it could happen for her because of her ability. With Garrett as her partner, anything seemed possible.

"Our kids?" she squeaked.

"What if we have three girls?"

She could see the wheels moving in his head. He wanted to take care of Rachel, and he was already worrying about kids they didn't have yet.

Yet... Yet!

The reality of her future was just hitting her. Rachel jumped up and threw her arms around his neck, kissing him long and deep.

As she trailed her kisses along his neck, he said, "I don't see how this is helping us find a solution."

"We'll figure it out," she whispered in his ear, then gave it a nip. "Someone made those earrings for her. I can make my own and sets for our girls."

Their girls!

Rachel leaned back and gave him a fake-serious look. "We get to have boys too, right?"

He lifted her up and she wrapped her legs around his waist. The smile on his face matched hers. He seemed as enthralled at the notion as she was.

"We can have as many kids as you want."

"Then what are we waiting for?"

They were going to do this right. Their children would be loved. So loved. Rachel's chest felt over-full, warmth and love washing away the pall of remembering such awful events.

"Okay," he said. "But afterwards, we're going to talk jewelry. Including rings."

Garrett grinned and carried her back to the bedroom.

Chapter Twenty-Three

"We're going to need a bigger house." Garrett couldn't believe they were already talking about kids. Lots of kids. His heart beat faster just thinking about it.

Rachel was sprawled across his chest after yet another round of lovemaking. She made a soft cooing sound and shifted her legs closer to his.

"You should design it for us," he said. "With plenty of bedrooms for the kids. Maybe one of those climbers like you see at playgrounds in the back."

She laughed and tightened her grip around his waist. "How about a pool?"

"We can plan to put one in later, but not right away. Not until they all know how to swim." The thought of a pool plus kids made his stomach sour. There were too many chances for them to get hurt. "Maybe not out in the country, either."

She pushed herself up on her elbows to look at him, her brow furrowing. "I thought you loved living out in the country."

"Too many wild animals." More variables he couldn't control.

"Cities have too many people," she said. "More people equals more ghosts."

"Right, I forgot for a moment."

He didn't want Rachel to be plagued by spirits. Or their girls, for that matter. His chest tightened at the thought of a flock of girls running around in the backyard in dresses, squealing in delight as they played.

"I like the look on your face right now," Rachel said.

He glanced back at her and smiled. "I'm not surprised. I suppose we can live in the country."

At least in the country the dangers were tangible. Rachel wouldn't be the only one who had to stand guard. He hated the thought that some ghost could be talking to his kids and he wouldn't know what they were saying or that they were even there.

"It went away," Rachel said.

"What?"

"The look on your face." She ran the backs of her fingers along his jaw. "It makes me wonder what I need to do to bring it back."

That mischievous expression gave him some pretty good ideas about what she had in mind. He could think about their future later. Like she said, they would figure it out. For the moment, he wanted to focus on her.

She was already sliding down his stomach when the room darkened quickly enough for them both to notice. Rachel rose to her knees, staring at the window.

"The storm's late today," she said.

"It rained a little earlier while you were sleeping. This must be another one."

Florida's humidity didn't just come from the ocean. The afternoon summer rainstorms did their part. It didn't rain long, and usually at the peak of the afternoon heat. Garrett glanced at the clock. It was already past five.

Thunder boomed in the distance and rain started to pound on the roof. Rachel stared at the ceiling.

"That's really loud. Did you ever pull your car into the garage?"

"No."

The noise above was rising, interspersed with pings and thuds that were unmistakably hail. Garrett jumped up and pulled on his pajama bottoms.

"I can bring it in for you," she said.

He leaned over the bed and kissed her for longer than he'd intended. When he finally was able to pull himself away, he said, "Darlin', there's no way I'm letting you go out in this."

She raised an eyebrow and smirked at him. "*Letting* me?"

"How about, 'I'd really prefer if you stayed inside.'"

"Fine. But I'm coming along to watch and help if I can."

She grabbed the T-shirt she had borrowed from him earlier and pulled it on. Garrett was mesmerized by the thin fabric floating down over her body, imagining the feel of it against her skin.

Rachel clapped her hands. "Let's go!"

Smiling, he trotted out of the room. His keys were on a table in the foyer. He picked them up as he opened the door to the garage and stepped through it. Rachel was right behind him.

"You don't have to come in with me."

"I'm okay," she said. Her smile was a bit strained. "I'm going to have to go into garages again eventually."

"But not now if you don't want to. You're already doing enough. You don't have to go so fast."

She crossed into the garage and stepped in close to him as she ran her hands up along his arms. "I like to go fast sometimes."

Damn. He was starting to tent his pajamas. He leaned down to kiss her again, deep and wet. Maybe he could give her some better memories to drown out the others.

There was a table next to the washing machine at just the right height to set her on. She could wrap her thighs around his waist while he rocked into her.

He was already reaching down to lift her from the ground when a thunderclap brought him back to earth. They both jumped. It probably wasn't the safest time to be doing anything too adventurous.

She smiled at him as she pulled away. "We should get the car in the garage before it's covered in dings."

"I suppose so."

She hit the button to open the garage door and the sound of the rain instantly intensified. Her smile faltered along with his.

Water ran into the garage from what could only be described as a torrential downpour. They walked as close to the door as they dared. Mist floated in and stuck to his chest. He couldn't even see the car.

"You need to go inside," he said.

"It's not that bad."

He shook his head. "I'm going to have trouble seeing. I don't want you here when I pull the car in."

"I guess that makes sense. I'll be waiting just inside the door, though."

"Okay."

She grabbed his hand and pulled him down for a quick kiss.

"For luck," she said.

He smiled and watched her walk away, waiting to turn around till she was safely out of the garage. Unlocking the door with his key fob, he took a deep breath, then plunged into the water.

It was always colder than he expected. In the middle of the summer, when the air was oppressively hot, the rain should match. But it didn't. And this storm was colder than most. It took his breath away.

Hail bounced off his shoulders and stung his scalp.

Running flat out for the twenty or so feet to his car, he was still soaked when he slid into the driver's seat. They were going to have to dry off the upholstery. At least the driveway kept him from getting sandspurs lodged in his feet.

The rain was even louder inside the car. Hailstones almost as big as golf balls pelted it. They seemed to be getting bigger. Nearby, a dark looming shape shook itself frantically back and forth—one of the palm trees in his front yard. The thing was practically bent in half.

"Jesus," he murmured under his breath.

He started the car, eager to get back inside—back to Rachel. The wiper blades did almost nothing to improve his visibility. Luckily, he knew his drive well enough that he made it into the garage without scraping anything. His car was definitely going to have some dings.

As soon as he was in, he killed the engine and stepped out, then closed the driver's side door. Rachel was standing in the doorway to the house, holding some towels.

"I wanted you to know I stayed safely inside the whole time."

"I appreciate that." He smiled at her as he slicked his hair back from his face, water trailing down his back.

She hit the button to close the garage door, then walked over to him and handed him a towel. He wiped his chest and arms, then went to work on his hair.

"I'm sorry you're so wet." She walked around behind him and started to work on his shoulders. "But I am really going to enjoy drying you off."

His teeth were chattering. "I think I'll enjoy it a lot more when I'm warmer. We should take a shower later."

She dabbed the water from his back with her towel. "What are you doing in five minutes?"

"You, I imagine."

She laughed, and he turned around and grabbed her, pulling her against his chest and lifting her feet from the ground. Her laugh deepened—the sweetest sound he'd ever heard.

So what if his car was all wet. He had a gorgeous, brilliant, incredibly imaginative woman to bed. He turned back toward the house with her already nibbling on his neck.

After one step, he froze. His heart was pounding, and the chill on his skin shot right through to his bones.

"What's wrong?" She tightened her grip on his neck and looked around.

Garrett couldn't breathe. On the floor between them and the door to the house was a snake—a snake with black, red and yellow bands.

A coral snake.

His stomach churned and his muscles felt both electrified and paralyzed. He had to move. He had to get her to safety.

"Oh, look at that," Rachel said. She sounded delighted. "It must have come in when the garage door was open to get out of the rain. Poor little guy."

"Get on the car."

"*On* the car or *in* the car?"

"Do it!"

She pushed away from him and he set her down. The car doors were unlocked. Maybe once she was safe, he'd be able to move again and could deal with this intruder. But instead of heading for the car, she took a step forward, between him and the snake.

"Rachel!"

"Stop shouting at me!"

The sharpness of her tone was enough to make him glance at her. The look she gave him then made him wonder what was the deadliest force in the garage.

She took a deep breath and let it out. "That is a scarlet snake. They're completely harmless."

"You don't know that."

"I do. I recognize the band pattern."

"Since when are you an expert?"

"I grew up here too. Knowing there's dangerous wildlife, I researched them. I can tell the difference between a scarlet snake and a coral."

His skin started to buzz when she said the word. His ears were ringing.

Shit—he had let it out of his sight. He looked back at it,

infinitesimally relieved that it was in the same spot.

If she knew about coral snakes, she knew how deadly they were. She knew you did not fuck around with snakes in Florida. Any snakes—even if you thought you knew for sure they were harmless.

"We can throw one of the towels over it and help it outside."

"No! We are not going near that thing."

He kept watching the snake, making sure it wasn't moving. It was coiled and seemed placid. But that could change in an instant. Especially with some asshole ghost prodding it.

Her voice was gentle when she spoke again. "Okay. You are obviously phobic about snakes. I didn't know. But don't worry. I've got this."

The blood rushed from his head and the room spun a little.

"That's the same thing…"

"What 'same thing'?"

"The same thing Dylan said. Right before he got bit."

"Dylan?"

"My brother."

"Your… Oh God, Garrett. I'm so sorry. I didn't—"

"He was sure it was a scarlet too." Garrett could barely force out the words. "He was wrong."

She gently touched his arm. "Listen to me. We need to get the snake out of the house. One way or the other. We can try to call a service, but the snake might move and find a hiding spot in the house before someone gets here."

What a nightmare. A snake hiding somewhere in his house?

If it made it inside… He'd have to burn the place down. They could stay at a hotel. They should move to Alaska before they had kids.

No, Alaska had bears.

Dammit!

"Can you trust me?" Rachel asked. "Trust me that I know what I'm doing here and can keep myself safe."

She didn't know what she was asking. Or maybe she did. He risked a glance at her and the earnest look on her face—the caring, the love—it melted some of the icy fear.

"I won't go near it," she said. "I'll treat it as if it's… dangerous. I promise. Please, Garrett. This is my chance to help you."

She had said she wanted to be his partner. He wanted to be hers too. That meant taking care of each other.

God help him. He nodded.

She took him by the arm and pushed him back a few feet closer to the car. He was tall enough that he could still see the thing, but if it went for his car, it could easily slither out of sight. Then again, if it went for his car, he could run the damn thing over.

Instead of going for a towel, Rachel walked toward the side door that led to the yard. As she opened it she said,

"We don't have the means to capture it and relocate it. Is it okay if I get it out into the yard?"

"I just want it out of the house."

"Okay."

The rain had stopped, thankfully. The patchy grass beyond glistened in the dim light. More rain might be on the way, but the snake didn't have to know that. Maybe it would go out on its own.

Rachel wasn't waiting around. She picked up the broom that was tucked behind the washing machine, then walked slowly toward the snake, giving it as wide a berth as she could.

It angled its head toward her. Garrett felt that tiny motion in his heart, a lurching tug of fear.

She was totally focused on the snake. Sliding the broom between the snake and the door to the house, she moved closer, but kept herself at least six feet back, her arms outstretched and her body arched away from it. What was the strike radius on that thing?

He would surely have a heart attack any moment. His chest was too tight to breathe.

The snake uncoiled and started toward him, but Rachel was right there, placing the broom sideways between them and herding it so it made a bee-line for the door.

Or the space underneath the washer and dryer.

Please please please... He willed the thing to keep going straight, to head outside.

It did.

He let out a huge breath as he watched it disappear into the grass. Finally, he could move. He jumped forward and slammed the door shut. He knew it was ridiculous, but he locked it, too, for good measure.

His whole body was shaking, only partly because he was freezing and still dripping wet. Rachel dropped the broom, then set her hands on his shoulders and turned him around. He leaned down, wrapping his arms around her and holding her tight. She stroked his hair and whispered in his ear—soothing words that only half-registered, he was so wired with adrenaline.

It could have bitten her. Scarlet snake or...not.

He wanted to keep her safe. But he hadn't been any help. When he had finally been able to do something, the threat was over. Again.

He couldn't live with himself if anything happened to her. Especially if it was because of him. Because of a lack of action. Because he was too late.

He thought about Finn's voicemail—the warning that might have come sooner if Garrett had kept pushing the investigation instead of telling Finn to back off at Elsa's request. The hours that Rachel might have spent free of Michael if only Garrett had listened right when the message arrived.

"Come inside." She took his hands in hers and walked backwards, leading him into the house.

Chapter Twenty-Four

As soon as they crossed the threshold, Garrett latched on to her again. Rachel needed to get him dry and warm.

His skin was freezing—still coated with rainwater. The blast from the AC couldn't be doing him any good.

"It's okay," she said. "We're okay."

Except Garrett wasn't. He was shaking, but she wasn't sure if it was from the cold. His reaction had seemed extreme at first, but the more she thought about it, the more sense it made. She kept her arms wrapped around his neck, giving him the time he needed to sort himself out as her mind filled in all the details for him.

His brother had been killed by a coral snake. And Garrett had been there when it happened.

Garrett had grown up in the country. He mentioned playing in the swamp a few times, but never gave many details. Coral snake bites were pretty rare and didn't manifest as many would suspect. They didn't hurt like a rattlesnake's. The neurotoxin caused respiratory failure.

Antivenom wasn't always on hand.

She couldn't imagine how terrified Garrett must have been to see that snake in his home, not knowing what it was or how dangerous. Scarlets were mistaken for coral snakes all the time. But she was sure the one in the garage had been a scarlet.

Still, she hadn't taken any chances. It was only about a foot long. Even if it had been a coral snake, she never came close to entering its strike radius. Better safe than sorry, and Garrett was right—she wasn't a herpetologist.

"I'm sorry," he said. She was so deep in her thoughts it took her a minute to realize he had spoken.

"For what?"

"Not helping."

"I'm glad I had the chance to help you for once."

"You help me all the time," he whispered. "Just by being with me."

"Garrett—"

She was going to try to laugh it off, to lighten the mood, but when she leaned back to look into his eyes, the tears streaming down his face made her stop. Her own eyes filled immediately, her heart lurching toward him, trying to give him comfort.

"You're the only one," he said. "The only one I've ever really felt I can be myself with. It's always been on me to take care of people. To be the responsible one. Even before it happened. But you... You're the only one who ever took care of me."

She couldn't take it. Seeing him bared down to his soul right in front of her, the wounds he kept hidden, the pain.

It was almost like seeing a ghost—seeing his soul through the shield of his body.

She lightly gripped his face and pulled him into a kiss. A slow kiss. Deep and long and healing. She let him sink into her through that simple connection, imagined her own soul wrapping around his and soothing him.

When she pulled back, he had a stunned expression. His eyes were wide as he stared at her. She wasn't sure what had happened, but she felt different. Strong. Empowered. She felt like…a healer.

"Tell me," she said.

He started to lean away, but she took his hands in hers again and looked into his eyes.

"Please."

Garrett cleared his throat before he began.

"He said it was a scarlet snake. That the bite didn't even hurt once he got the thing off him. We were out in the country. Too far to get help."

His eyes were unfocused as he watched his memories play out in his mind. The more he spoke, the thicker his accent became.

"Dylan was older than me. He was in his teens and I wasn't even ten." Garrett let out a short breath, not a laugh, but a release of energy. "I hadn't had my first real growth spurt yet, but he had. He always seemed so grown-up to me. Reckless, though."

Another wave of emotion hit him. Rachel felt it even as

she saw him wince, his jaw tightening and his eyes narrowed in pain.

"He saw I was upset. Wanted to reassure me that he was fine. So he said…" Garrett's voice broke over his words. "He said, 'Race you back home.' Then he took off. Just flew over the sand. God, he could run. It only made the poison circulate faster through his system."

He cleared his throat, then said, "I lost sight of him right away, but tore ass for home as fast as I could." He sniffed once and shook his head. "I found him in a fennel grove. Laying on the ground—so still. I turned him over and…"

Garrett pulled his hands from hers. He covered his face and tilted his head back. She gave him space to do it, but moved her hands to his chest. Her instincts told her she had to keep touching him. When Garrett looked at her again, he didn't bother trying to hide his tears or his pain.

"I had to get him home. He was so much bigger than me, but I got him over my shoulder somehow and carried him as far as I could. I had to drag him the last couple hundred yards."

Wave after wave of grief and guilt rolled through her. She tried to take the emotions in—to let them pass through her, channeling them away from Garrett and letting them sink harmlessly down through the floor. He had been carrying this for too long.

"My mom came out and saw that. Saw me dragging his

body. But it was the best I could do. I was screaming so loud. But the noise my mom made… I never knew what keening meant till I heard that sound. She fell to her knees, grabbed him up from me and held him and just rocked making that terrible sound."

He shuddered and another wave of energy flooded her. She opened herself to it, letting her heart feel his anguish, pulling it away from him.

"My dad came running out and grabbed Dylan—he had to fight my mom off to get to him. Dad was shaking all over, barely holding it together. He told me to call 911, but he already knew. He took one look at Dylan, and he knew it was too late."

Garrett looked back down at Rachel, dazed. His gaze slowly came back into focus. He covered his eyes for a moment, then wiped his face.

"Since then, I've always felt it was on me to protect everyone. I became a doctor so I would know what to do, how to help. But I don't always know. I can't always protect the people I care about, and that terrifies me."

She kept her voice as gentle as possible. "It's not your job to protect us, Garrett. We help each other out when we can, but we're all stumbling through this life together. All we can do is our best."

"It doesn't feel like enough. Not when people are still getting hurt. Elsa and Dante. You…"

"Don't. Dante was right. The only person responsible

for what happened to us is Michael. And I took care of him."

Garrett shook his head. "I guess you did. And that snake too. And the scorpion. I knew everybody else was underestimating you. Didn't know I was too."

"I think I've been underestimating myself. Or not estimating myself at all."

She was beginning to feel like she'd been sleepwalking through her whole life. But the jolt of what had happened to her, the trauma, had awakened parts of her she didn't even know were there.

Hearing ghosts? Yeah, she was used to that. Full-on empathic bonding? That was new.

The tether she felt leading from her to Garrett vibrated like the strings of a harp and she knew he was going to say something before he even took in the breath to speak.

"I've never told anyone else. We never talk about him. I've tried, but my folks just won't."

Rachel felt a hollowness inside of her. The loss of a sibling, so complete and utter that it was like he never even existed… It resonated within her somehow. Deep and echoing.

His parents should have talked to him about Dylan. They should be keeping Dylan alive by remembering the joy and love they all shared.

She thought about Misha again and tamped down the worry that bubbled up within her—just in case the connection with Garrett went both ways. Now was not the time to bring that up. Garrett was too vulnerable, too wounded.

But soon. She would have to tell him her suspicions soon.

She wrapped her arms around his shoulders and held him as tight as she could. He buried his face in the nape of her neck, his arms around her waist, holding her close.

"Thank you," she whispered. "Thank you for telling me."

When she leaned back enough that she could look into his face, he looked lighter. The lines around his eyes had softened and his brow wasn't as furrowed. She needed to build on that, to help them both get distance from the pain she hoped he was starting to leave behind.

"You can talk to me," she said. "About this—about anything. Always."

"I know. That's part of why I love you."

She smiled up at him. "It's nice to hear you say that when we aren't in bed. And when you're not mad at me."

"I'm sorry about that. I was really confused and hurting."

"And now?"

"Now…" He considered her words for a few moments, as if he was assessing himself. "I feel good. Lighter, I guess."

"Let me see if I can make you feel even better. Starting

by warming you up."

She led him to the master bath just off his bedroom. She started up a hot shower, then turned back to him and pulled her shirt over her head and threw it in the hamper. He smiled and slipped from his pajama pants, tossing them after her shirt. They held hands as they stepped into the water.

When she designed the open shower, she never thought she would have a chance to share it with Garrett. It took up a third of the room, filling one corner, with windows that let in the fading sunlight set high in the wall.

She nudged him under the water first, wanting him to get warmed up as quickly as possible. Jets sprayed their bodies from three sides. He put his hands on her hips, shifting them so she was enveloped in water and steam as well.

The hot spray first hit her shoulders, coursing down her spine and giving her goose bumps. She leaned into the water to wet her hair, then slicked it back. When she looked at him, he was staring at her.

"You are so beautiful," he said.

Those words had never meant so much to her. When she'd heard them before, it was always a sign that whoever was talking thought they'd already figured her out. The politician's pretty daughter. Nothing else to see but the surface.

Garrett looked deeper.

She ran her fingertips over his face, lingering on his lips. "So are you."

He grasped her hand and pressed a kiss into her palm, then pulled her closer, bending to kiss her. His hands followed the water's path down her back. He cupped her backside, as his tongue slid between her lips. Warm and wet everywhere.

She slid her hands over his chest, exploring the muscles, relishing his strength. The water coursed over their bodies, washing away their tension and all the residual negative energy.

Breaking off the kiss, he said, "Turn around."

As she did, he shifted so that she was facing the main jets. He moved behind her, pressing his chest against her back and pinning his shaft between them. Her hips squirmed and she rose on her toes without really thinking about it. All she knew was that she wanted him inside her again.

He kissed the side of her neck, lingering enough to leave a mark, then made his way up to her ear. As he nipped at her earlobe, her nerves lit up again.

He wrapped his arms around her, one hand lifting and kneading her breast and the other delving between her legs as he rocked his hips against her, rubbing his shaft on her backside.

The jets were lined up to hit all sorts of interesting parts of her anatomy. He shifted her again so they alternated between massaging her breasts and bouncing off the hand that shielded her most sensitive spot. When he moved his hand away, the intense stimulation almost set her off immediately.

"Garrett..."

"I know."

He bent down and grabbed the shower stool just outside the sprays of water, sliding it close. He ran his hand down the back of her thigh, then lifted her leg to rest her foot on the stool, opening her further to the jets. She gasped as the pleasure increased.

He reached for her again, kneading one breast while he lined himself up at her core with his other hand. Slowly, he inched himself inside, moving his hands to her hips as he slid all the way home.

Feeling her core tighten around him, his hips flush against her backside and his hands gripping her as the water pounded against her... Her head snapped back as her body started pulsing around him, so many sources of stimuli, she couldn't keep up with where the pleasure was coming from.

He held her up as she reached out to the cool tile, resting her hands against it to support her. She was still throbbing when he started to move.

The water was merciless, massaging her breasts and where they were joined as Garrett thrust into her over and over again. He would pull out almost all the way, moving slowly, then ram himself back in. He ran one hand over her raised leg, shifting her to reach deeper, to move faster without making her lose her balance.

Heat built in her, a diffuse inferno that ran beneath her skin like lava. He thrust faster, harder, his hands finding both breasts and holding them, using them to pull her tight against his chest, her back plastered to him.

She shifted her arms so that she only needed one to keep her propped up against the wall, wrapping the other around his neck and twisting so she could kiss him. He groaned against her mouth as her tongue slid into his. His pace increased, his shaft pulsing within her.

Her climax tore through her body, heat running over her skin. She had to be radiating light, so much energy coursed through her body. Even her eyes were tingling by the time he slid from her body and moved her from the jets.

He turned her around so that the water hit her back, his strong hands rubbing her shoulders as she leaned against his chest. She had never felt more relaxed or at peace. She had never felt as safe.

"Thank you," she whispered, her body yearning for his big bed and some sleep.

He held her tight. "Any time."

Chapter Twenty-Five

Waking up next to Rachel the next day was one of the happiest experiences of Garrett's life. He couldn't keep himself from smiling.

Her legs were tangled with his, one arm sprawled over his chest and the other folded against his side. She was as close to him as she could get and he loved it. Of course, his own arms were wrapped around her, holding her tight even as he slept.

He was never going to let her go again. He wouldn't have to.

His arms flexed around her and he kissed the top of her head. She let out a contented sigh.

"Morning," she mumbled.

"Good morning."

She yawned and nuzzled his chest. "I'm starving. Want some eggs?"

"Sounds like you need more sleep. Why don't I go make us breakfast?"

"Because then you won't be with me." She rose on her elbows to kiss him, erasing his thoughts of breakfast. But then she slid to the edge of the bed and stood. With a smile, she said, "Come on. Let's go."

Rachel standing naked in front of him—yeah, he'd go wherever she wanted. As he rose, she went to his closet and pulled out two T-shirts. She tossed one to him and put on the other.

"If we're going to be cooking, we probably shouldn't be naked."

"Good point."

He pulled the shirt over his head, then grabbed a pair of pajama pants from his dresser and put them on. Rachel waited for him—she didn't take off to get started on breakfast.

She took his hand when he reached the door, but he pulled her close instead of walking to the kitchen. He bent down and brushed his lips across hers, satin-soft and sweeter than honey.

After a good long while, he leaned back to see her eyes half-shut and her breathing quickened. He would have walked them right back into the bedroom, but her stomach growled. They both laughed at the sound.

"Sorry. My stomach is very opinionated."

"I'm the one stalling breakfast. Let's go."

They worked side-by-side in his kitchen, bumping into each other or at least brushing elbows often. No words were necessary. She made the eggs, he made toast and coffee.

As they ate at the counter, they kept smiling at each

other. He felt ridiculous—like he was a kid again, free-falling into that first love. Rachel wasn't his first, though. She was his last.

"I was thinking about the house," he said.

"The one we're going to fill with all those children?" The way she smiled as she spoke made his heart fill with warmth.

"That's the one. I was thinking we could build on a solarium, sort of like what Elsa has, only more detached. If ghosts are going to keep pestering you, we might as well make a sort of waiting room so we can deal with them on our terms."

"'Our' terms?"

"Partners in everything. I'm sure as hell not going to leave you to deal with this alone."

"I'm not sure how much you can do."

"Just because I'm not psychic doesn't mean I can't help." He would damned sure find a way. "I can make poppets, spray saltwater...look menacing."

She laughed at that, and he felt his smile deepen. His cheeks hurt, he'd been smiling so much.

"And I have resources," he said. "My friend Finn is a private investigator. You need to dig up facts on anybody who comes to you for help, he's your guy."

"Are you sure he'd be okay helping out a psychic?"

Garrett laughed and shook his head. Finn's secrets weren't Garrett's to tell, but the irony of her question was too much.

"He'll be fine with it. And he'll be more help than you can imagine. Finn's the best."

"A PI would be extremely helpful in many cases, I imagine. Tracking down descendents or lost items. Those are the main requests I get hit with. The ghosts want me to tell someone something or get something to a particular person."

"Why was Hiram hanging around?"

"'Scientific curiosity'. That's what he always said." Her smile softened as she spoke about him. "He wasn't done learning about this life when he passed on. He was the exception rather than the rule, though."

"I'm glad you had somebody to help you with all this."

"Me too."

"Speaking of helpful spirits, what about Misha?"

"What about him?"

"Do you think he might be helpful? Kind of act as an intermediary for you?"

That gorgeous smile of hers vanished, her eyes crinkling at the edges and the slightest line appearing between her eyebrows. She took a breath and held it, mouth open like she was on the brink of saying something. Something he was not going to like.

"What?"

"I...don't think Misha will be much help. I think he *needs* help. Closure of some kind. I haven't figured out what, though."

"I thought Hiram sent him to watch over you."

"That's what Misha said. But ghosts sometimes lie. And they talk to each other. He could have asked around, found someone who knew about my friendship with Hiram when I was a child."

Garrett's stomach soured. The idea of an entire network of ghosts using their knowledge to manipulate people... No wonder she had stopped listening to spirits.

"We're putting mirrors in the solarium. Lots of them." At least if she could see them, she would have a better idea of who she was talking to.

"That's...a really good idea."

Her gaze shifted from him, her demeanor intensifying. Her mind was carrying her away on that tangent. She was probably designing the room already.

"Do you have any idea what Misha wants then?" Garrett asked, bringing her back to the more immediate issue.

"I'm not sure." The pain and hesitance crept back into her expression. "But I don't think he's who he says he is. For one thing, he's younger than I thought."

Garrett's skin felt electrified. "He isn't... It can't be Michael, can it?"

"No, Michael was cremated."

She didn't seem as convinced as she had been. If it was Michael and he had somehow found a way to harass

Rachel from beyond the grave, Garrett would find a way to make him pay.

"He mentioned Dylan," she said. "Before you did. He said you had a brother who died."

How would a ghost know anything about Dylan? He'd been gone for thirty years. Misha might have asked around about Garrett, but why would he? Unless…

Garrett's heart started to pound.

"Wait, you don't think—"

She didn't have to say anything to give him his answer. The way her brow pulled together above her nose, how she leaned toward him as if ready to put her arms around him, to hold him together…

Yeah. She thought it might be Dylan.

Garrett's eggs threatened to come back up.

Imagining dead people hanging around was unnerving enough—serial killers or not. But Dylan couldn't be among them. He couldn't.

Garrett dropped his fork and pushed away his plate, then covered his face with his hands, leaning his elbows on the counter. His skin prickled, a sensation of warmth surrounding him like Rachel's arms.

But she wasn't touching him.

Her arms wrapped around him, giving the feeling a source. After-the-fact.

He dropped his hands so he could look at her. "What was that?"

"What was what?"

"I felt you touch me before it happened."

She started to pull away, but he caught her arms and kept them on his shoulders.

"Please don't," he said. "Don't pull away. Not now."

He needed her. Especially now that he knew Dylan might still be around—might have been lingering since his death decades ago. If so, Garrett had to help his brother find peace.

She took a deep breath, then let it out. Warmth washed over Garrett again, taking the edge off his pain and worry. She grasped one of his hands and pressed it against her chest just above her heart, then placed her free hand in the same place on him.

What he felt was indescribable. His mind still tried to put it into words.

Peace, happiness, contentment, hope, excitement—a kaleidoscope of emotions poured through him. He could feel his own emotions connecting to her and traveling through her as well, like they had closed a circuit by opening their hearts to each other.

He covered the hand she rested above his heart with his other hand. "What is this?"

"I'm not sure. It's kind of new to me. But if I had to guess, I'd say it's some sort of empathy."

"Is it part of your power?"

"I don't know. It's never happened before."

"When did you first notice it?" Damn, he sounded like he was starting an exam.

"It started after the snake in the garage."

Dread crashed through him, but even that ebbed quickly. "It's not because of…" He swallowed hard. "Dylan, is it?"

"Not directly. I think it was triggered by how upset you were and how much I wanted to help you feel better."

"So this is another thing you can do."

"Apparently."

It would probably come in handy when helping out ghosts. Starting with his brother.

The pain and guilt of it tore through him again. Rachel was right there, carrying it with him, easing his burden.

"Don't," Garrett said. "You don't have to do that for me."

"I know. But I want to. This is what you've done for me since we met. Helping me to feel less alone, more at peace with myself. This connection has always been there, I think. We're only just now exploring it."

He couldn't deny that. Since the first time their gazes met, he had felt it deep in his gut, in his soul. She was the one for him.

"What are we going to do about it?" he asked.

"I guess see where it takes us."

He wanted to see where it could take Dylan, how it could help him. With it being an unknown, a new power,

Garrett wasn't sure how safe it would be for Rachel, though. He didn't like the idea of her using any kind of empathic ability to connect with an unknown ghost.

"It's okay," she said. "You'll be right there with me."

"What, can you read my mind now? Because then we might be in trouble."

She gave a light laugh and said, "No, I could feel you worrying. And I can feel you wanting to act. We can see if I can help Misha, whoever he is. We can try to find out if he's Dylan."

Her voice trailed off at the end. She must have been waiting for another spike of dread or fear or guilt. But they were all overpowered by the one prevailing emotion he felt in that moment. Gratitude.

This gorgeous, generous woman was willing to walk into a situation that a few days ago would have terrified her, just on the chance that it was Garrett's brother. She wasn't running away from him. She was walking at his side, as a partner.

He didn't feel like he was out on a limb with her anymore. It was more like they were standing on a bridge that they were building together, one that would lead wherever they wanted it to go.

"That is…heady," she said.

"It's what I've always felt for you."

"I'm sorry I made you wait so long."

He shook his head. "It was worth it."

"If we aren't heading back to the bedroom now, we might want to try to tone this down."

The bedroom sounded really good. But if Misha was Dylan, Garrett couldn't let that go for another moment.

"What do we do?"

Rachel took a deep breath and closed her eyes. The warmth he felt from her lessened, but was still there. She moved their hands away from each other's chests, letting out a long, steady exhale. The feeling of connection faded till it was just a tingling along his skin, a calmness in his heart.

"Did that work?" she asked.

"You're the psychic. You tell me."

"I think that's as good as we can do with toning down the connection for now. Come on. Let's go talk to Misha."

Garrett was still nervous as hell, but he nodded and stood. She grasped his hand again and led him to the guest room.

Chapter Twenty-Six

It was hard to believe she was doing this. Willingly opening herself up to a ghost to help them. After everything she'd been through, the sacrifices she'd made to get them to leave her alone...

None of that mattered. Word was out about her abilities anyway. If Misha really was Dylan, she had to help him for Garrett's sake. But that wasn't her only reason.

She *wanted* to help Misha. Whoever he was. She wanted to help all the spirits that needed her and were aware enough to come to her for aid. First Misha, then the spirits of Michael's victims that were haranguing her.

If her mother had raised her in her family's traditions, this wouldn't have even been an issue. She would have been protected as a child and trained in how to use her powers. She would have been helping spirits for years by now.

Looking back wouldn't help anyone. She needed to be looking forward. To a future with Garrett. Embracing her abilities and exploring them more, honing her skills. She had the book knowledge. It was time to start putting it into a deeper practice.

"When we go into the room, be careful not to disturb the line of salt that's over the threshold." She pointed at the barrier she had made earlier.

"I thought spraying the door with saltwater was enough."

"Since there's already so much salt around in Florida, it generally is, but I wanted to be sure no one could get into the rest of the house. I left the door open and took the wards down from the window. With the window and the mirror, there are too many access points in there."

"The mirror is an access point?"

"Reflections are a link between this plane and the next. Mirrors are powerful enough that they can be used as doorways from the other side. They magnify and focus spiritual energy."

She hadn't talked to anyone about it since she was a little girl. When all of this was over, she was going to have a long conversation with Chloe and rekindle that relationship. In the meantime, she had to try to explain this better to Garrett.

"Ghosts can move around like people through doorways. That's the easiest way for them to get around. I think it's because that's what's most familiar to them from when they were alive. But they can also sort of teleport to different places by willing themselves to go there, especially the ones who are focused or have been around a long time and have lots of practice. They still need something to connect to. Either a person or a place they're familiar with. Hence hauntings."

"Okay, that makes sense."

"Good." She took a deep breath and went on. "Ghosts tend to think of themselves in terms of their human existence. Doorways and windows are obvious ways to get into someone's house. Warding them keeps ghosts from being able to enter and usually stops them from even seeing or hearing anything that goes on inside."

"What if a ghost doesn't see themselves as human?"

She shivered as she remembered her conversations about the topic with Hiram. Garrett was dealing with so much. She didn't want to burden him with yet more knowledge that most people never had to deal with.

"You don't want to tell me. I can feel it."

"I would rather protect you from knowing this."

"I think I've proven by now that you can tell me anything. I can handle it."

She nodded, then said, "If a ghost stops thinking of themselves in human terms, their soul devolves. Over time, they become what most people think of as demons. Different rules apply. They are much more dangerous than ghosts. Thankfully, it's very, very rare for a ghost to become a demon."

"Okay. That's a pretty scary thought."

"Sorry."

"Don't be. I'd rather know—be prepared for it if

something comes up."

"Well, hopefully we'll never need to worry about that. Anyway, Hiram told me that everything is kind of foggy on the other side. Trying to look through doors and windows is a little bit like looking through frosted glass. Unless it's warded, and then it's all opaque. But mirrors make everything crystal clear. And they glow on the other side."

"Do you like beards?"

She blinked at the sudden shift in topic. Her penchant for non sequiturs might be rubbing off on him.

"I guess they're okay."

"Good. Because I doubt I'll be shaving again anytime soon."

He gave her a small smile and she laughed, grateful for him easing the tension of the moment.

"So that's why you can see ghosts in reflections. Because those are the *real* windows from the other side?"

"Exactly. That's also why I have to be so careful around reflective surfaces. Mirrors especially can act like a sort of amplifier. Ghosts can use a mirror to get to a place or person they don't already know. I cover them so that I don't see anything disturbing and so they can't see me in a warded environment. If I tried to ward one and did it wrong…"

Her skin crawled at the thought. She knew some psychics used mirrors extensively in their work. With her already amplified abilities, putting any sort of energy on a mirror seemed like a colossally bad idea. Not until she had learned more. Had more practice.

Garrett squeezed her hand. She could feel him willing reassuring energy into her and welcomed it gladly.

"Then we keep the mirror covered and we don't mess up the line of salt. Got it."

"Are you sure you're ready for this?"

"Doesn't matter. One way or another, we're getting this done now."

She nodded, then turned back to the door.

Strangely, when Misha had been an unknown, she was less nervous around him. Not as much was at stake when she thought she was just talking to an easygoing ghost who was hanging around like Hiram had been.

But Misha wasn't like Hiram. She was certain of it.

Which meant one of two things. Either the ghost in the guest room was Garrett's brother Dylan and they were about to have an emotional reunion—or the ghost was a stranger pretending to be a friend.

As much as she hated the thought of Dylan lingering, the second was infinitely more frightening. One way or another, they needed to know.

With a deep breath, she stepped over the threshold. Garrett followed right behind her.

"Misha? Are you here?"

No one answered.

She walked deeper into the room, holding tight to Garrett's hand. "Misha, we'd like to talk to you."

After another few moments of silence, Garrett spoke up. "Dylan? Is that you?"

Still nothing.

"He might not be here," Rachel said. "I asked him to find the spirits of the women who are haunting me and tell them I want to talk. Maybe he decided to help with that after all."

"I'd like a few words with them myself. They need to stop stirring up bugs and snakes. Immediately."

When Garrett had offered to look intimidating, Rachel had laughed it off. Seeing the look on his face at that moment was anything but amusing. His jaw was set, brow drawn together and lips in a tight line. She could practically see lightning sparking from his eyes.

He might be able to scare ghosts after all.

"We should hear them out first. Try to talk. If they ever show up, that is."

She glanced around the room. No reflective surfaces to try to catch a glimpse of ghosts. No voices. Nothing.

"I don't want to have to do a summoning," Rachel said. "Those always ruffle the ghost's feathers, so to speak."

"I read a little about those in the books you loaned me. It sounded like an involved process."

"It can be. Or it can be a simple one, depending on how you go about it. I don't go in for show. My rituals are always simple and practical. Like the poppets and saltwater."

"I didn't know that qualified."

"If you do it in the right mindset, anything can be a ritual."

They could just wait for Misha to return, but who knew how long that would take. Rachel was already feeling antsy.

"Maybe I could use a rune…"

"Like a Norse rune?"

Rachel had always felt a pull to runes and collected volumes dedicated solely to their use. But they weren't mentioned in any of the books about ghosts she had loaned Garrett.

"How do you know about runes?"

He snorted, then gestured down the length of his body. "Witness my heritage."

She laughed, leaning into his broad chest. "Just because your ancestors were Nordic doesn't mean you've read up on them. And runes are a pretty obscure subject."

"With a last name like Wolfstrom, I was curious. I've read a bunch of myths. Runes came up from time to time. The stories made them seem powerful and dangerous."

"Anything powerful can be dangerous. The trick with runes is to use them with the correct intention."

"I stand enlightened."

She laughed again, until a sudden icy feeling shot

through her. Looking around the room, she sought out the threat.

"What is it?" Garrett asked.

"Misha?"

"I found them!" Misha's voice sounded even younger, a sure sign that he was in distress, even without the urgency in his tone. If this wasn't Dylan, it was someone who had been carrying a lot of emotional baggage when he died.

"Hello, Misha." Rachel tried to keep her voice calm. She wanted Garrett to be part of the conversation as much as possible, even though she also wanted to shield him from what might be said. "Thank you for finding the ghosts for me. I still want to talk to them, but I'd like to speak with you first."

"There's no time to talk. They're getting ready to act."

The near-panic in his voice confused her. He sounded as if she and Garrett were in imminent danger. What could the spirits possibly do to hurt them? Glancing around the room, she didn't see any animals or bugs. Unless the ghosts had found a herd of rhinoceroses to stampede into the house, they seemed fairly safe.

"The house is warded," Rachel began.

"They aren't just after you. They're mad at Elsa for escaping too."

"What?"

Garrett pulled Rachel closer. "What is it? What's he

saying?"

"Misha, what are the ghosts planning to do to Elsa? How are they going to harm her?"

"Christ," Garrett hissed.

"By going after Dante. He's in surgery and they're controlling insects that they've hidden in the room. They're going to startle the doctors while they're cutting him."

"Oh God…" Rachel shook her head. This was too awful.

Dante had already had one emergency surgery after Michael had shot at him. Even though the bullet missed, it hit nearby mason jars full of debris. The shrapnel had hit Dante in the face.

The only reason he needed surgery in the first place was because he tried to save Rachel. She didn't know he was going back under so soon. It had only been two months.

Her cell phone was on the bedside table. Rachel dove for it and dialed Elsa's number. Nothing happened. She looked at the screen and saw that there wasn't a signal.

"Garrett, we have to warn Elsa."

"Hold up a minute. What is he saying? Warn Elsa about what?"

"The ghosts of those women aren't just mad at me. They want payback against Elsa too."

"What! Why?"

"Michael wanted both of us. And we lived."

Garrett's forehead crinkled and she heard his teeth grind together.

"Tell me what to do."

"I don't know! I can't get a signal to warn her. Where's your phone?"

"In my bedroom." He had already turned and was headed for the door. In his haste, he scuffed the salt line in the threshold. "Dammit!"

"I'll fix it later. We don't have time to waste."

They ran to his room and he picked up his phone. As he looked at the screen, his shoulders slumped.

"No signal."

"Have you ever had that happen before?"

"No. Maybe one of the towers got hit in last night's storm?"

Rachel shook her head. Her stomach was doing somersaults. "It's possible that the ghosts are messing with the signal. But that's a good thing. If they're here messing with our signals, they can't be at the hospital."

"Hospital?"

The urgency in his voice had spiked. She hadn't filled him in on the vengeful spirits' plan yet.

"Misha said that Dante's in surgery right now. The ghosts are planning to hurt him by distracting his doctors at the worst moment. They've already herded insects into the room. But if they can block cell signals, they're more powerful than we imagined. Working together, they could do all sorts of things."

A single ghost that was this angry, this focused on revenge wouldn't need to make a bug fly into a surgeon's face. It'd be able to bump their hand, maybe even throw scalpels across the room. It could kill the lights, bite or claw at someone, give them a chill at just the wrong moment.

And more than one was after her. After Elsa.

All of the research Rachel had done on hauntings by angry spirits surged up from the back of her mind. All of her memories of her own experiences. She had shoved them away so that she wouldn't be too terrified to ever leave her house.

Garrett pulled her against his chest, wrapping his arms around her. "Take a breath and calm down."

He was feeding steady emotions into her. Calmer than her own, but tinged with fear. They still helped, and she let them in, using them like an anchor to keep from being pulled into the memories that clawed at her mind.

"They might be able to move things." Her voice was muffled by the fabric of his shirt.

"What?"

She stepped away and took that deep breath he suggested. As she let it out, she made herself focus. Solutions. That was what they needed.

"It's possible that one or more of them has become a

poltergeist. If so, they'll be able to move things. Nothing too heavy, but in a room full of surgical equipment…" She shook her head, her imagination taking her to places too dark to think about. "How fast can you get us to the hospital?"

"Twenty minutes. But Dante shouldn't be back in surgery for another couple of weeks. He has to heal before they can do anything else."

"Something must have already gone wrong, then. Misha says he's being operated on now."

"Shit." Garrett started to pace.

"We have to get to the hospital to warn them. We can ward the room to keep Dante safe while they work."

"No, *I* will ward the room. If these ghosts can throw around scalpels, they might have tricked Misha to lure you into a trap. Plus the hospital staff won't let you into the OR. They're not going to like me spreading salt in the doorways, either."

Garrett ran his hands through his hair, leaving them on top of his head so his bangs were pulled back from his face. "I don't know how to help him."

"If you can at least be there, maybe you can run interference. You'll know that something might go wrong."

He dropped his arms to his sides. "I won't leave you alone in the city. You'll be swamped by ghosts."

"Then I'll stay here. I can re-cleanse the house and put

the wards back up. Elsa and Dante will need a safe place to stay anyway. And Winston and Leo. When Dante is able to be moved, you can bring them all home with you. I'll keep trying to call so I can warn them. Maybe talk them through setting up some wards of their own."

She could sense how torn he was—wanting to help his friends and facing the overpowering urge to protect her. Pulling him into a hug, she said, "I'll be okay. Misha is here and seems to genuinely want to help. He can warn me if they start to focus on something more than blocking the cell signal."

Honestly, she'd be the safest one of them all. She hated the idea of staying behind, but at the same time, she didn't know what would happen if she went back to the city now.

All of her mental energy would be spent just sifting through the voices that would undoubtedly be piled on top of each other vying for her attention. And she doubted the ghosts of Michael's victims were the only ones savvy enough to make physical contact.

She remembered all the pinching and shoving, invisible hands grabbing at her wherever she went. She had to stop thinking about this. If Garrett sensed her fear, he'd never go.

Instead, she willed her determination into him. They were going to help their friends. She would make a haven for them when they returned. Garrett would make a temporary safe spot for Dante in the hospital. They could do this.

"I get it," he said. "Enough with the psychic pep talk. I'll go."

She followed him to the foyer. He quickly pressed his lips to hers in an urgent kiss. Then he grabbed his wallet and keys from the table and headed for the car.

Chapter Twenty-Seven

At barely lunch time, the sky was so dark it looked to be dusk. Clouds hung above—thick and heavy, and low enough he felt he could reach up and touch them. Garrett's grip on the wheel was turning his knuckles white. Twenty minutes to the hospital meant he was driving fast enough that there was no room for error.

The sky opened up as soon as he had the thought.

"Shit!"

Water hit the windshield like a tidal wave. His instincts told him to slam on the brakes, but he refused to listen. His arms tried to spasm from the jolt of adrenaline in his already saturated system. Years of training and experience helped him control his response.

Surprises happened in the ER all the time. Twitching could cost someone their life. In this case, it would be his.

He eased up on the gas pedal and let gravity and the weight of the car slow him down steady and safe. Florida might be full of bugs and snakes, but at least it was flat. Hills and ditches could have meant disaster.

Even though the road had to be slick, it traveled through the countryside in a straight line toward the city.

All he had to do was keep himself calm and let physics do the work for him.

When the speedometer was in a more reasonable range, he turned on his wipers and checked his bearing. He was driving down the center of the road, but at least he wasn't close to running off either side. Rain that thick would turn the ground to quicksand as far as his car was concerned.

The wipers swung furiously back and forth over the glass. The deluge instantly replaced the water they flung away. Lightning crackled right next to his car, bright enough to blind him briefly. Thunder pounded his eardrums right after.

"Fuck!"

This time, his nerves got the better of him and the wheel twitched to the side. The roads were as slick as he thought. The back end of the car swung around so that he was facing the wrong direction.

His momentum kept him going, coasting backward down the straight road. He used the passenger's seat headrest for leverage as he twisted around to look out the back window and keep himself on the asphalt.

He said a silent prayer of thanks that he lived far enough out of town that the roads to and from his home were deserted on weekdays. Gently hitting the brakes, he slowed the car to a crawl. He was planning to stop it, but was too stunned when bright sunshine dazzled his eyes.

Turning back to face the front of the car, he finally

stepped on the brake fully, his inertia making the seatbelt pull across his chest. Steam was already rising from the hood as the summer sun heated the water running down its surface.

Rain while the sun was shining wasn't new to him. But this... This was something else. Garrett put the car in park and stepped out so he could see the sky.

In front of him, a wall of dark gray clouds rose up through the atmosphere—a smooth wall that curved away from him. It was like the storm was centered right over his house. A house where Rachel was trapped. Alone.

Well, not exactly alone. She was with Dylan.

Or Misha...

A sick feeling filled Garrett's stomach, spreading out through his body. Something was very wrong. Beyond the bugs, the snakes, the storm, the pissed off ghosts behind it all. They were missing something.

Dante's doctors were at the top of their fields. Garrett had hooked Dante up personally, calling in every possible favor to ensure he received the best care. If Garrett could keep himself from wrecking during that freakish storm, Dante's surgeons could handle a moth in the face or a poke in the ribs. They were trained to deal with distractions, power outages, emergencies.

If Rachel had taught Garrett anything over the past few days, it was that he didn't have to be the one to run in and fix things. He pulled out his phone and saw a full-strength signal.

Letting out a huge breath of relief, he called Elsa.

"Hi, Garrett."

She giggled. Not the sound someone makes sitting in a waiting room while the love of her life was undergoing emergency surgery.

"Is Dante with you?"

"Where else would he be? Stop it!"

"Elsa!" Garrett didn't mean to yell, but he needed her full attention.

Dante came on the call, his voice low and filled with a quiet challenge.

"Good morning, Garrett. I trust you have good reason for speaking to Elsa in such a harsh tone that I could hear it even sitting next to her."

Dante sounded as pissed as he ever had, and Garrett was near giddy with relief. Hearing Dante on the phone meant that he was okay. It also meant he wasn't in surgery.

The ghosts that were after Rachel might have tricked Dylan—no, Misha—into leading them astray.

Or Misha had lied.

When Garrett didn't respond, Dante went on. "I will ask you to nonetheless forgo using such a stern tone in the future, as she is quite sensitive to it."

"I'm sorry." Garrett ran his hand through his hair. He had forgotten about Elsa's parents. Not that he had the full details on that. They could catch up later.

"Listen, we're kind of in a shitstorm here."

"I beg your pardon?"

Right. Dante was from the 1800s. *Shitstorm* probably wasn't used back then.

"A mess. Problems. Danger."

"What do you need?"

"First, I need to know that you're okay."

"We are both fine."

There was a pause, then Garrett heard Elsa say, "You're on speaker." Her voice was a bit colder than usual, but at least she seemed focused. "What's going on?"

Damned if he knew.

"Dante, are you due for surgery anytime soon?" Garrett asked.

"Not for at least several weeks. While the preliminary reviews have been promising, the doctors wish to see how well I have healed from the initial surgery before following up with additional procedures."

That was the first thing that made sense all day.

"Okay. Good. Listen, I don't know for sure what's going on here, but there are some ghosts that are threatening Rachel. They've even brought you both into it, trying to trick us and…"

And get Rachel alone.

The churning in Garrett's stomach intensified and a chill swept over his skin making his hair stand on end. When it came to the ghosts threatening Rachel, Garrett wasn't sure who he was talking about—Michael's victims or Misha.

Michael.

It had to be.

Michael had been enough of a narcissistic prick to call himself "Michael Angelo" as a painter. Going by Misha as he fooled Rachel into thinking he was a friend of Hiram's would be just the thing to play to his ego. She had said ghosts sometimes shared information. Michael could have learned about Hiram and…

Fuck!

Garrett jumped back into his car and pulled on his seatbelt. Who knew what was in store for him once he drove back into that storm. He had to be alive to help Rachel. He had to get to her.

He also had to warn Elsa. She was in even more danger than they thought.

"What can we do?" Elsa asked.

"I don't have time to explain, but Michael is back. I'm sure of it."

How the hell was he supposed to protect everybody? Rachel was miles away in the center of what was building up to a landlocked hurricane from the looks of it, Elsa and Dante were miles in the other direction, ignorant of the issue and how to protect themselves. Even Winston and Jazz might be on Michael's list.

"You know that little bookstore on Sunny Lane with the

dragon reading a book on the sign?" he asked.

"Bookwyrm. Yes, I did a signing there last year."

"Good. Then you know the owner."

"Chloe."

He relaxed the tiniest bit. "Call her. She's a medium and can help you. Tell her there's at least one poltergeist coming after you and everyone you care about. If you can't reach her—"

This was going to sound crazy, but he barreled on. "Make up some saltwater in spray bottles. Spray it on the windows, doors, any entry to the loft."

"Our windows are two stories high," Elsa said.

Shit! He'd forgotten about that. "Then make lines of salt across all your windowsills and the door to your place. And cover your mirrors. Make sure Winston and Leo stay inside too. And call Jazz and tell her what's up."

"How great is the danger?" Dante asked.

Lightning streaked from the sky and hit the ground less than a mile in front of Garrett. The thunder rolled in after like a warning. Or a challenge.

Garrett's jaws tightened, the muscles nearly cramping. He bit out each word. "Ward your place. I'll take care of the rest."

He ended the call, then dropped his phone in the drink tray and knocked the car into drive, flooring the gas. Once he was home, he was going to figure out a way to end this once and for all.

He felt the car hit the water like it was a solid thing, but then it gave and he was back in the downpour. He just had to keep the car going straight. And not miss his driveway.

The rain started to lessen. It made him more anxious. What else did Michael have up his sleeve? What was distracting him from trying to drown Garrett?

By the time Garrett neared his home, the rain had all but stopped. He started to turn into his driveway when something huge lurched up from the brush lining his property. Swerving to miss it, his car went off the drive and into the sand.

"Shit!"

He looked out his window to see an eight-foot alligator walking toward his car. He hit the gas again, but all his wheels did was spin, throwing up patches of grass and digging in deeper.

The gator opened its jaws and hissed. Rows of sharp teeth surrounded the pale flesh of its mouth. Its eyes should have been black, but they glowed bright blue.

At this point, it was just one more weird thing. He pushed it from his mind and focused on what to do next.

His drive was long. Maybe fifty yards. Gators were faster on land than most people knew, but if he had a head start, Garrett could outrun it.

He slid his chair back and climbed into the passenger's seat. As he opened the door to jump out, something slammed against it. The door hit him in the head with enough force to send him sprawling back, seeing stars.

The tip of another gator's nose came into view through the passenger's window.

His heart was pounding. He took a few breaths to calm himself. Looking at his hands, he saw they were okay. If they'd been in the door when it shut—hell, if he'd made it out of the car…

Best not to think of that.

He was a little dizzy and his forehead itched. He looked in the rearview mirror and saw blood flowing down along his temple.

The wound was superficial. Head wounds always bled more. He could fix it later.

At the moment, what he needed to do was think of a way out of his car. Crawling out the windows or using the doors wouldn't work. A gator could jump up and grab him easily. And if he hit the ground too close to one, the same thing would happen. They could strike like a snake.

His heart sank.

Please don't let there be snakes waiting out there too.

Surely gators were enough. Right?

One way or another, he was getting to his house. He would get to Rachel.

He looked around the car for a way to escape. There was no sun roof. Damn, he should have bought a convertible. He could pop the top off, climb on the hood, jump clear of the gators, and run like hell for the house.

Wait…

He turned around to face the trunk of his car. He pushed his chair flat and crawled into the back. The releases for the back seat were a little hard to track down, but once he did, he lowered it so he could reach into his trunk and dig out his tire iron.

He pushed the seat up again and took a deep breath, staring out the glass of his rear windshield as he tested the weight of the metal in his hand. He really wished he was wearing thicker clothes.

Covering his eyes with his elbow, he pulled back his other arm and struck the window as hard as he could.

Chapter Twenty-Eight

As soon as Garrett left, Rachel went to work. She lit incense in her censer and refilled the saltwater bottle, then headed to Garrett's room. Walking through the house, she tried to keep her focus. Her mind kept wandering to her friends.

Were they okay? Was Garrett putting himself in even greater danger by trying to help them?

There was nothing she could do about that. All she could do was make the house safe for them whenever they managed to arrive.

She also wanted it to be safe for Dylan. Or Misha. Whoever he was. She even still wanted to help the women who were haunting her, though at this point that probably meant helping them to cross over rather than resolving their issues. She couldn't believe how far they were going —how angry they felt just that she had survived.

Rachel's own issues were fighting against her as well. She made a line of salt in front of the garage door rather than cleansing it. Garrett would be returning through the garage and she'd have to cleanse the space again anyway after he pulled in, especially the way it was raining. She had never heard such a storm. Better to just block off the garage from the rest of the house for now.

When she reached the guest room, she paused again. Misha or Dylan—whoever he was—had seemed comfortable talking to her in this room. And she preferred the comparatively controlled environment to talking outside. There were too many variables in the yard, too many ways things could sneak up on her.

Plus, she liked the idea of letting Dylan stay inside with them. As Garrett's brother, she wanted this to be his home too.

She made a new line of salt across the threshold, then took the censer back to the kitchen and set it on a trivet on the counter. After hesitating for a moment, she set the spray bottle next to it. Walking into the room carrying the equivalent of a shotgun wasn't the reception she wanted for the troubled spirit—Misha or Dylan.

It was time to figure out who this guy was and what he needed. Rachel headed back to the room. She stepped over the barrier carefully.

"Misha? Are you here? I'd like to talk to you."

She listened intently for his response, but heard nothing but the rain pounding against the window. A shrill sound broke in, rattling around in her head. She jumped, heart pounding.

It was her phone. She had brought it back to her room before cleansing the house so that she wouldn't lose track of it.

Strange that it suddenly had a signal again. Maybe a tower had been struck by lightning like Garrett thought and repairs were just finished.

She ran to the bedside table and picked it up. The caller ID read *Jazz*.

"Hello?"

Without preamble Jazz said, "Are you absolutely sure that Michael is gone?"

Rachel felt a chill that shot straight through to her bones. Why did people keep asking her that?

"He was cremated." She sounded unsure, even to herself.

Jazz's voice kept cutting out as she spoke, like the signal wasn't stable.

"I know…if…found…connection…could…possess… someone?"

"Possession?" Rachel's stomach clenched again and the icy feeling in her bones intensified.

No way. He would still need an anchor, some physical remains. He couldn't—

Jazz said, "Oh God—" just before the call died.

The door slammed shut.

All the hair on Rachel's arms stood on end as the room dropped in temperature. She felt a cold breath on the back of her neck.

"Hello, Rachel."

She dropped her phone on the bed, then ran to the door and tried the handle. It turned, but the door wouldn't budge. She pulled as hard as she could, then threw herself against it, but nothing happened. Slowly, she turned around and took a few hesitant steps back into the room.

"Dramatic as always, I see."

She pinched her lips shut and closed her eyes, tears spilling down her cheeks.

Michael...

"You look lovely, my dear." Lines of cold traced down her arms like fingertips, lingering over the scars on her wrists. Michael let out a contented, *"Mmm..."*

"What do you want?" Her voice crackled as she forced the words out.

"You, of course. I have a little harem on this side, and you will be my crown jewel." He chuckled. *"I thought Elsa was the strongest one, but you... You surprised me, Rachel. When you* killed *me."*

The paintings on the walls rattled as the room shook. How was he so powerful? How was he even here? None of it made sense.

"It was self-defense," she whispered.

"It was selfish. Short-sighted. Like everything you do." The cold traced over her cheek, freezing the tears on her face. *"Don't worry. I forgive you."*

She turned her face away from his touch, just like she had done in his garage when he held her prisoner. It had been so long since she had felt a spirit's hands on her. Her flesh was crawling.

"My ladies can't wait for you to join us. They told me they warned you about what would happen if you killed me. But you didn't listen." He laughed again. *"Another of your strongest suits—only paying attention to yourself."*

Her heart broke at his words. She had been selfish for so long, focused on not hearing ghosts to the point that she didn't listen to her friends.

Elsa had warned Rachel about Michael, and she hadn't listened. Rachel had known Garrett loved her, but she'd ignored it instead of telling him straight out that they couldn't be involved or explaining the situation and discovering that they could.

She had wasted so much time. And she wasn't sure how much she had left.

"I'm grateful, actually. Death is much more fun than being alive. If I had known, I would have arranged this years ago. There are so many things I have to teach you, but I want to wait till you're here with me. I want you to feel everything I do to you—and you will feel it."

His hands were on her shoulders. She had nowhere to run.

"I've been practicing on the others," he said. *"Warming myself up for you."*

Bile rose in the back of her throat. Those poor women. She had to help them somehow.

"I've been experimenting on someone else too. Someone close to you, though you've never met."

What was he talking about? Hiram maybe? But Hiram had crossed over. She prayed it wasn't Dylan.

"He's been teaching me all kinds of interesting tricks— how to slip into bodies like a fine suit. When I'm done with him, I'm sure I'll have no problem finding another meat-puppet to play with. And another and another."

His cold breath brushed her ear. *"I will kill so many women, Rachel. In so many ways. Ways I haven't even imagined yet. And the men I use to do it..."*

He chuckled. *"They won't be able to stop me. I'll twist them around inside until they won't know where they stop and I begin. I will remake them in my image. And you'll be right at my side to watch. Forever."*

No. No no no. This was not going to happen. She would find whatever part of his body was left and destroy it. She would find a way to end his twisted soul permanently.

"I can see what you're thinking," he half-sang. *"I studied you, remember? I'm in your head as much as* his. *He just doesn't realize it yet. But he will. The moment I use his hands to crush Ms. Zhou's throat. When he hears me laugh while she dies and tries again to sort out his thoughts from mine."*

"Stay the *hell* away from my friends!"

Rachel dove for the reading chair and hefted it over her

head, then threw it at the window. Glass shattered, some of it falling into the room as a blast of rain-drenched wind hit her.

The chair lodged in the window. Rachel shoved it as hard as she could. It crashed to the ground on the other side. She hopped up onto the windowsill, ignoring the warning from her primal brain about the sharp glass that was scraping her arms, ignoring...

A low rumble sounded from the ground below. Instinct kicked in and she lurched back just as an alligator struck, its jaws clacking shut inches from her face.

She stumbled backward through the broken glass, not stopping when the backs of her knees hit the bed. Even though the alligator couldn't climb into her room, she kept moving away, crab-walking over the mattress. She was breathing so fast her vision was tunneling.

Calm. She needed to be calm. She couldn't help anyone if she was unconscious. And goddammit, she was going to protect her friends.

She took a few deep breaths, her body quaking with adrenaline. The sheets were sticking to her arms and legs where she'd been cut. Pain began to register.

She checked her wounds and found that most of them weren't too deep. Some still had small bits of glass in them. She steeled her nerves and picked them out, throwing them toward the window.

"Keep cutting." Michael's voice was right at her ear,

but she didn't flinch. *"That's a nice piece there. Use it on yourself. Maybe I'm haunting you, and it will stop me. Or you can have a go at me from this side."*

He nuzzled her ear, the cold almost burning. *"I would love to see you try."*

Rachel was adept at ignoring spirits. She used that skill, picking up the edge of her sheet and wiping away some of the blood on her arms. A flash of blue-green glass caught her eye and she quickly covered it back up.

The witch's ball. She had forgotten about it after taking it down and putting it under the sheet.

Her mind began to race. With Michael in the room already, using it would be the equivalent of a flash-bang grenade. He would probably be confused and startled at the least.

But he could retreat to the person he was possessing. Having a living body as a shelter in addition to whatever piece of him was anchoring him to the physical plane... That explained a lot about his strength and abilities.

He had been strong-willed and extremely charismatic when he was alive—his psychopathic focus was no doubt serving him on the other side. She had seen his type before in the prisoners her mother exposed her to. But Michael... He was even more dangerous.

From what he said and the powers he was already demonstrating, he was well on his way to becoming a demon—if Rachel didn't stop him.

Hiram and Chloe weren't here to help this time. She was on her own. All she had was the ball, and while it would distract Michael, she doubted it would affect the alligator outside her window.

Slowly, she rose to her feet, keeping the witch's ball hidden in the sheets she brought with her. She pretended she was using them to staunch the blood on her arms.

Pain from the cuts on her feet lanced up her legs. She didn't let that stop her from approaching the window, carefully avoiding more glass. Water was still coming in through the hole she'd made, wetting the floor. Her blood stained it red.

Peering out, she saw the alligator sitting on the wet ground. Its eyes glowed blue, the same shade as Michael's only lit with a preternatural light. She jerked back a few steps as it opened its mouth and hissed.

Michael laughed. *"Do you like my little pets? They certainly liked your friend Garrett."*

She turned her head toward the sound of his voice. Garrett should be at the hospital by now.

"What do you mean?"

"I mean he made them a substantial meal."

"No, Garrett left, he—"

"Do you really think after you strung him along for years, then finally let him rut in your body that he would be able to go? He turned around to come back. Of course, with this little storm I prepared for him, he didn't get far. I

made sure my friends gave him an exuberant welcome."

Michael clacked his spectral teeth together.

She was shaking again, but this time it was rage. Garrett couldn't be… Especially not that way.

Michael must have read her expression.

"The good doctor is dead. He is dead because he loved you. And love is the most dangerous thing of all. Women are not to be trusted. They will trap you and torment you. He learned this at the end. My gift to him."

The storm had stopped. She noticed it with numb detachment. The storm that Michael had used to kill Garrett… Only a gentle drizzle remained.

"It was my gift to you too, Rachel. I can do more than make you suffer. I wanted you to see I can make you happy as well. Give you what you want. Pleasure is an excellent appetizer for pain."

A chill breeze hit her ear again, creeping down her neck and along her back and arms. Michael was standing right behind her, running his hands along her body.

He was still playing God, only this time with her heart instead of her life. He had pushed her toward Garrett, made sure she had a taste of happiness greater than any she had ever experienced. And then he had taken it away.

"I am the only one who truly understands you," he said. *"Who you are, what you can do. We don't need to worry about anyone getting between us anymore. Garrett has already crossed over. He didn't even think to wait, to*

help you. But I waited. I'm here. For you. All you have to do is join me."

He wanted to break her, to control her. But instead of despair, all she felt was rage.

If she thought she had a chance of taking Michael out from the other side, she just might try. But with how well he could manipulate the physical world, she didn't want to think about what he could do to other spirits. He had always been a master manipulator.

Rachel was finished being his puppet.

She felt his hands on her shoulders as if he was urging her forward. His voice was gentle. *"Take your pick—my pet or the glass. I recommend the window. It'll be cleaner."*

"I recommend you go fuck yourself."

She dropped the sheet and held up the witch's ball, directing all of her rage and grief through it. The ball acted as an amplifier for her already enormous pain. She wanted Michael to hurt, like she was hurting. Worse.

The emotion blasted through the room. She could feel it. And even without that, the way Michael screamed let her know it was working. The remaining glass in the window exploded out into the yard.

That was unexpected…

Still holding the ball in front of her, she walked toward the empty space. Water and glass slid out of her way as she approached, pushed by the force of whatever the hell she was doing.

Outside, the alligator was already leaving, heading for the canal at the back of the property. She could sense that Michael had left—for the moment. Her heart was racing, but even that sensation was muted at the stark reality she was left to face.

Garrett was gone.

"Rachel!"

Rachel looked around the room. That was Garrett's voice. But he had crossed over... Hadn't he?

"Rachel!"

Someone was pounding on the front door.

Garrett!

She flung the door to the room open and ran through the house, chucking the witch's ball onto the couch as she passed it. Garrett was still pounding on the front door. It sounded like he was trying to break it down.

"Garrett! I'm here!" she shouted as she unlocked the door and threw it open.

Time seemed to pause. Garrett was standing on the stoop, his hair plastered to his face, rivulets of red streaking across his forehead and down his cheek. His clothes were pasted to his body and his chest was heaving as his gaze roved over her as well.

"Jesus..." he gasped.

He crossed the threshold and picked her up in one movement, crushing her to his chest as she wrapped her legs around his waist to hold on to him. He kicked the door shut and turned so that her back was against it, then he kissed her.

His lips crashed down against hers, his fingers firm against her backside as he held her tight. She wrapped her arms around his neck, returning his kiss, wanting to feel him, all of him, to know he was truly all right.

With their chests pressed together, their hearts were so close—only a few inches of flesh and bone between them. She could feel their energy mingling, merging.

She needed more.

Chapter Twenty-Nine

This didn't seem like the time to start something. Both of them were bleeding, though it all looked superficial. Who knew what kind of danger they were in. But Garrett could feel how much Rachel needed him, needed this. He sure as hell needed it too.

Her legs were wrapped tight around his waist, her tongue delving into his mouth and fingers burrowing through his hair. He pressed her against the door, grinding against her till she groaned.

How could this be happening? Gators outside, ghosts everywhere…

And Rachel opening herself up to him completely—heart, body, and soul. He could feel her fear, her relief, her grief. And a hell of a lot of lust and love thrown into the mix.

Just about the same as him.

But he was only getting the tip of the iceberg of what she was feeling. He sensed the weight of it lurking under her skin.

She arched her neck as he trailed his mouth along her trachea and down to her collarbone. Her hips were already moving on him. She was aching and hurting and needed an outlet for too many emotions. Quickly.

"Garrett…"

"I know," he murmured against her skin.

She hadn't bothered with underwear when they threw on clothes to make breakfast. Stretching his arm around her thigh, he pulled down his waistband and lined himself up. He plunged in deep, holding on to her thighs. Their gazes locked.

Her body relaxed against him as she let out a shuddering breath. And then another.

"Kiss me," she said.

"Any time."

A faint smile crossed her lips before he claimed them. He thrust his hips, her body warming him, sending frissons of pleasure all along his nerves. With the adrenaline already coursing through his system, he knew he wouldn't last long. Lucky for him, he could feel she was in the same boat.

Using her arms on his shoulders for leverage, she moved in synch with him, arching her hips away then back with each of his thrusts to get every drop of stimulation possible from their union. She sped up and he matched her, until the sensations were blurring together in a cascade effect.

All the adrenaline that had coiled in his body focused around where they were joined—on the primal energy of this act of love and longing. It gathered deep in his gut, pressure building until it burst through his body.

He felt himself shifting, like part of him was moving into her as they came and part of her merging with him. Something beyond the physical, something new and bright and full of possibilities. It left his skin tingling and his legs weak.

He leaned against her, pinning her to the door, while he pulled himself back together. She was still pulsing around him, holding him tight everywhere she could. When he slid from her at last, he lowered her feet to the ground, then reached down to pull his pants back up.

Her face was burrowed into the side of his neck, the vibration of her voice traveling through him when she spoke.

"I thought I'd lost you. He said…" Her voice broke. "He said you were dead."

"Look at me."

He waited for her to straighten up so they could look in each other's eyes again. Tears streaked her cheeks, tugging at his heart.

"Never gonna happen." He kissed her again, then rested his forehead against hers. "While you're here, this is where I belong."

She nodded and sniffed. He gathered her up in his arms and carried her to the couch in the living room.

After setting her down, he pulled his T-shirt over his

head. He should really get the First-Aid kit, but he couldn't leave her. At least the wounds were as superficial as he first thought. They must sting like crazy, though.

He knelt in front of her and dabbed at her legs with his shirt. "What happened?"

"It's Michael. He's back. He never really left."

Garrett nodded. "Yeah, I figured that out when he tried to drown me in that storm and sent some gators after me."

"How did you escape?"

"Broke a window and climbed on top of my car, then jumped off and ran like hell. They chased me farther than I thought they would, but when I reached the house, they sort of lost interest. Good thing too, because I left my keys behind in my hurry."

He chuckled and glanced up at her, hoping he could ease her worry even a little bit. Nope. There was a crease wedged between her brows and she was getting ready to cry again.

"I'm so sorry," she said.

"Michael's the one that needs to be sorry. And we're going to see to that next."

There had to be something in one of her books that would help them. Otherwise, they were trapped in his house with no way of calling for help. He didn't like the idea of that at all.

"How did he hurt you?" He could hear the change in his voice as he asked the question. The low tones almost hitting a growl.

"He didn't. I broke a window too."

"With your arms?"

They seemed to have taken the worst of the damage, but all the scratches were shallow. She had a few scrapes on her knees and the outsides of her legs, and needed to stay off her feet for a few days. Those were the cuts that worried him the most. None were deep enough to need stitches, at least.

"I used the reading chair in the guest room."

"I didn't know you had it in you."

"He said he was going to kill Jazz. The door to the guest room wouldn't open and I couldn't think of another way to get to her. God, Garrett, the things he said…"

Garrett held her face so she had to look at him. "We're going to stop him. Do you hear me? He's not going to hurt anybody else."

"But he already *is* hurting people. The women he killed —they were right. He's able to get to them again. He's torturing their spirits in the afterlife. And Jazz…"

Garrett's stomach curled in knots. "What about Jazz?"

Rachel gripped his hands and pulled them into her lap. "She called me right after you left. The signal wasn't very clear, but she was trying to ask me about possession. And then Michael told me that he's already taken someone. He's going to force the person he's possessed to kill Jazz if we don't stop him. That poor man… What he must be going through right now."

Garrett's thoughts were spinning. All his friends were in danger—again. And even though he knew it was happening, he had no way to get to them. No way to help.

"He'll go after Elsa next. He's going to kill everyone I care about to punish me. I know it." Rachel leaned forward as if she was getting ready to jump up.

"You need to stay off your feet."

"I need to get to my friends!"

Garrett let out a deep breath, knowing how upset she was going to be when he told her the truth about their situation. Knowing he had failed her again.

"The car's stuck in the sand. There's no getting it out. And I'm not sure how far away those gators went."

And his phone was in the car along with his keys. Shit. He didn't bother bringing up that cheery point. They would check her phone for a signal as soon as they could.

"For the time being, we're stuck here," he said. "And that means you stay off those feet."

"No. There's more we can do."

"Rachel, you're going to start bleeding again if you walk around."

"Good. I can use that."

His heart sank as he saw the determination in her gaze, felt it echo in his soul. There was no talking her out of whatever she was thinking, even if it meant more danger, more harm to herself. All he could do was make a stand with her.

"Tell me what to do."

Chapter Thirty

Blood magic was powerful. One of the most powerful magics.

Michael might have been a ghost long enough to figure out tricks and gimmicks, but Rachel had been studying the paranormal her entire life. She had just never opened herself up to her powers before. Powers she had grossly underestimated.

She remembered the water—red with her blood—moving away from her and taking the broken glass with it as she walked to the window. Psychokinesis.

Yes. She could use her blood. But she would need more if she was going to put a stop to Michael.

Runes. Definitely something with runes.

She wasn't naïve enough to think that she could get Garrett's car out of the sand. But she could make the wards incredibly stronger if she reinforced them with her blood. That helped her and Garrett, but no one else. Michael was still free to go wherever he wanted at the speed of thought.

She surveyed the room, taking stock of her resources. Censer with incense, salt, saltwater spray bottle. Those were small-scale compared to what she was facing.

If Chloe were there, she might be able to channel Michael's spirit into her own body and banish him. Rachel had heard of séances for that purpose. But she had never been part of one. Never been taught how to do it.

Sometimes, other people were used as receptacles for the spirit while the medium remained outside and could focus fully on banishing the ghost. Rachel looked at Garrett kneeling in front of her.

She knew he would have faith in her ability to keep him safe. He would jump at the chance to help, even putting himself through that hell. He was probably the most powerful resource she had, but she couldn't—wouldn't—use him like that. It wasn't safe. It wasn't right.

There had to be some other way.

She glanced down at the couch, her gaze caught by the witch's ball. Caught…

The tunnels of glass within the orb were meant to trap malicious spirits. What if she could lure Michael back and somehow trap him in the ball?

She picked it up, wiping her hand over its surface. How could she possibly get him into it? If she hung it back in a window, he'd simply stay outside or find another way into the house. He could wait them out, like a siege.

She couldn't stop staring at the witch's ball. It was the key. She knew it. But if she couldn't use it in a window…

"A mirror!"

Garrett started and fell over backward. His eyes were

wide, but he must have been encouraged by the smile she felt pulling on her face.

"Warn a guy next time," he said.

Her grin turned wicked. "Oh, there will be no warning. What I have planned will be a total surprise."

From the guest room, a tinny sound called out to them. Her phone again.

"Like that?" Garrett asked. He jumped up and started toward the room.

"Wait! I'm coming with you."

She ran to the counter, ignoring the pain in her feet and the way she slid on the bamboo floor as they started to bleed again. She grabbed up the container of salt and the spray bottle, pinning them to her body with the arm that held her witch's ball. She didn't dare drop it with what she had planned.

"Dammit, I told you to stay off your feet."

"I'll heal. Now let's go before we miss the call."

She pushed past him, running down the hallway to the guest room. Garrett was right behind her. She made sure they crossed the threshold together. Being trapped in the room alone with Michael once had been quite enough for her.

Her phone was still ringing, buried in the sheets that she had dropped near the window. Garrett threw them aside and picked it up, then hit the speaker button while Rachel set down what she carried on the bed.

He held the phone up between them and said, "Hello?"

"Garrett?" Jazz's voice. She sounded wrecked. "Where's Rachel? Is she okay?"

Rachel's stomach started doing flip-flops again. She had never heard Jazz sound so upset. Nowhere close.

"I'm here. I'm fine."

Garrett glared at her, but Rachel stared him down. Now wasn't the time to go into details. They could lose the connection at any moment.

"Thank God."

At the same time, Rachel and Jazz both said, "Listen to me," then paused.

"Me first," Jazz said. "He'll find me any second."

"Who will?"

"Finn. I mean Michael. I don't even know anymore! I'm losing him. He's losing himself. Michael is possessing him."

Garrett let out a breath like he'd been punched in the stomach. As if that and the feeling of loss and dread pummeling through Rachel from Garrett wasn't bad enough, Jazz sniffed loudly, her voice hoarse as she continued.

"He's coming for you and Elsa. You have to warn her. He's going to kill you and… You don't want to know what he has planned then. If I can't save Finn—"

"Stop," Rachel said. "We're saving everybody. And we're taking Michael out in the process. Permanently."

As in *eternity*. Michael was done hurting people Rachel cared about. He was done hurting anyone.

Even without their bond, she could see that Garrett was barely holding it together. With it, she could sense how much he cared. He loved Finn like a brother. She wouldn't let him lose another one. And whatever Finn was to Jazz...

"Where are you?" Rachel asked.

"I don't know exactly. I was knocked out. But I'm in a swamp. Probably somewhere near Clearview."

"Why Clearview?"

"Finn and I were trying to find out more about Michael's other victims. It's Michael's home town. We found the house where he grew up."

"Listen to me carefully. I am certain that Michael's body was cremated but there must be something of him left behind. Something acting as an anchor in the physical realm. With how powerful he is, it can't just be a lock of hair. It has to be something with more substance."

For a brief moment, she was actually sorry she and Michael hadn't been intimate. She hadn't had a chance to check him for surgery scars or find out if he'd ever had something removed. All those jars of *keepsakes* in his garage... Maybe one of them held an organ. Even his tonsils or appendix would be enough.

If Jazz couldn't find an anchor in Clearview, they at least had a lead on where to try next. In the meantime, Rachel had a plan to keep him contained.

"I think I know where it is," Jazz said. "What do I do with it?"

"Burn it. Can you do that?"

"Yes. But what about Finn?"

"Once you destroy the anchor, I'll be able to take care of Michael and Finn will be free. We'll be working from here to try to weaken Michael, but we need you to help Finn keep fighting."

If Finn was half as worked up about Jazz as she was about him, they stood a good chance.

"Jazz, you have to reach him," Garrett said. "Any way you can. He won't be able to live with himself if he hurts anybody."

"I know."

Garrett was frowning deeply, his brow lowered over his eyes. "Watch out for wildlife too. Michael can control snakes and gators and the swamp's full of them."

"It's good if he's spreading himself thin," Rachel said. "The more fronts we can hit him from, the better. Work on your connection to Finn. Try to reach him and help him to hold on."

Jazz's voice dropped to a whisper. "Hurry."

The call ended.

"Tell me your plan is going to work," Garrett said.

"It's going to work. But you're not going to like it."

"What do you need me to do?"

She wasn't entirely sure. She was cobbling things

together from all the different books she'd read, everything Hiram and Chloe had taught her. Mostly, she was going on instinct.

"I don't know. I'm not sure how this will play out. I just know I need you with me."

So much was at stake. She had never been more frightened in her life. If she failed, everyone she loved would die. And that was just the beginning. What Michael had planned, the lives he would take, the people he would destroy—

No. Just…no. She was going to stop him. Right now.

Garrett nodded. "What is it you're going to do?"

"Ask you to trust me."

She pulled him down for a kiss, lingering more than she probably should. A small part of her warned that it might be their last one. She pushed the thought away.

The witch's ball sat on the bed with her other supplies. She handed the container of salt and the spray bottle to Garrett, then picked up the glass sphere and headed to the bathroom with him right behind her.

This is where it had to happen. The mirror and the witch's ball were her best weapons. Plus her blood and her knowledge.

She made a line of salt across the door's threshold and another along the back of the sink's counter underneath the mirror, then handed the container of salt to Garrett. It was starting to feel disturbingly light.

"Mix up more saltwater, please," she said.

As he did that, she pulled some towels from the shelf and wrapped the witch's ball, then set it on the floor in a corner where it would be safe. When Garrett was done using the sink, she put in the stopper and filled it with warm water, then added more salt. Having the saltwater easily accessible would help with her work.

"Close the drain in the tub and then spray it down. Put a towel over the toilet tight enough that nothing can crawl out of it. See if you can find something to put on top of the toilet seat too. Just in case." She thought about that, then added, "Maybe make a salt line around the whole thing as well."

Garrett raised an eyebrow, but did as she said. He put a sturdy metal trash can on top of the seat when he was finished spraying and salting everything. Hopefully anything that might try to come up from the toilet wouldn't be strong enough to lift it.

"What next?" he asked.

"Spray me down."

He hesitated. "With those cuts, it's going to hurt like hell."

"I'll deal. And you're next, by the way."

She didn't let herself wince, even though the salt stung each and every wound. Turning in a circle and spreading her arms, she made sure he was able to get her covered in a fine coat of saltwater. Then she did the same for him.

It didn't feel like enough.

Using her blood to protect him was out of the question. Not only would he not stand for it most likely, but with what she had planned, it would make him a target. Their connection already opened him up to Michael more than she liked.

If he had her blood on him, it would act like a beacon—like the one she was about to set up. But a saltwater symbol on his chest would hopefully be lost among the others she was about to draw. She had just the rune for the job.

She dipped her fingertips in the saltwater in the sink, then lifted them to his chest and traced the shape of Eihwaz—like a backwards letter "Z"—a powerful rune of protection. She visualized him being surrounded by a bright golden light, strengthening his aura and keeping him safe.

She wished she could do the same for herself, but the saltwater spray would have to be enough. She didn't want to scare Michael off.

"Help me get the sheet down."

"Won't Michael be able to see what we're doing or use it as a door if we do?"

"The salt line should act as a barrier."

The way he scowled let her know that he didn't like the idea of taking down the sheet as clearly as the waves of apprehension flowing from him. Still, he moved to one side and carefully lifted the sheet off the corners of the mirror, making sure he didn't disturb the line of salt. He dropped the sheet on the floor behind them.

Rachel bent and picked up the witch's ball, then set it on the counter within reach but not too close to the edge.

"I'm going to need a few minutes of silence," Rachel said.

Garrett nodded and she went to work.

First Thurisaz—a straight standing line with a triangle jutting out from its middle pointing to the right. Thorn. She traced it in the top left-hand corner with the saltwater from the sink.

Upright, it was another rune of protection. As she drew it, she thought about herself and Garrett—all her loved ones, even the people she didn't know who stood to lose their lives if Michael was free.

Then she drew it in the corner opposite, with the arrow pointing to the left—a mirror image of the first rune. Reversed it meant ill-fortune, things not turning out as one hoped. She focused her thoughts on Michael.

The next rune was Sowelu, the sun. A symbol of victory. It had always looked like a lightning bolt to her. She thought of Michael's narcissism and played into that. Let him think this energy was for him—let it lure him in, make him feel secure.

But it wasn't for him. Or even for her. It was for Fate.

The next rune finished her thought. Jera—two arrowheads facing away from each other, touching so they defined a sealed space between them. It also looked a bit like a "Z", but with an open rectangular space in the diagonal line. The harvest time for karma.

"Reap what you sow," she murmured as she traced the symbol.

She continued to tell their story through the runes. Kenaz reversed, a single arrow-head. Darkness. Loss. Symbolizing both what she had felt during her time chained up in his garage and what Michael was about to experience at her hands.

Each rune flowed from her fingertips onto the mirror, her skin buzzing with energy, her arms crawling with it. Uruz, a little like an upside-down "U". The wild ox. Untamed. She wanted Michael to know he hadn't broken her.

In the mirror, she noticed her grim smile as she traced Tyr—justice. A single arrow pointing up.

She was placing the runes in a spiral pattern, visualizing a vortex, a spinning whirlpool of energy that would trap him.

And finally, in the center of the mirror, a single vertical line—Isa, the ice that held the whirlpool in check. The stick that held up the cage. The snare beneath the leaves.

It was ready. All she had to do was place the bait.

Her.

Chapter Thirty-One

The air grew heavier by the second, charged with energy like the moment before lighting struck. Goose bumps ran over Garrett's skin. With each design Rachel traced on the mirror, he felt it thicken.

And she was smiling.

That unnerved him most of all. The way she smiled into the mirror, like she was daring Michael to come. Daring him to do his worst.

Taunting him didn't seem wise. Almost everyone Garrett cared about was on the line.

What Finn must be going through, having that sick fuck playing around in his head. And Jazz trying to help Finn through it, sounding like her heart was being dragged across razorwire in the process.

Elsa and Dante were somewhere hiding behind a line of salt with Winston and Leo. Damn, even their cat wasn't safe. And it wouldn't end with his circle of friends. For Rachel, it might not end at all.

He could sense she was keeping things from him. Trying to protect him. But that just left him with his wild imaginings.

What if they failed and Michael managed to take them all out? Could he grab her spirit and keep it from moving on? She had mentioned Michael's other victims, that he was already tormenting them on the other side. There was no way Michael would let Rachel go if he had any say in it.

Garrett thought he might be sick, his nerves were so bad. He fought the bile in his throat back down. There was no way he would lift that toilet seat after what Rachel had implied. He imagined a rattler springing out and hitting him in the face, or dozens of scorpions crawling from under the lid.

The thought made him shiver. What Rachel did next made it worse.

Reaching out to the counter beneath the mirror, she drew her finger through the line of salt, breaking it.

Garrett shifted so that he stood behind her, ready to help however he could. Their reflections caught his attention. He outlined her perfectly, framed her smaller form, but didn't dwarf it. The result was harmonious. Balanced. It calmed him to think of how perfectly they fit together.

He had seen pictures of auras in her books. The image was almost the same as what he was seeing. It gave him faith.

He was going to protect her. They were going to get through this. All of them.

He rested his hands on her shoulders and sucked in a breath as their bond blew through him, electrified him. She was radiating power.

Garrett's eyes were tingling and he blinked a few times. The mirror was illuminated—all the symbols she had traced glowing with a faint silver light. He had no idea what they meant, but felt a tug, like he was looking into a pit instead of sideways into a mirror.

But not a mirror. Not anymore.

Their reflections and the room around them blurred and vanished. Instead, the glass was filled with gray fog and dark shadows.

Holy shit…

His disorientation grew worse as a silhouette emerged. The features were fuzzy, but gradually came into focus. Tousled blond hair, three days' stubble around a broad smile, straight nose, large eyes… Finn. But not Finn.

Those eyes were supposed to be gray. The same blue-gray as Rachel's, in fact. Instead, they glowed bright blue. Blue like the gators'. Blue like Michael's.

Garrett sensed Rachel's confusion. He shared it himself. If Michael had appeared, that would have made a sort of sense. Reflecting his soul and all that. But even possessing Finn, why would he appear that way?

Unless Michael was using more than Finn's body.

Shit! Why hadn't Garrett thought of that before? Finn was psychic too. And from what Garrett knew, Finn's powers made him a prime target for a ghost looking to jack someone's body.

If having some sort of special anchor already gave Michael a boost, what would riding around in Finn do?

Make it easier to get in people's heads. Or animals. Make it easier for him to charm people, to connect. Especially through his hands, one of which was lifted as he reached out toward Rachel, that disarmingly charming smile on his face.

Rachel lifted her arm in return. Garrett could feel some sort of feedback loop, energy rippling out from the mirror and from Rachel as well. There was some sort of connection there, a pull that neither of them understood. But Garrett did understand that she should absolutely not touch the mirror. He grabbed her arm to hold her back.

Finn's gentle smile twisted and another face lurched toward them. Garrett could still see Finn standing in the mirror, his expression pained and his hands reaching for the translucent *thing* coming out of him. Superimposed over Finn in a sick parody of Garrett and Rachel's reflections earlier, Michael's features took shape.

In life, Michael had been handsome by any measure. Death had wiped that out. His cheeks were sunken, dark circles surrounding eyes blazing with that unholy blue light. Straw-like strands of hair floated around his face, and his teeth were serrated like a shark's. His skin was waxy and bloodless.

"Hello, Rachel," Michael said.

He lunged at them, his face and shoulders coming out of the mirror. On this side, they looked solid. How was that possible? He reached out and locked his grip on Rachel's arms—and pulled.

She screamed, and Garrett tightened his hold on her, keeping her tight against his chest. His feet started to slide on the tile floor.

"What do I do?" Garrett yelled.

"The ball! The witch's ball!"

The...? Right. That glass ball she'd hung in her room. It was close enough for him to reach. He wrapped his arm around her chest, keeping her pinned to him, and picked it up with his free hand.

Michael let go of one of Rachel's arms. The pull toward the mirror lessened and Garrett gained some ground, bringing Rachel with him. But it gave Michael the opening he needed.

Laughing, he swatted the ball away. It hit the floor and shattered.

"Trinkets and baubles," he said. "Oh Rachel, I have so much to teach you once you're on the other side with me. Stop fighting it, love. We're all waiting for you."

Then Garrett saw them—dark forms lurking behind Michael in the mirror. The ghosts of his victims.

Their spirits looked like the portraits Michael had made using their blood. Distorted bodies, faces hidden or turned away. The pain and despair Michael captured on his canvases blew out from the mirror like a cold wind, freezing Garrett down to his soul.

Police had identified a dozen different victims from DNA testing of Michael's portraits. There were more than a dozen spirits in the mirror. So many more.

Rachel began to cry. Her right arm was turning blue where Michael's spectral hand held her.

"Rachel…" Garrett's teeth were chattering. "Rachel, sweetie, I need you to focus. I know you're scared. I am too. But everyone is counting on us. Including those women. We need to help them, remember? That was always the plan."

"The plan…" She sniffed loudly, then nodded.

Reaching up with her free hand, she dug her nails into one of the deeper cuts on her right arm. Blood welled to the surface.

Shit! He did not know this part of the plan. His stomach churned. He stopped himself from trying to staunch the blood that ran down her arm and dripped onto the floor.

Michael smiled. "Perhaps I don't have as much to teach you as I thought. But save some fun for me."

She let Michael pull her closer to the mirror. Garrett's instinct screamed at him to keep her away, to run, but he had to trust her—that she knew what she was doing.

When she was within reach, she slammed her hand onto the mirror, pushing most of Michael back into the glass.

His features became translucent again, superimposed over Finn's.

Garrett could see that Finn's eyes were closed, his eyebrows scrunched together. He was fighting Michael's control.

"Using blood…" Michael said. "You surprise me, my love. We're an even better match than I thought."

Rachel was gulping air. The mirror glowed where her hand touched it.

"Come to me," Michael said. He still had his grip tight on her arm. "Come to me and I may spare you one of your friends. You may choose. Any but the good doctor. He must die, of course, for tasting your forbidden fruit. But Elsa perhaps? That dear lovable butler of hers? The cat? Your—"

Whatever he was about to say, they didn't hear it. His face contorted in agony, mouth a wide "o" with all those teeth showing. Finally, he let go of Rachel's arm, his image retreating fully into the mirror.

Finn cried out, then his reflection vanished.

Garrett's breath rushed out of him in a sob. What had happened to Finn? Was he okay? Was he…

Rachel made a straight line down the center of the mirror—a streak of red that bisected it—then stepped back, pushing against Garrett hard enough that he staggered. He struggled to keep his hold on her.

She didn't lose her balance. Feet planted, she glared at

Michael in the mirror.

Michael glanced around as if he was searching for something—like maybe a way out. From how Rachel was laughing, Garrett didn't think he'd find any.

Garrett kept his hands on her shoulders as she approached the mirror again, matching his stride with hers. When Rachel spoke, her voice was eerily calm and filled with confidence.

"Ladies, find your peace," she said. "You are free."

Rachel ran her finger through the blood on her arm and then traced what looked like a large "M" on one side of the mirror's surface and a blocky "R" on the other.

The gray fog in the mirror began to move, forming a whirlpool. Garrett felt it pull at something deep in his gut, like his energy was trying to move toward the mirror. He felt it bump into Rachel, then settle back into him.

What the fuck...

But the dark forms in the mirror didn't have anything to block them. Some seemed to fight the current, while others swam with it. They all flowed into the center of that spiraling vortex, wherever it went.

Michael started to turn, but Rachel snapped, "Not you."

She smeared the "M" and "R" with the heel of her palm. The swirling stopped. Only Michael and the gray fog remained before them.

The mirror changed again, the room around them coming back into focus as the fog dissipated. Garrett still couldn't see their reflection, though. Only Michael's, as if his spectral form stood in the room instead of them.

Rachel ran her fingertip through the blood on her arm again. Her face angled enough so that Garrett could see that she was smiling. It was not a kind smile.

She traced over the line bisecting the mirror. Michael's pallor intensified and he started to shimmer as if shivering. Mist rose from him, like breath on a freezing day.

"You won't be hurting anyone ever again," Rachel whispered.

Chapter Thirty-Two

"Garrett, please hand me the trash can."

She pointed toward the toilet without looking. Her eyes were locked on Michael's in the mirror. If she looked away, she wasn't sure what would happen. She was scared to even blink now that she finally had Michael where she wanted him.

In her periphery, she saw Garrett pick up the heavy metal bin and set it on the counter. He didn't let go of it.

"Is he trapped in the mirror?"

"For now." For about the next thirty seconds—the last of his existence on any plane.

"Are Finn and Jazz okay?"

"I don't know."

"Shouldn't we find out before we do anything else?"

She had to blink—she couldn't stop herself. Michael stayed in the mirror. She let out a breath of relief. At least she didn't have that to worry about. But she could feel him trying to slip out of the mirror, trying to get away.

"I don't know how long I can hold him. We can't risk him getting away."

Garrett's voice was quiet when he said, "What are you

going to do?"

She didn't want to say. But she had to.

"I'm going to end him. Eternally."

"You freed the spirits of his victims. Can't you just—"

"I don't know where those other spirits went. I don't know what's on the other side. What if it's a revolving door and spirits are instantly reincarnated? What if he retains his memories, his personality?"

Michael smirked. "So many *what ifs* deciding my fate. I only have one question. What gives you the right to decide whether I cease to exist?"

That question could plague her for the rest of her days. But it wouldn't.

"When you chained me in your garage, you kept saying that you were God. That you decided when and how I would die."

"And now, you do the same to me." He made a clucking noise. "Love, we are so much more alike than I ever guessed. I truly found my match in you."

"*Met* your match. Not found. I am the one who will end you."

"You would really utterly destroy me? All I wanted was to immortalize those women."

"You wanted to control them."

"So now you control me. Does it feel good to hold my fate in your hands?"

"No." She shook her head. "It isn't in my hands."

For the first time, Michael looked uncertain.

"When I opened the gateway, it pulled in the other spirits," she said. "I felt it. Felt Garrett being affected too. But not you."

Michael's frown turned to a grimace, his lips pulling up from his teeth.

"I thought so." Rachel nodded. "You didn't have any trouble staying right where you were. I thought it was the rune at first. Isa—ice—holding you in place. But what I felt was warmth."

She smiled as she remembered it. Comforting energy. Restfulness and home. She hoped kindness was waiting for the spirits she had sent to the other side—a place that they could heal and rest. Maybe Hiram would be there to greet them—to help them on their journey, like he had helped Rachel.

"I felt it," she said. Something had guided her, something beyond her intuition.

"Not your hand but the hand of Fate? Is that how you'll absolve yourself of guilt?"

"This is my choice. Whatever that force was, I choose to help it."

She was finished sitting on the sidelines. She reached for the trash can and rested her hand on its lip. Garrett was right behind her. He hadn't said anything, but she felt the turmoil in him.

Softly she said, "You don't have to stay."

"No, he doesn't." Michael sneered. "But he will. He'll stay with you through the long years, thinking of how the woman sharing his bed and bearing his children was capable of destroying *a soul*. The most precious part of our existence. That you felt you had the right to decide not just between my life or death but my very existence."

Rachel's heart picked up. She knew it was a risk. Garrett was a doctor. Sworn to help people. What she was about to do... Even with what she had sensed from the vortex, the calm encouragement that this was the right thing, she knew she would wonder what Garrett thought of her after it was done.

"The doubt on his face is beautiful," Michael said. "The anger and the pain. And you are the one putting it there, Rachel. It's your masterpiece."

She gripped the trash can, but Garrett wouldn't let go.

"Garrett, please trust me. I know what I'm doing."

"I know," he whispered.

Michael spat out, "That won't change anything. He'll never truly trust you after this, after seeing what you're capable of. You aren't the one who gets to decide when I'm done!"

"No," Garrett said. "I am."

He pulled her tight against his chest as he lifted the trash can out of her grasp, then smashed it into the mirror.

Rachel saw the look of disbelief and fear on Michael's features just before it hit.

Lightning fast, cracks spread over the mirror's entire surface. They seemed suspended in place for a brief second—as Michael's ghostly form exploded into mist, dissipating almost instantly.

Then the pieces of the mirror fell. Her ears rang from the sound of them striking the counter. Garrett tightened his grip on her. She could feel his heart beating against her back.

They stared at the fragments for a few moments before Garrett asked, "Is it over?"

She nodded. "Yes. He's gone."

Chapter Thirty-Three

Garrett's heart was beating so hard it was painful. He had never been more scared. Life and death decisions he was used to. Immortal souls? Shit, that was outside of his depth.

All he had been sure of the entire time was one guiding truth—he trusted Rachel. And he could feel how certain she was, even with the pain of what they had to do.

He dropped the trash can and spun her around, pulling her into a crushing hug. He buried his face in her hair and kissed her neck.

"It's okay," she said. "We're okay."

Not entirely. Her arm was bleeding where she'd dug into her cut. His stomach churned at the memory.

He pulled her with him as he took a few short steps to the shelf and grabbed the First-Aid kit. His hands were shaking so bad she had to open it for him.

A cursory glance at the wound told him it still probably didn't need stitches. It might leave a scar, though. Another one from that bastard.

She set the kit on the back of the toilet and took out an alcohol wipe. Without pausing, she opened it and started on her arm.

"I can do that," Garrett said.

"I thought you weren't allowed to treat me." She grinned up at him.

How could she already be smiling? She wasn't even wincing while she cleaned up her wound.

She threw the bloody wipe into the bathtub and said, "I could use some help with the bandage, though."

Garrett cleared his throat. "I can do that."

Now that her cut was cleaned up, it wasn't as bad as he had feared. He let go of her long enough to open the bandage and put it in place.

She put her hand above his heart. "I really am okay. Are you?"

"Yeah."

"You didn't have to do that," she said. "I would have taken care of it."

"I wanted you to know that I understood. That I believed you. From what you told me about demons, I wouldn't be surprised if he was heading down the road to becoming one. And that guy with even more power… It's something the Universe doesn't need."

"I can't believe how much faith you have in me."

"I can. And I also…" He took a deep breath and blew it out. "Elsa told me she felt that she was being guided to save Dante. She knew she could pull him from his time and bring him here. What you said reminded me of that.

The way you trusted your power and listened to your intuition." He shook his head. "If something's out there, some force that wants to help good people and stop bad… Well, I'm in."

"I hope you're right. It would be nice to know we aren't alone in this."

"I've been trying to tell you—you're not alone. None of us are. Not while we have each other."

Rachel's phone started to ring in the other room.

"We should get that," she said.

"What about…" Garrett looked at the shards of glass coating the bathroom counter.

"We'll take care of that later. It's only broken glass now. But I'm thinking we should bury it in a salt-lined hole. Just in case."

"Maybe add some cement."

"You're thinking too corporeally," she said. "Come on."

She led him to the guest room, carefully stepping over the remains of her witch's ball. Sunlight was streaming in through the broken window, catching and reflecting on the broken glass along the wall below. Picking up her phone from the bed, Rachel hit the speaker button.

Before they could say any kind of greeting, Jazz screamed, "Are you guys okay?"

Garrett's heart picked up again. Finn had been the closest thing to a brother Garrett had since Dylan. He couldn't stand the thought of losing him. Not to Michael.

"We're fine," Rachel said, squeezing Garrett's hand tight. "What about you two?"

"We're okay."

Garrett blew out a huge breath. His eyes burned and he felt tears on his cheeks—and he did not give a damn. His body was shaking with relief. Rachel wrapped one arm around his waist, holding the phone closer.

"Finn, you SOB," Garrett said, wiping his eyes with the back of his hand and sniffing. "What the hell did you get my friend Jazz mixed up in?"

"Are you *crying*?" Finn's mocking voice came over the line—the best sound Garrett had heard all day.

"Shut up," Garrett said.

"Oh, I am never going to shut up about this."

Garrett laughed. He hoped so. He wanted Finn to give him a hard time about it for decades—for the rest of their lives, laughing and joking and poking fun at each other as usual.

"Ugh, bromance," Jazz said.

"I think it's adorable." Rachel laughed and squeezed Garrett's waist.

There was a silence on the line that made Garrett uncomfortable. "Finn, you okay?"

"Yeah, man. Yeah." But his voice was a little more serious than Garrett was used to. Gravely.

"Wait a minute," Garrett said. "Now are *you* crying?"

"You'll never prove anything."

Jazz laughed. "Don't worry, Garrett. I'll get some pictures."

The next sound to come out of the phone sounded suspiciously like kissing. Which seemed like a really good idea to Garrett. He kissed the top of Rachel's head. There would be time for more later.

"Look, we've got a mess to clean up here," Jazz said.

Garrett laughed. "Funny, I was about to say the same thing."

"Ours is going to take a while. We need to call the Clearview police—"

Finn broke in. "Already texted them. They're on the way."

"When did you text them?"

Jazz sounded supremely annoyed for some reason, and Finn instantly went on the defensive.

"As soon as you called Rachel!"

Garrett loved hearing Finn exasperated. It meant Garrett was right about the pair. Double-dates were in their future. He was sure of it.

"I didn't want them to check our phone records and see that we called our friends before them when—"

"Enough!" Jazz cut him off. Garrett could imagine her waving one hand in the air dismissively. "We can explain all that later. Bottom line is, you two need to call Elsa and Dante and give them the all-clear. We are all clear, right?"

"Yes," Rachel said. "Michael is gone—for good this

time."

"Thank you." Finn's voice had that somber cast again. Unnerving.

Garrett was used to his friend being worked up about cases or laughing about... Anything, really. This was a new side, brought out by whatever he'd gone through. Another scar for his friends, courtesy of Michael.

Yeah, Garrett wouldn't be losing sleep over ending Michael any time soon.

"We couldn't have done it without you," Rachel said. "We make a good team."

She looked confused for a moment, staring intently at the phone as if she was trying to see something. But then she shrugged and laughed.

"I'll text you after I call Elsa to let you know they're okay," Rachel said. "But I'm sure they are. We let them know what they needed to do to protect themselves and it sounds like we were all keeping Michael pretty busy."

A loud whirring noise sounded in the background.

"Okay," Jazz said. "The cops are pulling up."

"Is that an airboat?" Garrett asked. How deep in the swamp were they?

"Yeah. We better go. But we're headed your way as soon as we're done. And I'm bringing guests, so clean up."

"Guests?" Rachel emphasized the *s* at the end.

"Deal with... I know you can handle it," she said, then ended the call.

Garrett looked down at Rachel. One eyebrow was arced on her forehead. She shrugged.

"I'll call Elsa," Rachel said.

"One thing I need to do first." Garrett pulled her against his chest and kissed her. He meant it to be quick, but once he had her taste, he was lost.

Her mouth was so warm, her arms strong around his neck, pulling herself up to kiss him back. She lifted her thigh, sliding it along his leg.

Breaking off the kiss, he said, "Make the call fast and send that text."

"We still have a bunch of cleanup to do."

"Can it wait a few minutes?"

Rachel cast him a wicked grin. "I think we can make the time."

She dialed Elsa's number and hit the speaker button. Elsa seemed to answer before the ringing even stopped.

"Is everyone okay?" Elsa asked.

Rachel leaned into Garrett's chest and he squeezed her tight.

"Yeah," she said. "Everybody's fine."

Epilogue

A solarium wasn't quite right for Rachel's needs. She preferred the greenhouse they had built onto the back of their new two-story house. She sat at a round table nestled against the outer windows, watching Garrett run after the twins while Hiram, their eldest, wrestled with Dante and Elsa's daughter, Alexis.

Deirdre took a tumble and started to cry, but Garrett swooped her up into his arms, checking her knees for scrapes, then giving her kisses and tickling her till she laughed. Dylan clung to his leg, giggling madly.

Life was good.

Rachel turned her attention back to her notebook on the table. Elsa and Dante were planning a signing at the Bookwyrm to celebrate their latest collaborative effort—a children's book they had written together and Dante had illustrated.

Rachel was designing an exhibit for the paintings Dante had made for the book. They would hang in Jazz's gallery and tie in with the signing. All the proceeds were going to fund a new wing for the local hospital that would specialize in pediatric medicine.

A high squeal outside made her smile. Such a good cause.

The wind chimes hanging above her head sounded, a cold breeze stirring the pages of her notebook. Rachel planted her hand on the paper and let out a sigh.

"Rachel..." The voice was right at her ear.

In a calm voice Rachel said, "Yes?"

She took a sip of her tea.

There was a pause. Most spirits were confused when their introductions were met with nonchalance. The windows rattled in their panes. Great. One of *these* again.

Rachel frowned. "There's no need for theatrics. We're having a cookout this afternoon. Please don't make a mess."

"I will do what I want!"

The rattling kicked up and one of the plants scooted closer to the edge of its shelf.

"I can make your life hell. Make you wish you were—"

"Let me stop you right there." Rachel smiled as the ghost paused in its spectral posturing.

Rachel pulled on the cord that hung down next to her seat. It flowed through grommets set into the greenhouse's frame and ended on the far side of the space. The cord was attached to a gauzy cloth that covered a large mirror suspended high in the opposite corner. The lever that let her adjust the angle of the mirror was also right at hand. She took another sip of her tea, adjusting the mirror so that she could scan the room.

"Ah, there we are."

The ghost was standing next to her. They usually did. Rachel barely ever had to move the mirror at all.

This one was a woman. She might have been in her early twenties when she died.

"I'm sorry for your loss," Rachel said. "But that doesn't excuse such poor manners."

"I... You can't talk to me that way!"

"Oh sweetie..." Rachel smiled. "Let me tell you how this works."

She set down her tea and dipped her finger into the warm liquid, slowly swirling it around in a circle. As she did, the runes she traced in saltwater on the mirror every morning started to glow.

The ghost turned to face the mirror, eyes widening in her pale face as she saw her reflection. Gray clouds swirled around her, pulling her into the glass and trapping her there.

Rachel set aside her cup and flicked the tea from her finger. Her mother might not have taught Rachel how to handle her powers, but Lillian Montgomery *had* taught Rachel how to dominate social interactions. Rachel only cast an occasional glance toward the mirror, letting the ghost know that she was not worried in the least by the presence of a spirit.

"I hope the accommodations will be comfortable for

you while we work to resolve your issues. Please understand that I can't have ghosts who are willing to throw their weight around running freely near my home. There are children to consider. The safety of my family and our guests."

"How did you…"

"It's neat, isn't it? One of my friends used to be a set designer for a theater. He's a brilliant engineer, though he mostly paints nowadays. Set the whole thing up for me."

Dante had used cords and pulleys rather than electronic motors. The manual system was much more difficult for ghosts to interfere with and had a cool steampunk look.

"I understand that you might have lost touch with certain aspects of your civility," Rachel said. "But I must ask you to try to remember to treat me and mine with respect. I will do my best to reciprocate."

She paused to let that sink in with the ghost. Mutual respect or mutual antagonism. Those were the choices. Rachel wanted to be sure the ghost understood just what it would mean if she chose to make Rachel her enemy.

"You will remain in the mirror until I am certain that you pose no danger to anyone, living or dead. If you threaten me, my family, or anyone else…" Rachel stared at the ghost. "Ready or not, you *will* move on to the next plane, and whatever is waiting there for you."

The ghost shrank back from Rachel, becoming a bit more transparent. Good.

"But if you are willing to be courteous and explain your situation calmly, I'm willing to hear you out."

Rachel smiled.

"Now. Let's see what we can do for you."

—

Think you know everything? Think again! You can see what Jazz and Finn were doing during the events of *Whispering Hearts* as they face a new threat in *Lingering Touch*—and it's not just from beyond the grave. Secrets will be revealed that shock the group of friends to their core and show them that they're even closer than they thought.

Read on for a sneak peek of *Lingering Touch!*

Lingering Touch

The Summer Park Psychics
Book Three

Prologue

Summer Park—May 2015

Time travel was impossible. There was no such thing.

Finn had worked plenty of weird cases as a private investigator. This one might break into his top ten.

He picked the lock on the theatre's back door, then slipped into the building. The most recent production had wrapped almost three weeks ago. That meant only construction crews would be around. They'd be focused on the stage. Finn was interested in the theatre's seating.

All he needed was a few minutes in the box reserved for Elsa Sinclair—famous novelist and professional recluse. His best friend, Garrett, had hired Finn to figure out if Elsa was being conned by the guy she was living with—Dante Lucerne.

It seemed likely. For starters, Dante Lucerne had been dead over a hundred years. Finn turned up that little gem of information within an hour of working the case. The original Dante had been killed in a fire in London in 1881. Finn couldn't find any other men matching the name and description Garrett had provided. And it was a very unusual description.

Six foot tall, short dark hair, thin build, blue-green eyes, and scarring over a quarter of his face centered on his right temple. Oh, and he dressed like a guy from the 1800s…

who chose to wear a *Phantom of the Opera* mask.

Yeah, this case had definitely cracked his top ten.

Garrett had turned around and told Finn to drop the case right away, but it was too late. Finn's curiosity had been piqued. The more Finn learned, the more curious he became. He had even already brought out his secret weapon—psychometry. He'd used his psychic ability to read what had happened in the limo Elsa rented the night Dante appeared in her life.

Finn snorted and shook his head as he remembered Elsa telling Dante that she had basically teleported him from 1800s London to modern-day Florida.

Time travel. Yeah, right.

Finn could buy into a lot of things—psychometry and telepathy, for instance. His very personal experience proved those were real. But going back in time and bringing someone to the future? No way.

Dante had been really convincing, though. Not only had he been wearing the old-timey clothes Garrett had mentioned, but Dante had been covered in soot and sweat. He had the accent down, speech cadences sounding like something from a period piece.

Only one explanation seemed plausible—Elsa was researching a new book. She was going all out and had hired an actor to help her get into the spirit of things. For all Finn knew, this was how she researched all of her stories. It would explain why everyone talked about how real they felt. Hell, even Finn's dad was a fan.

Finn might have to read her next book. The horror novels he usually read right before sleep were finally getting to him. It had been decades since he'd woken up screaming from a nightmare. He was a grown man, for crying out loud. He couldn't quite remember what had happened in his dreams the night before, but he felt in his gut that it was somehow related to this case.

He'd never had an investigation get under his skin like this. He'd been on edge all day, jumping at the smallest things and feeling...honestly, kind of terrified. He didn't understand where it was coming from. He did understand that it needed to stop.

If sifting through the memories of the dozen or more people who had been in the limo since Elsa and Dante would help him figure out the mystery, it was worth it. Even the ones that were a graphic and unwelcome reminder of his last encounter with Jazz. They had broken up after a disastrous date in a limo.

That was Fate's punchline. Elsa wasn't just tight with Garrett—who was as close to a brother as Finn was going to get this lifetime—she was best friends with Finn's ex, Zhou Jazz.

Who was he kidding? Jazz wasn't just an ex-girlfriend —she was *the* ex-girlfriend. The only woman Finn had ever wanted to spend the rest of his life with. Their relationship had escalated so quickly, even though they'd only been together for a couple of months. He'd been certain she was the one he was meant for. Part of him still thought so.

Normally, he used his work to avoid thinking about her, letting himself get lost in the puzzles his investigations presented. With this case, everything reminded him of her.

He had even seen her a few times, talked to contacts that he introduced her to. For some reason, she was putting together a fake ID for Dante. If Dante was conning Elsa, he was conning Jazz too. Finn took a deep breath and willed his body to relax, his hands to uncurl.

If Dante was conning Jazz, if he tried to hurt her in any way... It would not end well for him.

Finn made his way to the box that Elsa had reserved for every single showing of the play. It was unlocked. Two chairs sat facing away from him. The curtains were already closed. Apparently, she insisted they were kept that way—yet another of her eccentricities. No one had bothered to open them yet.

It worked in his favor. He could check things out without being seen. Her memories should be all over the place.

Finn closed the door behind him and set to work. He held out his hands and shifted his awareness, letting the feel of the place soak in. A few deep breaths would open him to...

Holy shit.

The tiny room was bursting with energy. Finn felt like he was on a roller coaster, his stomach lurching and doing flip-flops. He staggered forward and grabbed one of the seats in front of him to stay upright. A jolt of energy lit him up like the Fourth of July. His eyes were electrified, his body tingling from head to toe. He blinked a few times, waiting for his perspective to shift as his powers kicked in.

Normally, he felt like he was floating above the place he was viewing—his awareness on the shoulder of whoever had touched what he was touching. This time, he was booted out of his body like someone rammed him in the gut. The vision was different too—the colors more vivid. Too vivid to be real.

He looked down from the ceiling to see Elsa standing in the same spot that Finn's body must be occupying. She was staring at...nothing. Between the no-blinking and standing completely still, she looked like a mannequin.

It would have been creepy if not for the ribbons of golden light whipping around, centered on her. They cast off little fireworks of energy that filled the space. Finn felt like he was inside a glitter-filled snow-globe that was being swirled around.

The light started to gather in front of her, taking on the shape of a man. Elsa's arms shifted so that she was embracing him, clinging to him. The light was painfully bright. In a final flash that made Finn wish he had eyelids to shut, Dante appeared in her arms.

What the fuck! What the flaming flying fuck!

Dante collapsed. It looked like he was convulsing.

"Dante? Dante, are you all right?" She grabbed a dark cloak from the back of the other chair. "I'm so sorry. I didn't think it would be this bad."

She draped the cloak over him, then dropped to the ground. She snuggled up against his back, spooning him and rubbing his arms and chest. He was shivering and breathing heavy.

"Stay with me. Please stay with me," she said.

Finn watched, dumbfounded. After a few moments, Dante's tremors subsided. He gripped Elsa's wrist and said, "I assure you, I have no plans to go elsewhere."

They sat up slowly. She knelt next to him, hovering like a hummingbird, her face pinched with worry. The pair finally faced each other, and damn, Finn could sense the chemistry even without his body. A much dimmer version of the golden lights was hovering around their bodies, linking them together like she was still holding on to him.

"How do you feel?" Elsa asked.

"I scarcely know where to begin."

"Are you hurt?"

"I do not believe so. For the most part, I am confused."

That made two of them.

"That's understandable. I'll explain everything as soon as I can. But right now, we have to go."

Elsa rose to her feet and offered her hand to help Dante

up. Of course, he took it. The two stood close, staring into each other's eyes like…

Like Finn wished he and Jazz would have. He groaned at himself, then forced thoughts of Jazz out of his mind.

"Where is it we are going?" Dante asked.

Elsa smiled. Finn realized he had never seen her look happy before. Not that they'd spent much—or any—time together. Jazz wasn't keen on incorporating Finn into her life.

"Home," Elsa said.

She stepped toward the door. The vision faded as she and Dante moved away. Finn blinked a few times as his awareness returned to his body. He was sitting on the floor where Elsa and Dante had been talking. When had Finn fallen?

The conversation Finn had viewed in Elsa's limo took on a whole new depth of meaning. She really *had* brought Dante forward over a century, had saved him from the fire that supposedly killed him.

Finn stood, careful not to touch anything. Once was enough for being pulled into the current of such a powerful memory. He staggered out into the hall, closing the door behind him. His thoughts whirled as he leaned against the dark wood, still clutching the doorknob.

Finn's hearing cut out suddenly, his perspective shifting so he was looking down at the door. Another vision? What the *fuck* was up with his powers today?

A blond guy was standing in front of Elsa's theatre box, stroking the door. Yeah, that wasn't suspicious at all.

Finn recognized him as one of the people he had sifted through when finding Elsa's memories in the limo she rented. He remembered the guy because he had just sat there, completely still, for a long time the day after Elsa and Dante rented it. That was too much of a coincidence.

Finn made a note of the guy's height and weight, his build, his clothes, anything that might help ID him later. The vision ended gradually, letting Finn sink back into the awareness of his own body again.

He had a call to make. Garrett needed to know that Dante wasn't the one Elsa should be concerned about. And after that, Finn would start looking for the blond guy.

—

You can get *Lingering Touch* now! I'd love to keep in touch. Join my newsletter to get sneak peeks and behind-the-scenes insight into my many worlds, and check out other ways to join my community on my website at cassandra-chandler.com/community. I really want to know what *you* think. If you enjoyed this book, please consider leaving a review at your favorite book review site. I'd really appreciate it—reviews help readers and authors alike!

Thank you for reading *Whispering Hearts!*

Cassandra Chandler

About the Author

USA Today Bestselling author Cassandra Chandler uses her vivid imagination to make the world more interesting, spawning the ideas she turns into her captivating Science Fiction Romances and enthralling Paranormal and Urban Fantasy Romances. Fast-paced and funny, lighthearted or filled with suspense, her stories will introduce you to characters you'll fall in love with and worlds you long to explore.

www.ingramcontent.com/pod-product-compliance
Lightning Source LLC
Chambersburg PA
CBHW072301020726
47501CB00002B/341